THE BEAUTY OF US

THE
BEAUTY
OF US

FARZANA DOCTOR

Published by ECW Press
665 Gerrard Street East
Toronto, Ontario, Canada M4M 1Y2
416-694-3348 / info@ecwpress.com

Editor for the Press: Pia Singhal
Copy-editor: Jennifer Foster
Cover design: Jo Walker
Cover photograph: Chad Madden via Unsplash

This is a work of fiction. Names, characters,
places, and incidents either are the product of the
author's imagination or are used fictitiously, and
any resemblance to actual persons, living or dead,
business establishments, events, or locales is entirely
coincidental.

LIBRARY AND ARCHIVES CANADA CATALOGUING
IN PUBLICATION

Title: The beauty of us : a novel / Farzana Doctor.

Names: Doctor, Farzana, author.

Identifiers: Canadiana (print) 20240357922 | Canadiana
(ebook) 20240364740

ISBN 978-1-77041-769-4 (softcover)
ISBN 978-1-77852-324-3 (ePub)
ISBN 978-1-77852-325-0 (PDF)

Subjects: LCGFT: Novels.

Classification: LCC PS8607.O35 B43 2024 | DDC
jC813/.6—dc23

This book is funded in part by the Government of Canada. Ce livre est financé en partie par le gouvernement du Canada.
We acknowledge the support of the Canada Council for the Arts. Nous remercions le Conseil des arts du Canada de son
soutien. We acknowledge the funding support of the Ontario Arts Council (OAC), an agency of the Government of
Ontario. We also acknowledge the support of the Government of Ontario through the Ontario Book Publishing Tax Credit,
and through Ontario Creates.

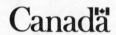

PRINTED AND BOUND IN CANADA

PRINTING: MARQUIS   5 4 3 2 1

For
Shamoon
and
Eileen Doctor

Fall Term,
September 1984

The light beckoned,
but I resisted,
couldn't cross over,
not yet.

Zahabiya

"Flushing!"

I turned over and away from the sunshine that pierced through the drapes. *Had I dreamt the scream?* When the second "Flushing!" drilled through the wall, this time in a higher pitch, I realized the yelling wasn't just in my head.

"What the fuck?" Mei grumbled from four feet away.

"She told us it'd be convenient to live beside the washrooms. She was full of crap." I sat up, put on my glasses, pushed my bangs away from my eyes.

"That bitch." Leesa, our roommate-for-a-day, had convinced us to move out of the upstairs triple dormer and into the first-floor double next to the washrooms. I'd felt bad for her when she'd asked us to switch with her two best friends so they could room together; Mei and I were strangers to her.

"Flushing!"

"Maybe she didn't realize?" I stared at the wall that separated us from the shrill shouting on the other side.

"Don't be naive. She knew. She set us up." Mei stretched her long arms over her head and whacked the wall with an open palm, her toes almost touching the twin bed's footboard.

Right at that moment, a bell rang. The dorm's collective alarm clock.

"Should we try to talk to someone? Our parents are paying a lot for . . . this." I gestured at the cracked plaster walls, scratched mahogany wardrobes, and warped-looking window, a room bruised by a century of living. I dismissed my own words almost as soon as I'd said them; my father wouldn't care about my complaints.

He was still mad that I'd ambushed him. To get to Thornton College, I'd gone to the library, searched its collection of Ontario Yellow Pages for boarding schools, requested application forms, and filled out six. When I'd presented him with Thornton's acceptance letter, he was shocked. Then he'd refused, saying it was too expensive. He'd finally and grudgingly agreed after weeks of lobbying and the intervention of his older sister, who'd advised him that a year away might do me — and all of us — some good.

"My parents won't give a shit. They wiped their hands clean of me when they dropped me off in that driveway."

Before I could ask what she meant, Mei bounced off her bed and leaned her head out the door, yelling, "Shut the fuck up!"

"Take it easy!" a girl shouted from the washroom. "It's to warn the girls in the showers, so they don't get scalded!" I stared up at the ceiling's swirly patterns.

"Great! This shithole has old, shitty plumbing, too!" Mei shot back, her voice like a foghorn through the thin wall.

I'd need to distance myself from Mei. I wanted to start the year off well and actually make some friends. At my last school, I'd always been on the outside of things, a product of being a year younger than everyone in my classes after skipping grade 5. That had marked me as just a little more different in a small town where I was already so different.

I swung my legs out of bed and opened the dust-streaked window. A black squirrel ran up the trunk of a nearby oak. He had a distinctive light grey stripe down his tail. Mei returned to our room, slamming the door behind her.

"Coming here might have been a mistake," I said, still looking outside. The squirrel leapt to a branch closer to my window. He stood on his back legs and stared at me. I tapped on the window, and he ran off, probably scared.

Nahla

"I'm sorry this is so rushed. And early." Mrs. Reeves, the headmaster's assistant, ushered Nahla into her office at 7:15 a.m. "We'd normally do this a week before classes started, but it wasn't possible under the circumstances . . ."

The job offer had come three days earlier, barely a fortnight since Mademoiselle Leblanc, Thornton's previous French teacher, had a heart attack and died in her sleep. *Well.* Nahla shuddered. *Not exactly in her sleep.* She shook her head, dislodging the image of her predecessor's brief and alarming middle-of-the-night awakening.

"That's okay, I'm an early riser," Nahla fibbed.

"Did Gerry get you moved in okay? Was everything ready for you?"

"Yes, he was very helpful." Gerry, the custodian, had shown her to her suite in the girls' residence yesterday evening. He'd hung around — giving her an extended tour of the kitchenette's supplies, a Noah's Ark of matched pairs of glasses, cutlery, and plates — and she'd wondered if he was flirting with her. He reminded her of Tom Selleck with his genial smile and playboy moustache. To get him to leave, she'd had to walk to the door, open it wide, and say goodnight.

"Good. We had him do a deep clean and a fresh coat of paint. The place really needed it. Did you know that Sylvie Leblanc — may she rest in peace — had lived there for twenty-five years?"

"He told me. But it looks brand new now." This was mostly true, but when Nahla had unpacked and settled in, she'd sensed Mademoiselle Leblanc's lingering presence. A solitary, long grey hair had trapezed from the shower head, slipping into her bath water. A perfect ring, where the older woman must have placed her glass each night, stained the bedside table. One of the mugs in the cupboard held a faint taupe lip stain.

"Glad to hear it. Now, here's your offer letter. Look it over, sign it, then we'll do a quick tour."

Nahla read through the two-page document, the terms of which Headmaster Lowery had discussed with her over the phone: teaching French to grades 7 through 13 and being a residence monitor. She signed and dated the sheets while exhaling a barely audible "alhamdulillah."

A bell rang, and Nahla startled. Mrs. Reeves said, "That's the second morning bell. It's kind of the 'hurry-up-and-get-dressed' warning. Don't worry; you'll start tuning out the bells."

Mrs. Reeves stood and gestured for Nahla to follow. They did a power-walk tour through the building, Mrs. Reeves pointing out science labs, classrooms, and offices. Nahla retained only half the information, distracted by the tall leaded windows, pointed arches, and vaulted ceilings. The school was grand, but also cool and uninviting, as though it begrudged its visitors.

"When was it built?" Nahla asked.

"I think the mid-1800s? It used to be a seminary."

"Ah, yes." It did call to mind a monastery she'd once visited, and with the hallways still empty, she could almost imagine the building's early inhabitants in the hushed passages.

"The boys' residence is next door. I'll take you there this afternoon."

"I am curious: Why is the girls' residence a block from campus?"

"Because Thornton didn't start taking girls 'til the '30s. Now, this is interesting: once upon a time, the girls' residence was the old town hall. It even had a courtroom and a police station downstairs. Of course, it's all chopped up into bedrooms now. And a new wing was added on a couple of years ago."

"That is interesting." Her own flat was on the old side.

"Your classroom is in what we call 'The Attic.'" Mrs. Reeves swung open a heavy wooden door, and they climbed a steep and slightly uneven staircase, emerging into a large open space with slanted ceilings. Sunshine radiated through the stained-glass windows, beaming blue, red, and yellow diamonds across the white walls. Caught off guard by the beauty, Nahla murmured, "Sahira. Charmant." Her brain cranked out Arabic and French before landing on her third language. "It's charming."

"Next to the chapel, it's the prettiest room here. But be warned: it's drafty in the winter. And, as you can tell, stuffy when it's warm."

Nahla walked between a row of desks. Most were covered in a fine coating of dust. And when she looked more closely, she noticed cobwebs lazily criss-crossing the ceiling.

"We'd better get back downstairs. I still have a couple of things to cover before breakfast. After that, there's an assembly during first period where you'll be introduced. Then we'll have a short memorial service — nothing fancy, we're Anglicans — for Sylvie."

"Oh, that's nice." But Nahla had no idea what she meant. She'd only ever been inside churches as a tourist.

Downstairs, Nahla thought they were doing the tour in reverse, but it turned out Mrs. Reeves was taking her through a different maze of hallways.

"Again, I'm sorry that you're being thrown in to the deep end like this. Maybe this will help. It's Sylvie's lesson plans." Mrs. Reeves handed Nahla a heavy weathered-looking binder.

"Thanks." Nahla's stomach clenched as she envisioned herself standing in front of thirty expectant faces at 9:45 a.m. She hoped her long navy skirt and ruffled white blouse made her look professional and fashionable. She'd worn her hair loose, but while Mrs. Reeves made photocopies, she reconsidered the choice, pinched a rubber band from her desk and corralled her curls into a tidy braid.

"Here's your timetable and your class and residence lists. You can leave everything here while we go get breakfast." A bell rang. "Speaking of which."

"I'm not really hungry. I think I'll take the next hour to review everything, if that's okay?"

"Of course. You have a lot to digest. We'll meet back here at 8:40 a.m. and head to the chapel together."

Nahla gathered her things and found her way back to The Attic. She sat at the teacher's desk and looked out at the empty room. The sun's angle had shifted slightly, and the coloured diamonds were now more faint. She scanned the list of sixty girls who lived on her side of the residence. She said the names aloud, their foreign sounds filling her throat:

"Kaley . . . Preethi . . . Rachel . . . Miriam . . . Fang . . . Dawna . . . Mei . . ."

So many of the names seemed to be from elsewhere, not what she'd expected from a Canadian boarding school.

"Nancy . . . Rachel . . . Barb . . . Marie . . . June . . . Zahabiya . . ."

She paused at the last name, wondering if the girl was Lebanese. She tried to remember all the Zahabiyas in her small community — which, by now, was surely circulating the scandalous news about an unmarried woman moving out of her parents' home — but came up blank. Not that any of them could afford a school like this.

"Simone . . . Cathy . . . Siobhan . . . Mallory . . . Jessica . . . Leesa . . ."

These girls were now her charges, although what this entailed, she wasn't quite sure. She wasn't sure of anything about this job; she prayed she wouldn't screw up her first real teaching position. No, she self-corrected. She could do it. She would succeed.

As she continued reading, a floorboard creaked. And then creaked again. The sounds were unsettling, but she knew the building was old and entitled to its rheumatic noises.

She checked the time and moved on to Mademoiselle Leblanc's binder, flipping through lesson plans, handouts, and test templates. She made notes for the day's classes. For the second time that morning, she whispered a grateful "alhamdullilah," and this time added on a whispered recitation of the "Al Fatiha" for Mademoiselle Leblanc's soul.

There was a cool breeze, as though someone had just thrust open a window.

"Call me Sylvie, ma chérie."

Nahla froze. She slowly turned her head, checking left, right, behind. No one was there. She told herself it was her imagination, fuelled by stress, but she knew otherwise, having grown up in a family of women who read coffee grounds, believed in spirits, and sought protection from the evil eye.

She hastened to Mrs. Reeves's office.

Leesa

Leesa took her seat at Table A3, the meal hall assignments pleasing her when she saw that Jason Anderson had the place across from her. He smiled deep dimples at the girl beside him, probably a ninth grader. Leesa watched his dark eyes twinkle, liked the way his brown hair had a tinge of red, as though an amber light shone from behind him.

She'd noticed him last year when he'd started at Thornton College. He was one of the brains. She admired the way he could articulate himself with confidence. In classroom debates, he answered teachers' questions well beyond the scope of the textbook's material, without being boring or arrogant. She often tried to add a caboose to his train of thought, after which he'd nod to her in reply.

The smart kids and her crowd rarely mixed, but it could be fun to flirt with him at mealtimes, to have an admirer her own age for a change.

While she'd always been a part of the elite circle, she'd never been close to its apex until last year. Before that, Jessica and Mallory, girls she'd known since grade 7, had only shown her a polite friendliness. But last spring, their best friend, Ashley, sprained her ankle, and too slow on crutches to keep up with them, Leesa had been invited to take Ashley's place in their trips to town or for ice cream. She'd worried that Ashley would reclaim her position after the summer once her injury healed and she'd be back to where she started, but a stroke of luck had secured her spot: Jessica and Mallory were assigned the cruddy room beside the downstairs showers, and she had the upstairs triad. She was perfectly poised to save them. She convinced the Indian girl and the Chinese girl to switch with Jessica and Mallory without any trouble, and they'd shown their gratitude by sharing their stash of Marlboros and flask of rum behind the building in the spot just out of reach of the motion sensor lights and prying eyes of the residence monitor. They'd quieted their boozy laughter when the new French teacher slid open her second-floor window to light her own cigarette.

Leesa spied Zahabiya and Mei hesitating near the dining hall doors like lost puppies. By now, they'd have figured out that the downstairs double sucked. Too bad. She'd been a new girl once herself and had to learn things the hard way. She turned her attention back to Jason Anderson.

"Did you hear that Mademoiselle Leblanc passed away?" She fluttered her eyelashes mournfully at him.

"Shocking, right? She had such a big heart. Sorry, pun not intended. Were you close to her?" His brown eyes were wells of concern.

"She was like family." If he'd reacted with indifference, she might have shared her real opinion.

"She . . . she was . . . a second . . . mom to . . . to me." The ninth grader beside him wiped her tears.

"Yeah." Leesa nodded, drawing the attention back to herself. "I was probably in her apartment at least once a week when I first came to Thornton." Leesa remembered the smell of Mademoiselle Leblanc's flat — a mix of Anaïs Anaïs and coffee — the sense memory so strong, it was like the woman was sitting next to her.

"Sad way to begin the school year. Here, Mimi." He passed the girl beside him his napkin.

A cowbell clanged, and Jason sighed and headed to the kitchen. Each student took turns being the table's waiter. Leesa counted her way around the table of twelve, calculating that it wouldn't be her turn until lunch on Wednesday. Lunches weren't usually that bad, except when they served carrot soup, vomit-coloured droplets of it splashing onto her hands as she ferried its terrine from kitchen to table. She'd complained to her mother — a class of '61 old girl — who agreed that the traditional chore was antiquated and menial. She'd promised to send a stern letter of protest to Headmaster Lowery, but who knew if she ever would.

Leesa surveyed the dining hall and spotted Jessica at A4 and Mallory at A2, good locations for being able to bring them extra johnny cakes or meatballs when she was waiter. But Ashley was at B3, also just one table over. *Keep your friends close and your rivals closer,* Leesa thought.

Zahabiya

My cue card–sized slip of paper read *Table B3*. Mei flashed her own meal hall card: *G2*.

"It smells like a mix of pancake syrup and sweat." Mei sniffed.

Yesterday, the dining room had been set up buffet-style, but today, there was a diagram at the door, showing the seating plan for the school year. We scrutinized the thirty rectangles to find our tables.

"Okay, see you later." I was relieved we weren't at the same table. I was already tired of her negativity.

The dining room was packed with students in Thornton's blue blazers, grey kilts, and grey dress pants. Students filed in from the kitchen carrying large platters. Sensing I was late, I hurried to find my table and wedged myself in the empty spot between two girls who, in the midst of conversation, leaned across me to continue talking.

"Our cottage is nice, but really boring. Oh well, at least my ankle got better, and I got to swim a lot and work on my tan." I shifted back as the girl to my left rolled up her sleeve and stretched it across my chest. Short, wispy blonde hairs stood at attention on her bronze forearm.

"You're, like, so lucky. My father made me do an internship at his company." The other girl rolled her eyes. "Said it would be good for my university applications."

"Geneva, right?"

"Yeah," the girl to my right took the passing plate of pancakes from the boy across from her.

"Do you want to switch, so you can sit together?" I asked.

"We're not allowed to do that," Cottage Girl replied.

"Headmaster Lowery has some kind of complicated system, so that different grades and new and old students sit together. It's to make everyone feel like 'family,'" Geneva Girl said, making air quotes with her free hand.

"Oh, okay. I'm Zahabiya, by the way. I'm new, grade 12." I forked a pancake off the stack and passed on the platter.

"Ashley. Grade 12 also."

"Giselle. Grade 13."

"Have you been here a long time?" I asked, not sure how to keep the banter flowing. I poured syrup over my pancake. It dribbled down the pitcher's side and a drop landed on my new kilt.

"Since gra — aaa — de 7," Ashley yawned like a lioness, showing off her perfect teeth.

"I started in grade 9." Giselle passed me a bowl of scrambled eggs.

"It must be cool to spend the summer in Geneva?" I attempted, while trying to nonchalantly rub at the sticky spot on my skirt.

"I guess."

The talk lulled as everyone ate. The eggs were bland, but I didn't want to ask Ashley to pass the salt. I met the gaze of a boy across from me. His skin was a shade darker than mine, and his glasses a tad thicker.

"I'm Cyril," he said, pulling a small bottle of hot sauce from his pocket and sliding it in my direction. "You might need this. I'm in grade 11, and this is my third year. I'm from Trinidad."

I returned his smile, grateful someone was being friendly, but then noticed that both Giselle and Ashley were snubbing him, even though he was smiling in their direction, too.

"Hi. No thanks. I don't like spicy food," I lied. He took back the bottle and put it in his pocket, squinting at me, as though trying to make sense of my words.

"So, Ashley, where's your cottage?"

I felt bad, but I was new, and first impressions mattered.

Nahla

"Bonjour, les etudiants! Je suis Mademoiselle Naim." Nahla pointed to her name on the chalkboard and was met with blank stares. The few attentive expressions that dotted the room were like dandelions on a green lawn.

"D'accord. Nous allons nous presenter." She explained that they should share their names, where they were from, and one thing they loved in the world. This was grade 12 French, so her request was within their capabilities, but still, her words didn't rouse them. "Ne vous inquietez pas. Don't worry. If you've forgotten over the summer, I'll guide you."

She scanned the room, armpits prickling, stopping at a girl in the second row who was busy whispering to her neighbour. Her blonde hair, the colour of white gold, fell around her shoulders in cascading curls that she must have spent all morning cajoling into form. Nahla self-consciously tucked her own unruly frizz behind her ears.

"Veuillez commencer." Nahla gestured to the girl, who, in flawless French, reported that her name was Leesa, originally from Toronto, but she lived in Paris for many years because her parents were executives at a major cosmetics company. This garnered gushes of admiration from a few of the girls sitting nearest Leesa. Nahla wondered why she hadn't been enrolled in a Parisian school, given her strong language skills, but before she could ask the question, Leesa looked at two girls on her left and said, "J'aime mes amis. Especially my two besties."

"Well, we know that's true, don't we?" A girl near the front muttered.

"Voulez-vous continuer?" Nahla pointed to her.

"Je m'appelle Mei. This is my first year here. My parents are not important people in the least — dentistes en Ottawa. What do I love? I dunno. I guess j'aime Siouxsie and the Banshees." She crossed her arms in front of her chest and leaned back in her chair, her long legs stretching into the aisle. Nahla translated the English words verbatim and asked her to repeat them before gesturing to a boy at the back. They continued this way, around the room, until just one girl was left.

"Je . . . m'appelle Zahabiya. Sorry, I read and write better than I speak. J'habite à Brock, about two hours — deux heures — away. Je suis une etudiante nouvelle ici and, so far, j'aime Thornton." The girl said this with a self-conscious laugh, but there was also a sadness lurking under her words. Nahla began a translation, but the lunch bell rang midsentence, and the classroom rumbled into alertness as students stood and filed out.

Nahla turned to look at the long list of places she'd transcribed onto the chalkboard. Mrs. Reeves had informed her that Thornton had an outreach program that recruited foreign students. Still, the vast geography these students had traversed struck her; there were children of immigrants whose families lived a few hours away, foreign students from Ghana, Hong Kong, Haiti, Barbados, St. Lucia, Kazakhstan, Nigeria, Trinidad, Brazil, and white Canadian teens with parents transplanted in France, Italy, Egypt, Japan, Kuwait, and Saudi Arabia. *What was it like for parents to separate from their children in this way?*

A flush of compassion rose for her own parents who'd protested her move from Montreal to take this job. Her father had even blocked the open door like an angry sentry, only relenting when the cabbie came up the walk. Perhaps their disapproval hadn't been just a desire to control her, to enforce their values and social mores on her, as she'd believed. They'd made an arduous journey together, a family of five escaping the war in Beirut and settling in Montreal.

She knew she was an outlier; no one in their community had a daughter who had moved out before marriage. Her flight from their suffocating love must have frightened them, fractured their vision of security. She'd have to find a way to repair the rift she'd created. But she also wouldn't give in. No she was determined to keep her new and hard-won independence.

She hastily tidied her desk and opened a bottom drawer to store away the heavy teaching binder. As she shoved it in, something blocked the way. She pulled out a small grey notebook and flipped it open. On its first two pages was a list of dates and times scrawled in what Nahla now recognized as Mademoiselle Leblanc's handwriting:

04/18/84	?	*quelques semaines ont passé déjà??*
04/25/84	9h02	*marche vers le nord*
04/25/84	9h57	*de retour*
05/02/84	9h03	*vers le nord, mais rentre dans un char bleu*
05/02/84	?	*observe L dans l'espace commun à 9h15*
05/09/84	9h03	*marche vers le nord*
05/09/84	9h58	*de retour, visiblement perturber*
05/16/84	5h00	*rencontre avec L, l'interroge sur ses plans. Pas prévu.*
05/16/84	10h00	*de retour pour le* bedcheck
05/23/84	9h02	*demeure dans l'espace commun jusqu'au* bedcheck
05/30/84	9h02	*dehors avec M & J aux tables pique-nique*

What did all this mean, these descriptions of someone walking north, coming home, going somewhere in a blue car, spending time in the common room? Who were L, M, and J, and why was Mademoiselle Leblanc keeping track of them? Nahla fanned open the notebook, confirming that it was otherwise unused.

She slipped the book into her handbag and headed to the dining hall.

Leesa

Leesa waited near the library for Friday's mail call. Although the post arrived daily, it was delivered to students on Mondays, Wednesdays, and Fridays by a tenth grader who wheeled a squeaky metal cart from Headmaster Lowery's office to the library doors. Mrs. Reeves sorted the mail, and from time to time, when parcels arrived looking worse for wear, rumours circulated about the secretary pilfering from them. Leesa wasn't sure she believed them, but just to be safe, she brought the secretary a tin of langue-de-chat biscuits at the start of each school year.

A dozen or so girls were congregating, eager for word from home. Leesa felt a damp hand on her elbow.

"Is this where the mail pickup is?" Zahabiya asked. Leesa pulled her arm away. Everywhere she went, the Indian girl seemed to follow.

"Yup." Leesa studied the girl's face. She'd be almost pretty if she wore a little makeup.

"I probably won't get anything. My family's not like that, you know?"

"No?" Leesa mentally plucked and shaped Zahabiya's eyebrows. Despite herself, she was curious. Most Thornton families *were* like that, sending cards and care packages with regularity, a way to soothe anticipated homesickness. Or parental guilt. Many of the mothers would have done this two to three weeks ago, calculating delivery times to ensure arrival the first week of school.

"I went to camp two years ago. I never got a single piece of mail the whole month." The Indian girl adjusted her bra, which looked to be one size too big, someone's hand-me-down.

The mail monitor rounded the corner, and the girls rushed her.

"Wait your turn!" the tenth grader cried, forcing her body between the cart and the throng. "Okay . . . Anna Johansson! . . . Barb Eaton! . . . Carrie McDonald!"

She handed out envelopes in various sizes and colours. A girl named Deena got a two-foot-by-two-foot cardboard box. Her friends exclaimed over its contents: cookies and candies and chocolate. Other girls, early in the alphabet but without mail, sauntered off, deflated.

"Giselle Marovic! . . . Hannah Bloom! . . . Lana Ramsingh! . . . Leesa Allen!"

She sprung to her feet.

"Wow, it's heavy!" she said, setting down her box in front of her. It *was* heavy, filled with ten pounds of the best French chocolate that she'd picked, packed, and mailed herself fifteen days earlier.

"I wonder what my mother sent me this time?" She smiled and blushed for the remaining audience as she ripped through the two layers of tape she'd carefully applied. She handed bars to Jessica and Mallory, then closed it again.

"That's quite a haul," Zahabiya said with an unimpressed look, which probably was just jealousy.

"I guess I'm just really loved."

Zahabiya

After walking the wrong hallway, the same confusing route I'd taken each day that week, I finally found my locker. I gathered binders and textbooks from my morning classes and dumped them in my already-bulging bookbag.

"You taking the whole damn library home with you, girl?" Two lockers away stood a girl weighed down by her own sagging duffle.

"Why so much homework the first week of school?" I banged my locker shut.

"It's some stupidity about getting us into routines. They do it every year. Don't worry, tomorrow's Saturday, only a half-day of school." The girl kissed her teeth, and her big brown eyes shone with mirth. I couldn't help but laugh along, my crappy mood evaporating.

"Yeah, it's weird we have school Saturday mornings."

"Yup, weird. It's to balance out Wednesday afternoons off."

"Are you from Jamaica?" I asked. Over the week, I'd met students from all over the world, the opposite of my old school, where you could count the number of brown and Black kids on one hand.

"No. Someplace way better." She took a bow. "The Bahamas."

"Oh, I've been there. But only for a day, my family went on a cruise before my . . . anyway, the beach was amazing."

"Yeah, we get lots of those boats parking their big asses by our town. Where are you from?"

"Brock. It's a town two hours away."

"No, I mean where are you *really* from?"

Usually, when I got asked that question, it bugged me. But that's because it was always white people asking.

"India. I mean, my family's from there. I was born here."

"That's what I guessed. I'm Lavinia, by the way."

"Zahabiya. How long've you been here?" By now, I'd picked up that seniority was a big part of Thornton identity.

"This will be my fourth year. All of high school."

"I'm new."

"That's not news, girl." Lavinia said this with a straight face, but then unable to contain her own amusement, she threw her head back and laughed.

"Oh." *Was she making fun of me?*

"Don't be so serious. I'm just joking. Have you been to the ice cream shop yet?" I shook my head. "Then let me be your tour guide."

We walked a block to the residence, separated at the lobby, agreeing to reunite after dropping off our bags. I slid open my desk drawer, where I'd stashed all the cash I had — a ten-dollar bill — until allowance would be disbursed on Sunday. I'd only asked my dad for ten dollars a week, the middle of Thornton's suggested range that started at three and maxed at fifteen, but he'd shaken his head and told me I'd have to get by on three. Over the summer, I'd worked part time at his office and had already drained my earnings on new clothes and shoes. *How was this going to work?*

Back at the front doors, Lavinia was waiting for me, and we headed toward a residential area.

"Over there's Headmaster Lowery's house." Lavinia pointed at a Victorian home with an expansive front lawn and manicured gardens.

A tabby with a purple collar stepped in front of us, and I crouched to pet him. He purred and pressed his cheek into my palm. I looked up to see that Lavinia had taken a big step away from us.

"You don't like cats?" I asked her.

"They creep me out. I don't really get why people want them in their homes."

· "Yeah, my dad feels the same way. But I love animals. I want to be a veterinarian." I thumbed the cat's tag: *Clement.*

"Well, at least you know what you want to do. I'm still not sure. The curse of being good in all my classes." She laughed.

We carried on to the ice cream store, which operated from a window on the side of its factory. The building hummed like a refrigerator. Single scoops were only a buck, thank God.

"Welcome back, girls. We always miss you Thornton students when you're gone." The server piled an extra scoop of chocolate on my already-toppling cone.

We thanked him and continued walking, Lavinia pointing down a long hill behind the dairy. "There's a supermarket, a couple of okay clothing stores. A pharmacy, a few restaurants — nothing West Indian. I really miss my mom's cooking when I'm here."

While Lavinia described the weekly dining hall menu and how the leftovers of one day became the disgusting soup of the next, I calculated that my first trip home to Brock wouldn't be until mid-October, almost five weeks away, a stretch of time that made the ice cream thick in my throat. *Was I homesick after only a week?* I hadn't considered missing my room, our house in the new subdivision, the small town surrounded by farmers' fields. Yet each night since my arrival, I'd dreamt of all those things. I didn't know I'd be such a big baby.

"The soccer pitch is a shortcut." Lavinia pointed to the field on the edge of campus. "But watch out, it can get muddy in the middle — I found out the hard way, got a loafer stuck once."

I imagined the field like something alive and hungry, swallowing students' shoes. But the weather was sunny and dry that day, so Lavinia led me through it, offering her own rendition of the new students' tour I'd been given the week before.

"See that building beside the school? With the turrets? That's the boys' dorm." With the sun silhouetting the building, the front-facing windows were like dark, blank eyes.

"Oh, and you've probably been told the gym is brand new and the library is too. Don't they look like glass bookends next to these ancient buildings?"

"I thought the same thing the first time I saw them. It's like they're trying to cheer the old building up but—"

"It's not quite working? Yeah. Oh, and next year, we're getting a new domed running track." She pointed behind the gym, to where a few guys were shooting hoops.

We circled back to the residence's rear door.

"And our tour ends at the manor."

"The manor?"

"It's what we call the girls' residence. Makes it seem more high-class, I guess. This back door is locked, usually at curfew. Have you seen the jail cells in the basement yet?"

"What? You're kidding."

Lavinia led me down the stairs, past the common rooms and to a dark section used to store extra mattresses and desks.

"See." She stood on the other side and clasped the iron bars. The cells reminded me of Victor Newman's dungeon on *The Young and the Restless*, and I imagined a tired prisoner sitting in its musty corner, watching us.

"Why does a boarding school have jail cells?"

"This was a police station, like, a hundred years ago. They didn't tell you that on the tour?"

"They obviously skipped the interesting stuff."

"If these walls could talk . . ."

When we went back outside, the sun was lower on the horizon, and a flock of geese honked overhead. It was close to dinnertime, so Lavinia and I headed back to the main building. For the first time in a long while, I felt like I could belong somewhere.

Nahla

With the lunch-hour bell, Nahla's grade 12 students filed out. It was Saturday, the end of her first teaching week, and the steep learning curve that she'd been trudging up had left her weary.

"Helloooo!" Maeve McKinney breezed into her room. "Want to join me for lunch downtown? It's cold cuts and pea soup here." She opened her mouth wide and mimicked vomiting.

"Sure, thanks." Nahla smiled at the English teacher's antics. She'd run into her a few times in passing, the woman always enthusiastically friendly, with a tendency to stand just a little too close. Now, she squeezed Nahla's shoulder.

"How's your first week going? I remember what it was like for me last year, trying to figure out all the rules and students' names."

"Honestly? It's been hard. I was a teaching assistant in university, but this is my first time teaching young people."

"You'll be fine. I don't even know how I got this job. I wanted to teach science, and I hate reading! But this was the only job here, so I thought, *just apply!*, then I did. Well, I just follow the curriculum anyway. What did you study?"

"I did a master's in French literature."

"Ooh la la! You're way more advanced than that, plus perfect you're teaching them!"

They stepped out. "Still so warm!" Maeve gathered up her long red hair into a ponytail, the elastic snapping with each go around.

"Reminds me of home." Nahla shrugged off her cardigan.

"Montreal?"

"Beirut."

"There's a war on there, right? I saw something about that in the news. Christians and Muslims fighting each other?"

"Well, it's more complicated than that." Nahla tried to stifle the irritation that inevitably rose when this subject came up with Canadians.

"And how long have you been in Canada?"

"We came when I was a teenager."

"You know, I can't imagine. Except for teachers' college in Toronto, I haven't been anywhere. My parents have a farm an hour away. I live just over there," she pointed to a tall apartment building a couple of blocks south, "with Joanne. Have you met her yet? She teaches health and phys ed."

"A few days ago." Joanne had greeted her with a handshake and a "bonjour, ça va?" that gave Nahla the urge to move in for a double-cheek kiss, but of course she'd abstained, having learned long ago that while Lebanese and some Québécois greeted people this way, most Canadians didn't.

They stopped at Wong's, a Chinese-Canadian restaurant. The place was half-full, and Maeve waved at a trio of men at the back, who beckoned them over. Maeve smiled and shook her head. "Another time. Today is girl time!"

Nahla would have liked to have joined them, but she followed Maeve to a table near the front.

"They're all science teachers, right?" Nahla had been introduced, but all the information was jumbled in her brain.

"Neville Thompson teaches biology; Krish Patel, chemistry; and Frederick Wolfe, geography. And I just saved you from dying of boredom," Maeve whispered. So far, Nahla had noticed that Neville, who was Black, and Krish, who was from India, were the only other teachers who weren't white. She'd connect with them later.

"It's slim culinary pickings in this town, but this place has the best sweet-and-sour chicken balls and moo shu pork." A waiter dropped off menus with a numbered list of specials, each with an egg roll, fried rice, and meat. Nahla chose number five, stir-fried chicken with vegetables. She hoped Maeve wouldn't order pork.

"They offered me the residence monitor role after Sylvie died, but I said no. I heard from Margo Jones — she took the job on the new wing after her divorce last year — she says they're always knocking on your door and getting into all kinds of shenanigans. How's it going?"

Nahla sipped her water. She and Margo had done study hour and bedchecks together the first night, but Margo hadn't mentioned any "shenanigans."

"I'm hoping the free room and board will be worth the trouble. And, so far, there hasn't been any." She knocked on the laminate table and then blushed when Maeve raised her left eyebrow at her superstitious habit. "Just a couple of the very young ones have come by to chat — homesick, poor things. I feel bad for them. I can't imagine being twelve and away from family."

"Yeah, but I bet some are better off at Thornton. I've heard stories. Some of their families are completely absent. I think the residence monitors end up being like stand-in parents to some of them."

Nahla thought about Sylvie's grey notebook, which she'd tucked into her handbag; she liked to pull it out to study the strange list from time to time, compelled by the mystery of it. "If you don't mind my asking, what was Mademoiselle Leblanc like?"

"Well, they say you shouldn't speak ill of the dead, but, to tell you the truth, I found her bossy. Opinionated. She was a fixture, and yet I don't think she was close to any of the staff."

"Oh, that's too bad." Nahla rubbed her arms, feeling the chill of the restaurant's air conditioning, and slipped on her cardigan. She cast a glance to her left, where her bag sat on an empty seat. For a second, she thought about showing Maeve the notebook but was distracted when she felt a light pressure on her right shoulder. She turned around, but no one was there. Across the room, Frederick Wolfe met her gaze and smiled. She waved to him and turned back to Maeve.

"Oh, good; here's the food." Maeve smiled at the fried orange balls the waiter placed before her.

Nahla said a silent bismillah over the non-halal meal. The pressure lifted from her shoulder.

Leesa

Leesa and her two roommates sprawled on the residence's front lawn, which was against the rules; "loitering" there had been prohibited ever since the uptight neighbours across the street complained about the students' noise. The backyard, however, had been taken over by the Caribbean girls, who, slathered in baby oil, liked to suntan topless when teachers were not around. Strangely enough, no one from the building directly behind the manor had made any complaints against Thornton's girls.

"What do you think of her?" Jessica pointed her chin at the new residence monitor, who was coming up the walk.

Leesa tipped down her sunglasses and smiled at Miss Naim as she passed. Before the teacher disappeared through the doors, she called, "Girls, please move to the backyard." They waved and ignored her directive.

"She's okay, I guess. Nicer than Leblanc. Younger," Leesa said, glancing at the flab pushing out from the waist of Jessica's acid-washed jeans. She'd spent the summer at her cottage and had complained about gaining weight from her mother's cooking. Maybe Leesa could restart the aerobics club to be supportive. Mallory, on the other hand, was almost gaunt from being on diet pills.

"Where is she from? India?" Mallory asked.

"Our next-door neighbours' daughter looks just like her. They're from Kuwait. Megarich. I think her father's a prince or something," Jessica answered.

"I bet Lebanon," Leesa said. "Lots of immigrants from there. And her French is good."

"We should probably be friends with her," Mallory suggested. "It's never a bad idea to get the monitor on-side. Remember how Leblanc was always having such a cow?"

"Omigod, yeah! She almost caught Lorrilee Manning selling me and Mallory weed." Jessica laughed.

"Wow," Leesa said.

"I'm not surprised she had a heart attack. Like, stress can kill." Jessica rolled her eyes.

"True." Leesa rummaged through her backpack and handed each girl a chocolate from last week's self-sent care package. Soon the girls shifted to talking about the candy's fat content. Leesa didn't want to think about Mademoiselle Leblanc.

"Leesa, do you like Rodney Davidson?" Jessica asked.

"Yeah, he's cute, but isn't he with Ashley?"

"They broke up over the summer," Mallory said.

"Newsflash, they're back together again," Jessica corrected. "But not for long. Thomas told me that things are, like, très rocky between them."

"Really? Evan hasn't said a word," Mallory said in a mock whisper. Both she and Jessica had Thornton boyfriends, as well as secret summer boyfriends who had their own regular school-year girlfriends.

Thomas and Jessica had been together, on and off, since grade 10, and Mallory and Evan since grade 11.

"Oh my God! It would be so awesome if you dated Rodney, Leesa! Then we can triple date," Mallory said.

"Exactly, that's what Thomas says, too. Like, things are just so awkward with Rodney dating Ashley, and none of us talking to her anymore," Jessica added. Leesa didn't know the reason for Ashley's shunning, but didn't want to jinx things by asking.

"Well, if they do break up, I'm open." Leesa tried to sound cool, but of course that would be perfect.

"Have you *ever* had a boyfriend?" Jessica laughed. "Like, no offence, but we used to think you were a lesbo."

"I love you, you love me . . ." Mallory sang.

"Homosexuality! People say that we're just friends . . ." Jessica joined in, an octave higher.

"But really, we are lesbians!" Mallory and Jessica harmonized, and the two of them convulsed into laughter.

"I've had summer boyfriends," Leesa protested. That was kind of true, if you counted the third cousin who asked her out two years ago and her building's young janitor, with whom she fooled around a bunch of times this past summer. "No offence, but the boys here are so juvenile. I've just never connected with any of them."

"You're right. I love Evan, but he is immature. My summer boyfriend was nineteen and so much sexier." Mallory fanned herself theatrically.

"Mine was twenty-one!"

"Omigod, that's, like, illegal!"

Leesa laughed along with Jessica and Mallory, but wondered silently: *What would they think of her having dated a man twelve years older?*

Zahabiya

"Ali! Ali! Accept the charges! Ali! Ya Allah!"

I arrived at Miss Naim's half-open door and started backing away when I heard her yelling, but Miss Naim hung up the phone and beckoned me inside.

"Come in. This line only does local calls, and my brother does not seem to understand . . . never mind. What can I do for you?"

"I wasn't sure if I should bug you on a Saturday night." I'd searched for this information in the long list of residence rules, but hadn't found the answer.

"I'm here whenever any resident is upset and needs to talk about—"

"Oh, it's not like that! I had a question about the homework." Now I felt bad for disturbing her, but I'd been blocked about this assignment for days.

"Please, go ahead." Miss Naim collapsed in her chair and gestured for me to sit, too. With no makeup, and her curly hair in a messy bun, she didn't look much older than my sister, Zahra.

"Okay. My question is: Will we have to present these in class?" I felt my face go warm.

"No, it's for my eyes only," Miss Naim answered.

"Oh, okay. That's good. That's all I needed to ask." I stood.

"Zahabiya, if there is anything else . . . I'm here." She looked at me with concern. I had a sudden urge to flee.

"Thanks."

Back in my room, I sat before a blank piece of paper, pen in hand, stumped. Eventually, I began:

> *Ma famille est normal.*

What else? I decided to switch to English, so I could get this started. I could translate later.

> *I have an older sister, Zahra, who is in first year university.*
> *My father is a gastroenterologist. My mother—*

I didn't like to share personal things. I hated how people's expressions shifted from discomfort to pity when I did.

> *My mother My parents are from Bangalore, and we've travelled there many times, because my grandparents live there, as do many uncles, aunts, and cousins.*

What else would Miss Naim want to know?

> *My family is Muslim but not really very strict about it. I think of myself as more agnostic.*

Was Miss Naim a religious Muslim?

I am also a believer in animal rights and, therefore, I am mostly vegetarian.

I was probably going too far off-topic. I counted the words I'd written so far — fewer than a third of what was needed. I reread the passage, realizing that Miss Naim would likely notice my omission. People talked about mothers and fathers and siblings, not just fathers and sisters. I reminded myself this was a first draft and continued:

My mother died almost four years ago, of cancer. Everyone says, "Oh, you were so young!" I guess it's true. But I don't feel that way. When I realized she was dying, it was like I became older. Not adult, exactly, but not twelve.

I didn't have a lot of friends, but after she died, it felt like the ones I did have kind of drifted away. Or maybe it was me who drifted. Here at Thornton, maybe I'll have a fresh start.

My dad remarried last year. I guess he needed a fresh start, too.

What would Miss Naim think of all of that? It was way too much detail. And now I had to translate it all.

"*Watership Down* is about to start downstairs. Coming?" Mei rushed past me. I folded the sheets and slipped them into my desk drawer.

"Oh, hi."

"It's about nature, so you'll probably like it." Mei pulled a bag of candy out of her cupboard. "There's popcorn. And licorice." She dangled a red vine in front of my nose.

"I'll feel better if I make a dent in this work. Anyway, I've seen it already; my mom took me to see it when it came out." I grabbed the licorice from her hand.

"Oh, yeah? That's cool. Well . . . I'll see you later." Mei pushed out her lips and tilted her head to the right. I call this "side head," and it's usually accompanied by a sigh. But to her credit, she didn't sigh and left me alone.

On our second night here, Mei had talked about her life at home — constant fighting with her mother, a father who was always away at work — and then she'd asked me about my mom. I gave her the shortest summary: "She died, and my father remarried." And then I pretended to fall asleep.

Alone again, I pulled the French assignment out from my drawer. Sucking on the red vine I added:

> *Just before she died, Mom and I saw Watership Down at the Brock Cinema. It was just the two of us. She was really sick, but we'd both been looking forward to seeing it. She was practically a walking encyclopedia about birds and animals and insects, and she taught me everything I know about them.*

I put down my pen. My chest felt heavy, as though I'd inhaled molasses. Cancer. I hated the word. I also hated the way people said it in only hushed tones, the way they said "divorced" or "alcoholic." It was just a disease, and my mom hadn't done anything wrong to get it. She hadn't smoked. She'd gardened and hiked and jazzercized.

I folded the papers again. Maybe I'd translate them the next day or maybe I'd write something else entirely.

I heard a bird call from just outside, and from its song, I could tell it was probably a mourning dove. I went to the window and peered into the darkness. The bird called again, and it wasn't until it flapped its wing that I spied it on the lawn. *Was it injured?* I opened the window to get a better look.

My mom once told me the folklore about spotting a dove at night, that it means a deceased loved one is visiting you. I'd laughed, said it was ridiculous, but I could tell she liked the idea. Now I wished for it to be true.

"Mom?" I whispered. But I felt foolish. The dove flew away. I shut off the lamp and went downstairs to watch the movie.

Nahla

After two weeks of awful Thornton dinners — today was chicken fingers with mashed potatoes and soft carrots — Nahla realized that she'd have to find another way to feed herself. If she wanted to save money to get her own place, she could only afford one or two restaurant meals per week. She put in a request for a second hot plate to Gerry, who delivered one later that day.

"Found this in storage." He placed it onto the counter, his biceps bulging. The appliance took up most of the available space.

"Thank you."

"But listen, it can't be plugged in at the same time as the fridge and the other hot plate. Only two of the three can be plugged in at the same time." He gave her a demonstration, miming disconnecting and connecting the various appliances in tandem.

"I understand." Sensing he might linger, she took a few steps toward the door.

"The whole building is like that. You don't know how many times a Lean Cuisine in the basement microwave has shut off the lights. I swear I drop by here a couple of times a week to fix stupid things like that. But . . . I don't really mind coming by to help." He smiled and winked at her.

"Oh, that sounds unnecessary and inconvenient. Why don't you show me where the fuse box is, so I can reset it if needed?"

"You know how?" His eyes roved over her body as he sized her up.

"Of course. Our house in Montreal is very old. I've had to do it many times." She opened the door and led him out into the hallway. As she followed him down the two flights to the basement, she thought about the two-bedroom bungalow her family rented in Montreal. It had always galled her that Ali, six years her junior, had his own, albeit small, bedroom, while she and her two sisters slept in the living room, their beds converting to couches during the day. Thornton's tiny suite was like a mansion in contrast.

Nahla and Gerry passed a common area, where six girls, arranged in two rows, exercised in front of a large television, doing the *:20 Minute Workout*. With their matching leotards, headbands, and glossed lips, they looked like the dancers onscreen. She tried to remember their names. *Leesa from her class, and was it Melanie? No, Mallory. And Jessica and Barb*. She didn't recognize the other two. Gerry stood, transfixed, watching them. She prodded his elbow, and they continued down the hall.

Next door was a lounge, where a dozen girls squeezed onto two couches and the floor watching *Diff'rent Strokes*. She knew three of their names: Zahabiya, Mei, Preethi. The rest were probably from Margo's side. She glanced back and frowned. A chorus of laughter erupted from the room.

"Is it like this at the boys' dorm, too? The visible minority students in one room and the rest in another?"

"*Hmm.*" Gerry paused, taking a second look at the lounge, then backing up to the room where the girls jumped and stretched. Nahla waited between the two. "I never thought about it before. Maybe they just have different interests? You know, *Diff'rent Strokes* for different folks?" He laughed. Nahla didn't. They carried on to the utility room.

Leesa

"Gerry is such a perv. He just ogled us," Mallory huffed, as she reached left, in sync with the dancers onscreen.

"Really?" Leesa craned her neck to see, but he was already gone.

"Who was that with him?" Lauren asked, starting elbow twists. "Miss Naim?" Lauren was the number one worker to the grade 12 queen bee triad of Mallory, Jessica, and Leesa. Barb and Carrie were number two and three workers, respectively. Without anyone saying so, the queens took the front row during workout time, while their acolytes filled the second. Just a year ago, Leesa was in Lauren's spot, right behind the ousted Ashley.

"Yeah," Jessica replied, twisting to the left.

"She seems okay." Barb twisted right.

"Hipper . . . than the rest of our . . . decrepit teachers." Mallory bent to a flat back, chest heaving.

"True. I wish we had Miss McKinney as residence monitor on our side instead of Miss Jones." Carrie reached for her left foot.

47

"I've always thought Miss McKinney would be a good match for Mr. Stephenson. He's so hot!" Lauren touched her right toe.

"No, no, Miss McKinney's too tall for him. Mr. Wolfe's a way better match for her." Barb, reaching up to describe his height, fell out of step.

"Duh! Miss McKinney is a big lesbo!" Leesa lunged to the left. She intentionally used the word Jessica had called her the previous week.

"What, that's . . . not . . . true!" Mallory lunged to the right.

"Mallory, everyone knows Miss McKinney and Miss Robertson are, like, together." Jessica started jumping jacks.

"Miss Robertson, our gym teacher?" Carrie missed a beat and flapped her arms twice to catch up.

"You okay, Mallory?" Leesa asked. Mallory was not only winded, but also clearly out of the loop and probably struggling to save face in front of the other girls. Leesa followed the dancers into double-time jacks.

"It's . . . the . . . diet pills. Make . . . my heart . . . beat faster when . . . I . . . exercise. It's a . . . good thing . . . burns more . . . calories." Mallory slowed to a sway.

"Well, you look amazing." Leesa stretched skyward as the music slowed for the cool down. She glanced at Jessica, who reciprocated with an eye roll that expressed disapproval of Mallory's diet pills. Leesa took note. She was still the third in their triad, but she had an entire year to fix that.

Zahabiya

"Damn! Can you believe we've been here three weeks already? Actually, three weeks and three days. Seems much longer. A fuu-cking eternity." Mei stared at her calendar, filling in assignment due dates and absent-mindedly slipping gummy bears into her mouth.

"It hasn't been that bad, has it?" I was trying to stay positive.

"It's different for you. You chose to be here. Went out of your way to be here. My mother announced my eviction two days before school started and packed my bags for me. I'm still in shock."

"I guess that makes sense."

A few years ago, Zahra showed me a book that listed the stages of grief: shock and denial, anger, a couple stages I couldn't remember, acceptance. Mei seemed to be see-sawing between shock and anger.

Then, the stages hadn't made sense to me. I'd bumped around the empty house that first summer after Mom died; that was probably shock.

By the fall, everyone had moved on, including me. We returned to work and school, and then later Dad met Tara, and they married. There wasn't any anger or any of the other stages. How could you get angry at someone for dying of cancer? We'd all had to arrive at our destination — acceptance — quickly. We didn't have any other choice.

"I've been wondering: What really made you choose this place anyway? Do you have a wicked stepmother? Or just a masochistic streak?" Mei passed a candy bag to me, and I chose an emerald-green bear. I studied its tiny face, half-hoping it would answer the question for me.

"Tara isn't wicked. We're not best friends or anything, but she's okay." I bit the bear's little legs, its arms, then its torso. I stared at its indifferent, mute head.

"What's the problem, then?"

"Everything just . . . changed after they got married. And now my sister is away at university . . . but that's not why I applied to come here. I just . . . wanted to be able to *do* something? To take charge of something." I popped the green head into my mouth.

"I don't get it. How is this taking charge? Living under the dictatorship of bells? Sharing a bedroom when you had your own at home? I'm terrific company, but, I mean . . ."

"I dunno, it's like my house, my family, my life stopped being mine. I couldn't stay. I needed to be somewhere else. It's hard to explain." Trying to articulate it made me feel stupid.

"I get it." Mei gave me side head, this time with a sigh.

The study bell trilled, warning that we had five minutes to get to our desks with our books. Mei gathered up her calendar and binder and dropped them onto her desk with a thud.

"I'm studying on my bed today. The chair is so uncomfortable." I crossed my arms over my chest.

"Ha! You big rebel, you."

Nahla

Study period annoyed Nahla. She had to walk the old wing twice between 7:30 p.m. and 9 p.m., interrupting her own lesson prep and grading time. And the list of rules she was supposed to enforce was stricter than even her own parents could have devised:

1. *Students must sit at their desk during study period.*
2. *Study period is a silent ninety-minute session. Students may not work in pairs or groups during this time.*
3. *No eating or drinking or gum chewing during study period.*
4. *Headphones may not be worn during study period.*
5. *Students may not ask dormitory monitors for study help during study period.*
6. *Students may wear casual dress or uniforms during study period.*
7. *The common phones must not be used/answered during study period.*

Over the month, she'd noticed that the girls mostly complied with the rules, which was good because she felt silly policing teenagers' homework time. When there were so-called infractions, she half-heartedly redirected the students and moved on.

She did like getting a quick look at the girls' spaces. The rooms on her side were long and narrow with built-in wardrobes and two or three beds and desks. Whoever had converted the building in the 1930s had divided it into mostly similar rectangles, but some were slightly irregular, with odd little alcoves or rounded corners.

The girls had individualized bedding and were allowed posters on their walls. Most had male pop stars (Duran Duran and The Police were the favourites, with a few Culture Club and Wham! mixed in) or landscape scenes from their countries of origin. Her own walls were still bare.

Last week, the Bell telephone guy finally came to hook up a line, and she'd tried calling home twice, each time getting someone — *her father? Her brother?* — who'd immediately hung up on her. She shook the thought away and continued her rounds.

Near the end of the hallway now, she passed the first-floor bath-room and heard a flush. She was supposed to herd the girl back to her desk, but she refused that kind of meddling. She reached the last room and looked in. Mei frowned over a notebook, while Zahabiya lounged on her bed, reading. Nahla felt a pang of pity for the girl, recalling her recent assignment. While her report about her family had meandered, her French writing was excellent, and she'd marked it 9/10.

"Zahabiya, you're supposed to be at your desk."

"I concentrate better when I'm more comfortable."

"Yep, these chairs are pretty hard," Mei chimed in.

"Fine," Nahla whispered and carried on.

When she reached the upstairs triad, all three girls were sitting on Jessica's bed, focused on a fashion magazine and sharing a bag of chips.

"Girls . . ." Nahla interrupted them.

"Sorreeee." Mallory returned to her desk and offered Nahla a smug smile. Jessica followed, muttering about being treated like kids.

"What-ev-er," Leesa said, rolling her *r* in an odd way. She sat, then swung her legs up onto her desk, then looked back over her shoulder at Nahla. Their antics were childish, and Nahla barely cared whether they did their homework, and yet a sudden anger rose up in her.

"You all have detentions tomorrow." Nahla's heart raced, and she knew that she'd just stumbled into a clumsy power struggle.

"What! Like, that's not fair!" Jessica exclaimed.

Nahla turned on her heels and rushed through the rest of the floor.

Back in her suite, she shut the door and opened her window, then lit a Marlboro, exhaling out the window. *What was it about Leesa, Mallory, and Jessica that so bothered her?* Of course, they were arrogant, but she'd encountered spoiled, popular girls before, girls who believed themselves to be superior because their families had money. But something about this felt different, worse. She replayed the interaction in her mind — their dismissive gazes and gestures. And then it hit her — Leesa had tried to mimic *her* accent with her "whatever."

She inhaled deeply on her cigarette and expelled smoke out the window, batting at the air to make sure it all went outside. She extinguished it and marked ten assignments. When the 9 p.m. bell rang, she realized she'd neglected to do her second loop around the hallways. *Would anyone have noticed?*

She lit another cigarette at her window and stared out. The back door shut, and someone walked toward the road. She squinted, spying golden tresses bobbing up and down in the darkness. She pulled Mademoiselle Leblanc's grey notebook from her bag, tracing her finger along the entries. *Was Leesa the mysterious* L? *And were* M *and* J *her roommates?* She stood at the window to see if the girl would return, but after five minutes, she gave up and resumed her marking. It wasn't her problem; curfew wasn't for another hour.

Leesa

"How was your summer?" he finally asked. Except for their stilted "hellos," they'd both been quiet until they'd pulled over under the large maple on a country road a few miles out of town, their usual spot. He tended to be nervous until they had privacy, so Leesa was accustomed to the silence. Still, it had been many months since they'd met in this way, and when she'd phoned him from the manor's basement phone nook that Wednesday at 7:15 p.m., as she'd done ever since they'd started, she hadn't really expected him to pick up.

The sun had set, and she couldn't make out his expression in the car's dim interior. *Was he glad to see her?* They'd agreed — well, actually, he'd decided — that they had to stop meeting last spring, after she'd told him about Leblanc, and how she'd been asking questions about where Leesa went most Wednesdays from 9 p.m. to 10 p.m.

They'd also spent some Saturday evenings and Sunday afternoons together, but Leblanc hadn't seemed to notice that. Leesa had tried to convince him that the stupid bitch would soon get distracted by another student, but he'd been worried. She'd suspected that he was really just growing bored with her and was using Leblanc's prying as an excuse to let her down easy.

"It was okay. I met someone — a guy in Paris — and we dated most of the summer," she said with an exaggerated shrug. She didn't add that Gilbert was a janitor — *would he find that funny?* — or that all four of their "dates" were rushed make-outs during his shifts, culminating in her mother catching them naked in her bedroom, and Gilbert being redeployed to an office building in Sèvres.

"Well, I can't say I'm happy to hear that, but we were broken up." His tone was smooth, unruffled, maybe an act. *And did he want to get back together now?*

"It was just fun. Nothing serious." She turned and looked out the passenger-side window. The farmer's fallow field was a grey empty space at night. During the day, a single horse sometimes grazed near the road. They'd named him Charlie, their inside joke.

"I worried about you. It was the first time we hadn't talked in, what, two years?"

"Two and a half." She *had* missed their talks, which had begun near the end of grade 9, when he'd found her alone and crying after school. He'd shown concern, and she'd told him about her parents' divorce. How amazing it had felt when he'd passed her a tissue and shared about his own family troubles. She could tell that he was listening to her, really listening. After that, she found a way to cross paths with him as often as she could.

In time, and without discussing it, they started taking long drives and walks together, always far from the campus. By the beginning of grade 10, they'd both confessed deeper feelings, and he'd said they had to stop before things got "inappropriate." For two weeks, she stayed away, as he'd requested, but knew, deep in her heart, that it wasn't what either of them wanted. His resolve didn't last.

She could tell him anything, everything, and he'd listen. It was the best part. They'd hold hands, talk, kiss, talk, grope, talk. They had sex for the first time right before she told him about Leblanc's questioning. And then a second time after. And then he broke up with her, saying he was afraid Leblanc would figure it out and report him.

"I missed you this summer. I kinda wish I hadn't worried so much about Leblanc. And I wish we hadn't waited a month into school to reconnect."

"Why didn't you give me a sign?"

"I wasn't sure if you'd come back after the summer . . . different."

"Well," she heard the vulnerability in his voice and swatted his arm, "you're the one who's different. What's with the moustache?"

"You like it? My barber says it's trendy now."

"It's not bad."

"I'll shave it off if you don't like it." He smiled and reached for her hand, and she let him take it. She pulled him close, and they kissed.

Forty minutes later, he dropped her a block from the manor, and she made it inside the front lobby a second before the 10 p.m. bell. Out of breath from the short jog, she collided with the Indian girl.

"Sorry! Hey, are you okay?"

"Fine . . . why?"

"I dunno. You look . . . flushed. Or something."

Leesa turned and checked her reflection in the lobby's mirror. Her hair was mussed, her cheeks pink.

"I'm fine." She headed for the stairs, combing her fingers through her hair.

In their room, Mallory and Jessica were changing into pyjamas.

"Where've you been?" Mallory asked. "You disappeared after study period."

"I just went for a walk. I like to clear my head in the evening sometimes."

"Wait . . . you look different." Jessica studied her.

"Oh my God! She has sex hair! Jessica, doesn't she have sex hair?" Mallory squealed.

"*Shhh*," Leesa said, shutting their door. "Listen, I did go for a walk . . . and then . . . I ran into someone . . ."

Leesa cringed inwardly. *What was she getting into?*

"You ran into someone?" Jessica asked.

"Whowhowho? Tell us everything. Every single detail," Mallory demanded. Leesa hesitated. Of course, she knew she couldn't tell the truth. But now she had to tell them something.

"Um, Jason Anderson . . . near the soccer field. We . . . hung out . . . and made out a bit . . ."

"Why didn't you tell us you two were an item?" Mallory asked.

"Because we aren't. We've only talked and flirted a bit. It was sort of a surprise meeting him tonight. Totally unexpected. And listen. You can't tell anyone. No one can know."

"But why?" Jessica asked, eyes wide, clearly enjoying the drama.

Leesa hesitated, thinking hard. "Because . . . he's in a relationship."

"Well, that's not going to work." Mallory shook her head.

"He says it's over and he plans to break up with her, but she's really vulnerable, and he's . . . he's afraid she might fall apart if he does." The lie tumbled from Leesa's mouth; it was a version of a whispered phone conversation she'd overheard her father make years ago, before the divorce.

"Who's the girlfriend? Someone from Thornton?" Mallory asked.

"No, a townie."

"Oh, right. He's a *day student*," Jessica muttered. "Day student" was code for "middle class."

"*Uh-huh*." This wasn't the best lie. She did have a little crush on Jason, but he wasn't exactly the kind of boy that would ensure her solid — or advanced — standing in their group.

"What are you going to do?" Jessica asked.

"I'm okay with playing it cool for now. And maybe this was just a one-time thing."

"He is kind of a nerd," Mallory said.

"True, but cute, right?" Could she drag this out a while? It might be helpful to have a cover if things continued.

57

"Right, even if he is a brain, the secret affair might be fun," Jessica agreed.

"Promise not to say anything? This stays among the three of us?"

"Of course. Just the three of us." Mallory nodded, her lips curling into a smile.

"I really hope Rodney dumps Ashley's ass soon, so that the two of you can hook up. He's a way better option for you," Jessica counselled. "I wonder if we can speed that along somehow?"

"That would be way better. In the meantime, I might just have myself a little fun." Leesa flopped down on her bed.

Zahabiya

The library was where I felt most at home at Thornton. In contrast to the main building's sombre architecture, it was newly constructed, with floor-to-ceiling windows that let in the early October sun.

When I'd come for my interview the previous spring, I'd walked into the building, my nervousness dissipating as I breathed in the books, the stacks wafting hope and possibility.

Then, I could only guess at the lives of the neatly uniformed students hanging out there. I'd imagined them to be more sophisticated than the kids at Brock High School. I knew better now. They were just more travelled and rich. They clung to the same types of cliques as everyone else.

I still wasn't part of one, but Lavinia had continued to be my "tour guide" and introduced me to people. Now, she waved to me from a desk in the middle section of the library. Around her were Cyril, from my dining hall table, Jason, a guy in some of my classes, and Marie, a girl from across the hall who'd I'd said hello to a few times.

"Hey! Join us! You met my little Trini brother, Cyril?"

"Yeah, we sit together in the dining hall." He looked over coolly, in a way that told me he wasn't impressed with me. I couldn't blame him. Since the first day of classes, I'd barely acknowledged his presence and had instead tried to make friends with Ashley, who'd warmed to me after I'd let slip that Leesa had scammed me and Mei to move downstairs.

"And this guy here is the Big Brain of the school, Jason? And Marie, Thornton's resident artiste," Lavinia said.

"Hi." I gave them an awkward little wave.

"Everyone, this is Zahabiya, lover of animals and ice cream. She's also super smart, sweet fifteen, and already in grade 12."

"I'll be sixteen in December," I hastened to add.

"Don't you love how Lav introduces us?" Marie's hazel eyes studied me with a measured curiosity. Funny, I'd assumed Marie was a jock, not an artist, with her tall, strong frame, messy ponytail, and always-askew tie.

"Accurate, though, right?" Lavinia asked, hands on hips.

I took the empty chair beside Lavinia, avoiding the seat across from Cyril.

"Hey, Zahabiya." Jason turned to Lavinia. "We have French, English, and art together."

"I'm thinking about dropping art. I'm ahead a credit and I can barely keep up with all the homework."

"Not a bad idea," Marie said.

"Find something else to drop. Art's a bird course. An easy A."

"Everything is an easy A for you," Cyril said.

"I do like it." I got an $A+$ on my first assignment, and Mr. Stephenson had written a note on the back, "Excellent technique, Z! Welcome to Thornton!" Except for Miss Naim, he was the only teacher who'd made an effort to be encouraging.

"I liked your drawing from last week. It was a pug, right? Pugsquisite." Pugsquisite. What a dork. But also a good-looking dork. Lavinia raised her eyebrows. I smiled uncomfortably.

"Thanks. It's my neighbour's dog, Stanley." I turned away from Jason's gaze. "So, Marie, how come you're not taking art — since you're into art?"

"Into art! She's a genius. Show her your notebook." Before Marie could pass it over, Lavinia had pulled it from her hands and laid it out in front of me. Something told me to wait for Marie's nod before opening its cover and turning its pages. She shrugged her assent, maybe out of modesty, or because no one could say no to Lavinia.

"My dad got me a private art tutor in town. She's from my community and she's won a bunch of awards. I got permission to get my art credits that way." Marie picked at her down-to-the-quick fingernails.

"It's obvious why." Lavinia pointed to the notebook. Inside, there were photos and pen-and-ink drawings of Thornton's students and buildings.

"These are really good!" I meant it, but I also said it because I sensed that Marie had a wall up.

"I take photos, then try to draw them sometimes, but mostly I take photos." Marie brushed off the compliment.

"Where's this from?" Cyril pointed to a photo of an old house surrounded by tall trees.

"My reserve, two hours north of here." She looked at me, her expression hard to read. "I'm Indian."

"Me, too!" I looked more closely at Marie's features, growing confused. I heard Cyril's quiet scoff.

"No, girl, not *East* Indian like you, First Nations. Native." Lavinia laughed. Marie rolled her eyes.

"Oh, right. Sorry, Marie," I said, my face growing warm. I almost blurted that I hadn't ever met someone Native before, but stopped myself before putting my foot in my mouth a second time.

"You know, the kind Columbus found when he got lost on his way to India." Jason grinned at me.

"And don't forget he found us, too, in the process," Cyril said, pointing to Lavinia and himself. "That dude needed a better map." I noticed Cyril's cheeky smile for the first time.

"That's funny." I was a little out of my depth and tried to keep up with their banter. I made a mental note to find a book about Native people and maybe another about the Caribbean.

I turned the page of Marie's book.

"Oh, hey, here's Lavinia," I said. Marie's drawing captured her confident spirit through her wide smile and upward tilt of her chin.

"That is good." Jason peered over my shoulder, so close I could feel his warm breath on my cheek.

Just then, I looked up to see Leesa gazing at me from the detention area, a section of tables about thirty feet away. Her roommates, Mallory and Jessica, also seemed to be staring. My stomach tightened, and I nodded in their direction.

"You friends with them?" Marie asked, her tone telling me she wasn't.

"Nope."

"Why are they looking at us, then?" Marie asked.

"Who knows why those girls do anything. Snobs," Cyril muttered.

"They're superficial. It's the problem with being filthy rich," Jason said, then looked to Marie. "No offence."

"Hey, before my dad's business took off, I would have needed a scholarship, too. Don't put me in the same category as those bitches."

"Right, it's not just about having money, it's about thinking you're better than everyone else because you do," Lavinia added.

I thought about that. In Brock, my family was among the most well-off, although not on the same scale as the rich kids here. I hoped I'd never made friends back home feel inferior.

I turned away from our watchers, distracted by a tickly sensation of an orange ladybug crawling up my forearm. I examined the tiny beetle's spots.

After a moment, she lifted away, and I followed her flight toward the detention area. Leesa was still looking our way, but now it was clear that she was focused on Jason, who'd returned to his seat.

He and Cyril were in the midst of a conversation about the distinctions between Caribbean and Canadian wealth.

"Even though our parents can afford to send us here, we'll always be seen as second class in this country. Colonial subjects." Cyril shrugged. Now I felt really awful for having snubbed him, for trying to fit in with the white girls at our table.

"True." Lavinia nodded. "At least in this school, race trumps everything."

"I think it's like that for families like mine who immigrated to Canada. And, of course, for Native people, too. We'll never be seen as equal," I said. Cyril made eye contact and looked at me with less guardedness than before.

Marie ignored my comment. "God, they're still staring!"

I felt the ladybug's six tiny feet again, this time on my hand.

"Yeah, I think Leesa is actually staring at Jason," I said, glancing her way.

"At me?" Jason squinted in her direction, which caused Mallory and Jessica to giggle. Leesa smiled and turned away demurely.

"Weird," Cyril said.

"No! It's interesting," Lavinia said. "Jason is being selected to join Thornton's top tier. Ha! You might get a nice all-expenses-paid trip to Paris out of it."

"Never in a million years." Jason shook his head, cheeks reddening.

"I should take you outside." The ladybug now rested on my thumb.

"Are you talking to a bug?" Marie asked, eyebrows raised.

"Is it 'bugging' you?" Jason joked.

"But does it talk back?" Cyril asked. "That's the question."

"I wish," I joked back.

I cradled the ladybug in my palms to the library's outside door. At first, she didn't seem to want to go. I knew ladybugs were seen as symbols of good luck, so I waited for her to be ready. After a bit, her two sets of wings unfolded, and she flew away, free, with the breeze.

Nahla

The copy machine squeaked and clunked, coming to a dismal stop. Nahla pulled at a jammed piece of paper, but unwilling, it tore in half.

"Son-of-a . . ."

"That's an appropriate name for it." Michael Stephenson laughed and went to work, pulling open various doors and latches, liberating the stuck page.

"Thanks." She pressed the green button, and the photocopier resumed its mechanical hum.

"These mandatory midmonth tests are a waste of time. Especially for art." He shook his head and held up his pages to be copied.

"It takes forever to mark them. Plus, there are the assignments. And the class prep!" She extracted the last warm pile from the tray.

"Everyone is overwhelmed since Lowery came on a few years back," he said, feeding his own test papers into the machine. "You could switch to multiple choice, like I do. Then administer the test at the beginning of class and make the students swap and mark them. Then you just have to record grades."

"I would have never thought of that." Although they'd made small talk many times over the past two months, she only now noticed the distinctive blue-green shade of his eyes. He looked like an older version of Tom Cruise but with a five o'clock shadow.

"It's not technically against the rules, but I wouldn't broadcast it, if you know what I mean. We've all had to find time savers like this."

"Have you been teaching here long?" Under the thin material of his long-sleeved shirt were the outlines of strong shoulders, pectoral muscles. She averted her gaze, hoping he hadn't noticed her long study of his chest.

"Five years now. But I'm an artist, a painter — that's my real passion, and this job pays the bills. And you: How's your first term going so far?"

"It's hard to believe it's November already. It's been tough. Teaching seven grade levels, plus all the girls in my wing of the residence . . ." Her gut churned as she silently added, *moving to a new town, and except for one brief chat with my sisters that abruptly ended when my father came home, radio silence from my family.*

"How's it been living in Sylvie Leblanc's old place?"

"It's comfortable. Gerry did a great job fixing it up." She gestured to Gerry, who was filling his coffee mug.

"Thanks." He turned and saluted her like a soldier.

"It's odd, but even after five years, I barely knew her," Michael said.

"She wasn't all that friendly. Always seemed angry about something." Gerry shrugged.

Did the old French teacher have any friends? Nahla held the photocopies to her chest, a wave of emotion cresting: hazin jidana, si triste, so sad.

"With her sudden death, you really must have had to hit the ground running in September."

She took a breath, focused on Michael and Gerry again.

"I did. But I have her teaching materials, thank God." The grey notebook came to mind just then, but something told her not to mention it.

"And how are you handling the students? Most are great, but some can be challenging, right?" Michael shook his head and smiled.

"Well, there's one who gets under my skin. Leesa Allen. Grade 12, long blonde hair, arrogant attitude. Know her?"

"I think so . . . " He tapped his chin. "Taught her a couple of years back."

"She's a contradiction. My top student, fluent in French. But she spends most of the class talking to her friends. So disrespectful." She shuddered slightly.

"My theory is that the ones with good, loving families are easy. And the ones with bad family situations are not," Gerry said, surprising Nahla with his serious tone. She was used to him cracking jokes and making suggestive comments.

"That sounds about right," Michael said.

"*Hmm*. Leesa certainly doesn't show her vulnerable side."

"I guess you can't judge a book by its cover, right?" Michael countered.

"I should try to be more understanding. Thanks for those insights, guys."

"No problem," Gerry said on his way out the door.

"Always happy to help a newbie." Michael patted her shoulder, the touch spreading heat down her arm. "Hey . . . some of us — the younger crew — get together once a term. We were thinking tomorrow night. You should come."

"Hellooo." Maeve sauntered in with Frederick Wolfe. Standing side by side, they looked like siblings, with their light skin and similarly lanky frames.

"Maeve, Frederick, are we still having our 'quarterly meeting' tomorrow? I was just telling Nahla." He rested his hand on her shoulder once again. Nerve endings lit up like sparklers all the way down the length of her arm to her fingertips.

"Oh, yeah. I meant to tell you, Nahla! It's a last-minute thing. I so need to blow off steam — *gah*!" Her eyes popped out, and she mimed her head exploding. "We're meeting at our place."

"Great! See you all later, then." Michael took his photocopies and left.

"Can you make it, Nahla?"

"I'd love to."

"How about you, Frederick?"

"I'll try to come for a bit." He emptied his mail cubby and headed out. "See you later."

"He won't come," Maeve said in a stage whisper. "He's married, and they have a three-year-old and a newborn. But, hey, did I pick up on something between you and Michael just now?"

"Oh, no, no! I'm sure he was . . . just being friendly."

"I think you like him," Maeve singsonged, lining up her pages on the machine.

"Maeve are *you* interested in him? You'd make a good couple." Nahla didn't want to step on her new friend's toes.

"Oh, gosh no! Not my type." Maeve waved the idea away. "But just look at you! You're obviously smitten!"

"Oh, no. No, I'm not." Nahla shook her head, rubbing her warm cheeks. But Maeve was right. Her body was light and tingly. She hadn't felt this way since Baashir.

"Okay, okay. Um, just one thing about tomorrow . . ."

"Oh, yeah, what can I bring?"

" . . . um . . . whatever you like to drink."

"Sounds good." Nahla rushed away before Maeve could start up her teasing again.

Back in her flat, Nahla reviewed Sylvie's test questions, considering how to convert them into multiple-choice format. But soon she was distracted by the memory of Michael's touch. She closed her eyes, gave in to the sensation.

What does it mean?

a) *He likes her.*
b) *Canadian men touch women in casual ways, so it means nothing.*
c) *She likes him.*
d) *It's been almost a year since Baashir, and it feels good to be touched.*
e) *All of the above.*

Baashir. Her first real boyfriend and heartbreak. He'd been her teaching assistant in third year. Both shy, their initial flirtation was through extended intellectual conversations about the readings during his office hours. These talks moved to the campus coffee shop, then to the cinema, their rationale that the films were vaguely related to the course content.

They kept their relationship secret, even after he was no longer her instructor because her parents couldn't find out she was dating. But a part of her knew his family wouldn't approve of someone from outside their community, even if they were both Muslim. In the end, he couldn't (*or wouldn't?*) oppose an arranged marriage to a second cousin in Pakistan. Her parents, too, had been busy attempting matches for her, but she'd held them off with the excuse that she needed to finish her education first.

She'd been miserable for months after the breakup, losing her appetite and her excitement for French literature. But there was also a measure of relief; she'd had to tell 101 lies to be with Baashir. Without that burden, she was calmer at home, an ease that came from being a "good daughter." And now, she'd lost that ease. She doubted she'd ever get it back.

Nahla felt a rustle and a cool breeze. Of course, when she looked around, she saw nothing. This had been happening for two months already, so she took a deep breath, steeled herself. Her teta back in

Lebanon used to talk to spirits. She tried to remember how she went about it.

"Hello, Sylvie. Is there something you need?"

She waited, felt foolish. But then heard a voice, raspy but clear, "Merci, ma chérie. Mais pas tout de suite."

Nahla sat like a statue. *Not yet?* She waited, the air returned to normal, and she sensed she was alone again. She thrust open her window and lit a cigarette.

Leesa

Leesa followed Jason into the library after lunch on Saturday. She'd tried to talk to him a few times over the previous weeks, but he'd always seemed in a hurry. During meals, even, their interactions were brief, cordial. *Was he just shy around girls? Or was it her?*

This was probably a huge waste of her time. Sure, she was halfway interested in Jason, and he was handy for keeping Mallory and Jessica off the trail when she slipped away in the evenings. She hoped those dates would continue, but after last year's breakup, who knew?

Maybe, with a little tweaking (Jason needed a haircut and better shoes at the very least), he could fit in with her crowd enough to stop her being a fifth wheel to Mallory, Jessica, and their boyfriends. Or worse, a seventh if they ever made up with Ashley.

Jason sat at his usual table in the library's centre. Today he wasn't with his geek buddies. With the afternoon off, most students had left the school, as though evacuating a building on fire.

"Doing homework?" she asked, then silently chastised herself for her boring opener. His lack of interest was chipping away at her confidence.

"Yeah, just need to get a couple of things done." He barely looked up from his French textbook.

"Hey, if you ever want help with French, je parle français."

"Thanks, I'm all right."

"Mind if I sit here?"

"Yeah, no problem." He scribbled something into his notebook. Needing a prop, she pulled out her French textbook. She felt pathetic. Two minutes passed.

"Actually," he said, "I am a little confused by this. Have I used the correct temporal preposition here?" Leesa shifted to the seat next to his.

"Um, temporal preposition?" She barely paid attention in class, coasting on her oral and written fluency. She leaned over his notebook, making sure that he could smell the scent of her strawberry shampoo.

"It's this sentence here." He slanted away, passed her the book, and pointed to the passage in question.

" . . . est ouvert depuis le 1er novembre." She read aloud, "Yes, that sounds perfect." She put her hand over his arm, squeezed.

"Okay, thanks." He slid his arm away.

"So, do you live near here?"

"Not far . . . Look, I really need to get this stuff done."

"Oh, yeah, no problem! I'm happy to help with French any time you need." She blushed, collected her things, and hurried out of the library. Why were her overtures being rebuffed? She was one of the prettiest, smartest, and most popular girls at school.

She considered a fake breakup story for Mallory and Jessica, who everyday asked about the relationship. Tonight, she could tell them that she was having second thoughts, that he was a terrible kisser, or something. And then she could figure out how to find someone new, maybe one of the more promising jocks.

As she passed the parking lot, she saw her real boyfriend getting into his car, and her mood lifted.

"Hey, there!" she called.

"Oh, hello, Leesa. How are you today?" He gave her a stiff wave. She knew he was being weirdly formal on purpose.

"I have a question for you!"

"All righty!" He lowered his passenger-side window. She leaned in.

"Can you meet me at our regular spot in ten minutes?" Even though the parking lot was deserted, she kept her voice low.

"Yeah, but it's gotta be quick. I've got somewhere to be in half an hour." He checked his watch.

"Then tonight instead? Curfew is at 11 p.m."

"Sorry, Leesa. I've got a family thing. How about tomorrow?"

A family thing? He never talked about his family anymore — *had something changed at home? And hadn't he just said on Wednesday that he wanted to go to a hotel with her?* Maybe he was full of crap, was stringing her along, was going to dump her again.

"What the hell?" Leesa felt her throat tighten, heard her pitch rise.

"Leesa, we can see each other some other time—"

"Fine, then, let's just forget it." She stomped away from the car, the gale force of two rejections adding speed. She yelled over her shoulder, "This is never going to work. Maybe we should just end this once and for all."

She'd hoped he'd follow her in his car, but when she turned around, he'd driven off in the opposite direction. Her eyes welled up. She held it together until she reached her empty dorm room. Then she cried for him, for her family, herself, for being so alone. She remembered going to Mademoiselle Leblanc years ago when she was like this, and for the briefest moment she wondered if she should talk to Miss Naim. *But what could she say? How could she explain these feelings?* She dried her tears, and, bit by bit, a numb resolve, like cotton batten, filled her. She washed her face and reapplied her eyeliner and mascara.

Zahabiya

"I keep telling them, year after year, that they need to stock Black beauty products at this drug store, but they never listen." Lavinia pointed at the shampoo shelf and shook her head.

"So, Lav, I saw something odd today." Marie's tone was conspiratorial.

I looked up from a row away, where I stood in front of a small-town selection of maxi pads, a single brand of the chunkiest kind, no wings.

"Oh, yeah?"

"Leesa Allen was freaking out at a guy in the parking lot today. Like, freaking out."

"At who?" Lavinia asked.

"I'm not sure, exactly," Marie said. "After she stormed off, he drove away, so I didn't get a good enough look—"

"Is she dating someone?" Lavinia asked. "I can never keep up with Thornton soap operas, but I have to say, I enjoy watching them."

"I thought she liked Jason?" I asked, not sure if I should join their conversation. I had a feeling that until Lavinia had taken me under her wing, it had been just the two of them.

"I don't know. She yelled, 'Fine! Let's just forget about it!' and then said something about ending things."

"Girl, you've got the what, when, and where, but you're missing the why and who." Lavinia shook her head.

"True. Anyway, Leesa Allen is not worth a minute more of our time." Marie walked to the back of the store.

Marie's words made me think of that day, weeks ago, when I ran into Leesa coming in late. She'd seemed off somehow. Maybe it was connected with what Marie had seen. She'd probably been rushing back from being out with some guy that night. *Why was she flirting with Jason while also being with someone else?*

I let the gossip go and refocused on the pads and my mental math.

My period had lasted a full month, and I was almost out of supplies. I could have called my dad for a little extra money, but I was intent on dealing with his ridiculously low allowance with stubborn self-reliance. By some miracle, I'd managed to save a dollar a week, so I had twelve bucks on me. But I was supposed to join the girls for fries after the pharmacy, so I'd need to put aside a few dollars for that. I could afford one package of maxis for now.

"That time of the month?" Marie sidled up to me.

"Yeah. It's been a long month." I confessed my unusual menstrual issues to Marie and Lavinia.

"Must be the stress of first term," Lavinia said.

"Yeah, mine didn't show up this month at all. Must be stress."

"Or maybe you're pregnant. Might that be the reason?" Lavinia kept a straight face, but then they both cracked up.

"I'm just messing with her," Lavinia explained to me.

"Inside joke. I have a loser love life." Marie shook her head.

"Oh, yeah?" I asked, curious to know if it was as loserish as my own. I knew Lavinia was interested in a grade 13 student, Paul Jeffrey, and they'd teased me about Jason, but I didn't know anything about Marie.

"It's the classic doomed love story. Like Romeo and Juliet. She loves this boy, but her father is super protective."

"More like a super snob. He wants to keep me and Rob apart. He's worried I'll end up 'pregnant at age sixteen with some riff-raff's baby' — his words."

"And your mom?" I asked.

"She died giving birth to me. At age sixteen. With some riff-raff's baby."

"Oh," I said in a low voice. "Sorry."

"It's okay. I'm used to it. And anyway, I told him I'd never let a guy get me pregnant. I got on the pill a long time ago. I take care of myself."

"And rubbers! You never know about STDs," Lavinia said.

"That's true." Of course, I'd thought about these things, but only theoretically. I still hadn't kissed a boy yet, let alone had sex with one. But when it happened — and I hoped it would happen sometime soon — I'd make sure to not ruin my life by getting pregnant.

"Condoms should be free," Marie said. Then she pointed at my pads. "Pads and tampons should be free. They're all essential health items. It's sexist that they're not."

"I'd vote for that," I said.

"True enough. Hey, you two done? I'm starving. Let's go get some fries. Or maybe poutine! That's the Canadian thing, right?" Lavinia headed to the cash.

"I could go for some poutine," Marie said.

At the counter, I silently recounted the money I had left, calculating how much more poutine would cost. I stuffed the meagre bills and coins back into my wallet when I noticed Marie watching me from the door.

We crossed the intersection. I stopped to pet a beagle sitting on the sidewalk, leash-less and person-less. Marie bent beside me to rub his ears.

"What is it with you people, always touching animals?" Lavinia shook her head.

"He's not wearing a collar." I looked into the dog's watery eyes. He yawned wide. "But he doesn't seem stressed."

"Oh, sweetie, are you lost?" Marie asked.

"Toby! Tobeeeeee!" We turned to see Jason running down Main Street, leash and collar swinging from his hand. Cyril followed, a few feet behind.

"I didn't know you had a dog." Jason hadn't mentioned it in the few brief and awkward conversations we'd had.

"He's my neighbours'. I walk him a few days a week."

"He's got a talent for slipping out of his collar when Jason's not watching," Cyril said.

The dog lay down on the sidewalk, seemingly satisfied with himself.

"Hey guys, we're going to the Quinte. Wanna come?" Lavinia asked, exchanging glances with me, as though I was part of whatever plan she was hatching. I held my thin plastic drug store bag behind my back.

"Sounds good." Jason looked at Toby. "I'll have to take him home first."

"I think you can bring him. They just enclosed their patio in one of those clear plastic tents," Cyril said.

"You want to bring a dog to a restaurant? And won't it be cold?" Lavinia protested.

"You'll be fine!" Marie linked her arm through Lavinia's. "They have heat lamps."

We got a patio table with high stools beside the sidewalk, and Jason tied Toby to a table leg. I studied the menu. A plate of fries was two fifty, while poutine was five.

"I think I'll just have fries." I put down my menu and sipped water. The others had ordered colas.

"Yeah, me, too. I only have a few bucks on me." Jason dug into his pocket, pulling out a wrinkled two-dollar bill and three singles.

"Listen, it's my treat today," Marie said, looking at me.

"Oh, thanks . . . but I'm okay." I unzipped my coat to let out the flush of heat that came with her offer.

"No, really, let me. My dad upped my allowance to fifteen per week, plus he lets me use his credit card."

"My parents still insist on ten, so that I'll 'learn responsibility with money.'" Lavinia warmed her hands near the heater. I imagined the relief I'd feel with ten dollars a week.

"Still? I argued inflation with my parents and got twelve fifty," Cyril said.

"Well, you're both lucky, because my 'allowance' consists of what I earn from walking Toby. Plus, I do relief shifts at the bakery, but those paycheques are for university," Jason said. "What about you, Zahabiya? Your parents stingy or generous?"

"My father chose the bottom of the range," I said, looking down at the patio stones. "Three. Maybe I should find a dog to walk, too." The waiter arrived, and Marie ordered us five poutines. I smiled weakly at her.

"Wow, I can't get over your three bucks," Lavinia said. "I don't know anyone who gets fewer than five."

"Three bucks can't go very far." Cyril gave me a sympathetic look.

"He's mad at me." I explained my secret Thornton application process and his half-hearted assent.

"Girl, that sucks. But it sounds like your dad didn't want to let you go. He must really love you," Lavinia consoled.

"But three bucks!" I felt simultaneously like a spoiled brat and a victim.

"What about your mother?" Jason broached.

"She died a few years ago," I answered, trying on Marie's coolness. But I'd just taken a sip of water, and it went down the wrong way. Jason patted my back while I coughed and hid my face in my napkin.

"Wow, a dead mother *and* a pissed-off father." Marie appraised me as though putting together a puzzle that had been missing some of its pieces. I nodded.

Thankfully, the orders arrived. Cyril pulled his bottle of hot sauce from his pocket and shook it over his plate.

"Could I try some?" I asked.

"I thought you didn't like spice?" He raised an eyebrow.

"It never hurts to try new things." I smiled and took the bottle. I put a cautious dime-sized blob in the corner of my plate while Cyril watched with amusement.

"Be careful, that stuff burns," Jason warned.

I dipped the edge of my fork into the sauce, speared a fry, and took a bite.

"It's good." The prickly heat worked alongside the salty gravy. But more importantly, I could tell from Cyril's slight smile that I'd made up for my past mistakes.

Leesa, Mallory, and Jessica passed us on the sidewalk. Toby barked once, and I tensed.

"Hey, Jason," Leesa called, "did you finish the French assignment?"

"Yeah, it's all done," he said politely, then picked up his fork.

"Oh, really glad to hear that. Let me know if you need more help." Leesa knocked on the clear plastic sheet that enclosed the patio.

The girls continued walking, and I overheard Jessica ask, "Okay, Leesa, that was weird. What's the story?"

"Did you see what they're eating? That's, like, two thousand calories per plate!" Mallory said.

"She's an enigma," Marie said, once the girls were far enough away.

"I thought she was seeing someone?" Lavinia set her fork down, plate still half-full. "Or according to your gossip, just dumped someone."

"Man, it's like she's stalking you. She's literally everywhere," Cyril said.

"Plus, she's at my table in the dining hall! I've started eating breakfast at home, so I only have to see her at lunch."

"I kind of feel bad for her." The words had escaped before I could make sense of them.

"Why?" Marie's pretty face turned ugly as she grimaced. "She's awful. So awful."

"I dunno . . . I guess it's because I can tell she's lonely." *The way I'm lonely*, I silently thought. Toby lifted his head, howled, got up, and resettled himself at my feet.

"See?" I laughed. "He agrees with me."

"Interesting. You might be right. They say bullies are just insecure and desperate for love and attention." Lavinia looked satisfied, having sorted out Leesa's psychology.

"If only they learned how to be nice people — a much better way to get love and attention, right?" Jason shook his head.

"Nah, it's about power. Bullies just want control," Cyril said.

"I just avoid her as much as I can. Honestly, I'm glad she convinced me and Mei to move to a different room."

"Yup, you dodged a bullet there. But, Jason, you'd better watch out," Marie said, frowning. "Girls like her, they get whatever they want."

Nahla

Nahla clutched a bag of chips and a sweating bottle of ginger ale and approached a six-storey building nestled behind a stand of trees. A ten-minute walk from Thornton, it was close, yet far enough from her claustrophobic world; she hadn't yet seen a single student on the streets that led to Maeve and Joanne's place.

Two blocks away from the building, a car slowed beside her, and Gerry rolled down his window.

"You going to Joanne and Maeve's? Hop in!" She didn't want to get in his car, but she also didn't want to be impolite. After all, Gerry had been by only a few days earlier to drop off a space heater. When she got in, he leaned over to give her a half-hug, which she half-reciprocated, his damp cheek rubbing against hers. His aftershave was overpowering, and even after they'd parked and got out, she still smelled it on her coat. He grabbed a guitar from the hatchback.

"You play?" she asked.

"Yeah, I'm in a local band. Just a hobby. I also DJ weddings sometimes. And all the school dances."

"Really?" She pressed the *Robertson/McKinney* button, and while they waited for the buzz and click that permitted their entry, she studied him, this new information rounding him out. He wore jeans that weren't paint-splattered and a heavy sweater that looked hand-knit. They took the elevator to the third floor where Maeve was waiting, door flung open, the Eurythmics' "Sweet Dreams" escaping from the apartment.

"Welcome to our humble abode!" She reached for Nahla's jacket. "Don't you look nice. And, Gerry, you brought your guitar!"

Nahla realized she was overdressed in her long skirt and silk blouse. Maeve wore a Cotton Ginny tracksuit. At least Joanne had on brown parachute pants and a matching velour turtleneck.

Nahla followed everyone into the large living room, which walked out to a cement balcony that faced the street's tree canopy, already orange and sparse.

"You have a lovely apartment." Nahla took in the weathered couches and dining table that reminded her of her family's modest home.

"It's fine for now. We're saving up to buy a little house," Joanne said.

"May I ask how much the rent is? I might get my own place next year."

"Three fifty per month," Maeve said.

"For a two-bedroom? Cheaper than Montreal!"

"It's a one bedroom," Joanne clarified. "Like I said, we're trying to save up."

"Oh. Still, a good price." Nahla noticed the tension, like a silent fart, wafting among them.

"See over there?" Gerry opened the sliding glass door and beckoned her onto the balcony. "That's Thornton and the girls' residence."

Nahla could see tiny figures, like ants, going out the front door. The buzzer rang.

"Oh, that must be Michael!" Maeve announced. "Let's get the party started!"

Joanne paused their Trivial Pursuit game to empty an overfull ashtray and to refill the chip bowl. Maeve changed the record.

"I love this song." Maeve set down the needle, the vinyl crackling before the music began.

"Anne Murray is a talent. She does a great version of this one," Joanne agreed.

Gerry strummed his guitar and crooned along to "Daydream Believer," his baritone harmonizing with Murray's alto.

Michael swayed to the music, bumping Nahla slightly, who sat beside him on the couch. She liked that he, too, had dressed up a bit, wearing a green polo shirt and a crisply ironed pair of trousers.

"I read somewhere that she's from Nova Scotia." Nahla wondered from which recesses of her brain this bit of trivia had emerged. She hadn't been able to keep up with the others' acumen and had only one green pie slice, her childhood geography, history, and pop culture references a mismatch to the game's.

"Hey, so am I," Joanne said.

"I hear that's not the only thing you and Anne have in common." Michael laughed.

"True," Maeve interjected, not joining in the laughter. "They both love golf."

"What's so funny?" Nahla asked.

"Maeve, I think it's fine." Joanne looked to Maeve, who nodded. "Nahla, what our juvenile friend here is alluding to is that Anne Murray is rumoured to be gay, which I doubt is true. But anyway, Maeve and I are lesbians, and we're a couple."

"Oh! So that's why you have a one-bedroom, oh my goodness. I can be a little clueless about these kinds of things, but don't worry, I'm cool with it, really. I had a friend in university who was gay, we took three classes together, and now I just seem to be rambling on and on and making a fool of myself, asfe. I mean, je suis désolée." She shook her head and took a breath. "I'm so sorry!"

"It took me a while to catch on, too." Gerry leaned across the table and touched her knee, which just made her tense up more.

"It's okay, Nahla, we told you because we like and trust you. It's kind of an open secret among the staff, but it's not public knowledge," Maeve explained.

"Because there's still a lot of discrimination against gays and lesbians," Joanne added. "Many people still believe we're pedophiles. We've had friends lose jobs because people think it's not safe for kids to be around us."

"And they think we're vectors of AIDS, which, by the way, isn't even a thing among gay women. Thank God," Maeve added.

"Yes, I understand. Thank you for trusting me." Nahla silently chastised herself; she'd foolishly believed that myth about AIDS, too. And, even worse, she'd been holding a slight grudge about Maeve's ignorance of *her* world.

"Whoa, that's a relief. Glad we got that over with. Now we can really chill out," Maeve said, downing her glass of wine. Gerry refilled it and his own from a bottle that left a red ring on the glass-topped coffee table.

"Can I get you some more ginger ale, Nahla?" Joanne picked up Nahla's empty glass.

"Or how about some wine?" Gerry offered.

"Ginger ale is fine. I don't really drink alcohol."

"Like, ever? I tell ya, before the first term is over, you'll be a full-blown alcoholic!" Maeve said.

"Maeve! *Muslims* don't drink," Joanne said.

"Oh! Did I just put my foot in it? Are you religious?"

"Well, I wouldn't call myself religious." Nahla fidgeted with her watch strap. She was a believer, perhaps a lazy one, but lately, she'd been forgetting her prayers. Her parents would say that being a bad Muslim meant she wasn't Muslim at all. Same with her brother, and probably her sisters and nearly every Muslim she knew. She took a breath and concentrated on the four pairs of eyes focused on her. "I mean . . . I've tried wine a few times, and it was all right . . ."

"Well, maybe you just haven't found the right drink yet," Gerry suggested.

"Like I just haven't found the right man yet?" Maeve rolled her eyes.

"Here, try a sip of this. A screwdriver, vodka and orange." Michael passed his glass to Nahla. She looked at his lips as he spoke. For the first time since her breakup with Baashir, she wondered what a kiss might taste like.

"Hey, don't pressure her," Joanne said.

"It's okay." Nahla took Michael's glass, raised it to her nose, sniffing a combination of rubbing alcohol and citrus. Never mind what her parents and siblings and everyone else thought of her. *Wasn't she here, in Belltown, to find her own way?* She took a cautious sip. The vodka made the juice brackish. "Not bad."

"Just a sec." Before she could turn him down, Michael was in the kitchen mixing one for her. "I'm making yours weaker than mine."

"Hey, whose turn is it? I've lost track," Gerry said.

"I think it's mine." Maeve picked up the six-sided die.

"Here you go." Michael's fingers grazed hers, warm and rough. Painter's hands. A sip warmed her throat and esophagus, a strange sensation combined with the chill of the juice on her tongue. A gulp made her shoulders relax. When Michael let his arm rest against hers, she didn't shift away, and his heat soaked through her blouse's silk until it was difficult to perceive a barrier between their skins.

An hour later, Joanne won the game, the bottles were empty, and the gathering lost its verve. They said their goodbyes, and Nahla followed Michael and Gerry to the parking lot.

"Want a lift?" Gerry asked.

"I'll take her, you're going the opposite way." Michael opened the passenger side for her.

"I don't mind walking." A blush of shyness overcame her.

"Don't be silly, get in." She waved goodbye to Gerry, then sat in Michael's car. He closed the door for her. The gallant gesture made her giggle, but then, that single screwdriver had left her feeling lighter, happier than she'd felt in a long time. It was like she'd been wearing a grey woollen cloak for months, and then the strings around her neck were untied, allowing it to slip off her shoulders.

"Are you okay to drive? The laws are strict nowadays, aren't they?"

"The cops rarely patrol here." He started the car and it seemed, to her, drove extra carefully through the quiet residential streets. Perhaps he, too, didn't want to rush the end of their evening.

He pulled over across from the girls' residence and shut off the engine. He glanced at the mostly dark building, and said, "Looks like nearly all the lights are out."

It was almost 11:30 p.m., but the reality didn't alarm her. "Oh, well, I'm a half hour late to do bedcheck. Thanks for the lift."

"It was fun tonight." He leaned over and kissed her cheek.

She turned toward him, and he kissed her mouth, his lips warm, tentative. He tasted like cigarettes and oranges, as she probably did. He abruptly pulled away.

"I shouldn't have done that. I'm sorry."

"Oh?" Now she was sober.

"It's just that . . . I have a rule about not getting involved with co-workers. It can get awkward. I apologize."

"Okay . . . I guess you're right." A confused shame settled over her. "Goodnight."

She stepped out of the car but hesitated on the sidewalk, wanting, needing something more from him. "Bye, Michael."

He waved stiffly and pulled away, and she crossed the street, lit a cigarette, and smoked it on the front steps. The damned bedcheck could wait a few more minutes.

Leesa

Now that she'd had all day to stew, Leesa regretted her mistake. *Why had she lost her temper like that?* Calling to apologize felt urgent, a necessity. She'd been waiting until after bedcheck to sneak downstairs, but it was nearly 11:30 p.m. *Where was Miss Naim?*

Jessica was hunched over *Seventeen*, headphones leaking Cyndi Lauper, and Mallory was probably in the bathroom upchucking. They'd cover for her.

She slid her feet into her slippers and hurried down the stairs to the basement payphones. She pushed a dime into the slot, dialled his number and held her breath. After four rings, a woman answered, and she knew to hang up. She waited three minutes, then five, then seven; he had the numbers for the three phones and was supposed to call back. But none rang.

She trudged up the steps, knowing that she'd need to take one of the sleeping pills she'd stolen from her mother's medicine cabinet.

When she reached the first landing, Miss Naim was coming through the front doors.

"What are you doing out of bed this late, Leesa?"

"Nothing." Too many words crowded her brain. She walked past the teacher, their shoulders lightly grazing, and felt a hand on her forearm.

"Is anything wrong, Leesa? Do you need something?" The question was gentler, softer than the first one, and so Leesa hesitated, met the teacher's gaze, exhaled. Then she caught a whiff of aftershave. *Was it Polo?* She couldn't be sure because Miss Naim's perfume and cigarette smoke intermingled, masking it.

She studied Miss Naim's face and saw that her lipstick was slightly smudged. Yes, that was Polo. But that didn't mean anything; lots of men wore that scent. And he had a family thing tonight.

"Leesa, tell me what's wrong."

"I said it's nothing."

Leesa returned to her room to find her roommates in bed. She opened her bedside drawer, found a valium, and swallowed it dry. She clicked off her bedside lamp and slunk under the covers. Her racing thoughts slowed, and an older sadness crept forward.

The company had transferred them to Paris when she was eight. Before, back in Toronto, her parents would leave for work by 7:30 a.m. and didn't return home until late, relying on their ever-changing housekeepers to look after her. Paris had brought a welcome shift.

During their first month in France, the three Allens spent full days with a French tutor, growing their vocabulary. Ginette arrived each weekday at breakfast, and until late afternoon, she immersed them in French conversation, newspapers, and films. Weekends, her parents slept in while she watched cartoons until 10 a.m. Then they'd take a drive, go shopping, or play board games.

Of course, her parents' hectic schedules resumed after that, but it seemed to Leesa that they were happier than when they'd lived in Toronto. Or that's what she'd hoped. By the middle of her tenth year, she noticed her father's absences and overheard the private and strained discussions between adults she didn't yet fully comprehend. At age eleven, she picked up the extension phone and eavesdropped on her father whispering his loyalty to Ginette.

No one explained the separation, but Leesa understood when her father's side of the closet had been emptied. Then he announced that she would soon have a baby brother. For a time, it was like her parents could only speak to her in half sentences, ellipses, and incomprehensible emotional outbursts. Julia, their housekeeper, was the one who filled in the gaps and translated her parents' story.

The summer Liam was born, she was twelve, and her mother pulled out an old yearbook and showed her where she'd be going to school. It wasn't in France, but rather her mother's old boarding school in some hicktown in Canada. Leesa didn't complain or argue because maybe, just maybe, Thornton would be better than home.

Now, in bed in her mother's old boarding school, she cried for her eight-year-old self, that stupid, hopeful kid. And as she'd done since she was twelve, she dried her tears and put away the feelings.

She focused on the present, resolving to apologize to him for being such a cow today. She wouldn't jump to any conclusions and would bury her illogical suspicions. Within moments, her mind was foggy, her body heavy, and she let herself sink into the quicksand of medicated sleep.

Zahabiya

"My head is going to explode. I can't memorize another fucking French phrase." Mei rested her head on the library's long wooden table. We were all exhausted, but at least after the French exam, there was only biology to cram for.

"I like the alliteration of that: 'fucking French phrase,'" Jason mused.

"Groupe de mots en français fucking, doesn't have the same ring," I joined in.

"Zahabiya, did I just hear you curse? And with a French accent?" Mei looked impressed.

"Fucking growth," I answered, rubbing my tired eyes. When I opened them, Leesa was at our table. She ignored Mei and me and said to Jason, "Puis-je vous parler seul une seconde?"

"Yeah, okay." He followed her a few feet away.

"What do you think she wants?" I whispered.

"I dunno, but he's looking très uncomfortable."

"Très *inc*onfortable," I corrected. We watched as Leesa's face fell for a second before turning haughty and then pleasant again, like a salamander swiftly camouflaging herself.

"What did Miss Maybelline want?" Mei asked when Jason returned.

"She asked me to the winter formal." He looked at me. "But I said no."

"Good. No one needs more Leesa Allen in their lives," Mei muttered.

I was glad. Over the last couple of months, Jason and I had become friends, and I found myself looking forward to seeing him. Lavinia and Marie insisted he had a crush on me, but I still wasn't sure. I knew he didn't like Leesa, but it dawned on me that someone else could like him and ask him out, and I'd lose my chance.

"Jason, us girls," I broached, "Lavinia, Marie, and I were planning to go together . . . you know, dateless . . . I mean, we'd be each other's dates, I guess? Mei, you can join us, too, if you want." It was clumsy, but the best I could manage. I'd never been to a formal before. I'd even avoided the non-formal high school dances back home.

"I'm going with Kwame Matthews. He asked me today," Mei answered.

"Why didn't you say anything?" I didn't know she liked Kwame.

"It's not a big deal. We're just friends, but I thought having a date would make the experience less horrific." She shrugged.

"So, um, Jason, do you want to go with us?"

"Sure," Jason said, but I still couldn't get a read on him. *Was I being obtuse? Was he?* The bell rang, and we rushed to class to write our exam.

A few days later, I slipped on the green satin dress I'd borrowed from Lavinia. It had puffed sleeves, a dropped waist, and a billowing skirt. She applied blush and eyeshadow and a thick coating of blue mascara for me, which made my lashes feel like chemical butterflies.

"It's not too much?" I said, looking in the mirror.

"No, it's like Samantha in *Sixteen Candles*."

"*Ugh*, I can't stand Molly Ring-worm," Mei grumbled. Tonight, instead of candy, she was passing around a two-litre bottle of cola she'd spiked with three airplane-sized bottles of rum. She'd bought them from a grade 13 student who offered the "service" before every dance.

"That's because you're more like Morticia Addams." Marie laughed, reaching for the bottle. She took a swig and handed it on to Lavinia, who took a dainty sip, before passing it to me.

"I'll take that as a compliment." Mei leaned into the mirror and darkened her eyeliner.

"I can barely taste the rum." I took another big gulp. Zahra had introduced me to rum and coke last year, raiding the liquor cabinet when my dad and Tara were on their honeymoon.

"Yeah, it's weak. But go slow, Molly."

We tromped through the snow to the main building where we ditched our coats and boots and put on pumps. Linking arms, we entered the dining hall, and I marvelled at the magic the dance committee had created; the tables and chairs had been moved aside, replaced with white archways and a centre gazebo. Gerry DJed from the stage. Sparkly, plate-sized snowflakes hung from the rafters.

Our group mostly danced in a circle, and during the first half, Jason finally arrived, Cyril in tow. Jason wore a grey suit. I was used to seeing him in our school uniform's jacket and tie, but that night he looked older, more solid. More handsome.

Gerry played a lot of fast songs, and when he interspersed them with slow dances, we cleared off the floor. Once in a while, Lavinia and Marie were asked to dance, leaving me as a wallflower. I looked around for Jason, psyching myself up to ask him, but he seemed to disappear during the slow songs.

At one point, Lavinia motioned toward the punch bowl, where Ashley was gesticulating and yelling at Leesa, who stood arms crossed and smug-looking. We all neared the periphery of gawking bystanders. The girls started pushing and shoving one another, their fancy party dresses going slightly off-kilter. I wondered if we should do something, try to intervene. But pretty soon they got pulled apart, Gerry walking Leesa off to the stage, and Miss Naim escorting Ashley outside. Rodney Davidson, Leesa's date and Ashley's recent ex, didn't seem to know where he was supposed to go.

"Whoa, that was a lot," Lavinia said.

"I can see why Ashley went after her. She and Rodney have been together since grade 10, then they break up, and *boom*, he's here with Leesa," Marie said.

"I heard a rumour that Rodney found out that she'd been cheating on him," Lavinia said. "I wouldn't have expected that from Ashley, but who knows."

"Ashley says someone is making up lies about her. I believe her." Ashley had been upset for the past two breakfasts, lunches, and dinners.

Gerry put on *Breakdance*, and Lavinia left us to dance with Paul. We watched as they dominated the dance floor. Mei and Kwame looked pretty in sync, too.

"Don't you think it's just too convenient that all those rumours happened in time for Leesa to swoop in and grab Rodney?" Marie yelled over the music.

"You think?" I asked, remembering how Jason turned her down only a few days ago. Marie raised her eyebrows and laughed.

"Oh, Zahabiya, you're cute." She slung her arm across my shoulders. Until then, I really wasn't sure if Marie liked me or only included me on account of Lavinia and I being friends.

The song came to an end, and the opening bars of "What a Feeling" came on.

"Yes!" Marie yelled. We headed to the centre of the floor and belted out the lyrics as we danced. Cyril took Marie's hand and spun her. Jason joined us, swaying stiffly to the music. I shifted to dance closer to him.

The song ended with the squeak of the record player's needle.

"All right, last song," Gerry announced into his mic. "As usual, we finish off with the classic 'Stairway to Heaven.' And I get my smoke break!"

This was my last chance. I looked at Jason, and before I could ask him to dance, he held out his hand to me. I'd been waiting all night for this. I held his shoulders, and he palmed my waist, and we maintained a shy inch between our bodies. It was kind of strange — awkward but exciting — to be touching him in this intimate way. I caught Lavinia's approving nod as she danced near us with Paul.

During the semi-fast electric guitar interlude, all the couples separated and swayed faster, and Jason and I followed suit, not making much eye contact. Then we stepped closer for the last slow twenty seconds, and he leaned his head down against mine. His breath tickled my ear, and I was too warm, but I didn't pull away because it felt good to be close to him. I pulled him in tighter.

When the song finished, he thanked me for the dance, and I thanked him back. Not sure what to do with all my nervous energy, I waved goodbye and caught up to Marie and Lavinia, who were waiting for me near the doors.

Nahla

"I used to hate school dances," Maeve crabbed to Nahla, "but I hate chaperoning them even more."

They stood near the doors, surveying the students. So far, they'd only had to confiscate one bottle of vodka and intercept a couple of non-students not on the guest list. Nahla thought the students looked so grown up in their party dresses and suits as they glided around the dance floor.

"I was never allowed to go, so this is a new experience for me." Nahla sighed, reminded of the frustration and lack of fairness she'd felt each time her parents had withheld permission for a dance, excursion, or party.

"You didn't miss anything. Let's just hope there isn't any drama tonight." Maeve checked her watch.

"Drama?"

"Some girl always leaves in tears. Teenagers." Maeve rolled her eyes. Gerry sauntered over from the stage. He'd left Madonna's "Like a Virgin" to play on the turntable.

"Ladies, you look ravishing tonight. Like the music?" Before they could answer, he began singing along with Madonna's lyrics. Nahla backed away from him, but Maeve joined him in a duet. Near the song's end, he rushed back to flip the record.

"Wasn't Michael supposed to work tonight?" Nahla asked, attempting to sound casual.

"Yeah, he had to cancel. That's why I'm subbing in." Maeve regarded Nahla with sympathy. "So, no new developments?"

"No, it ended before it even started. But he's right; it's best we remain friends. We have to work together, after all." Nahla parroted back the sensible yet disappointing words he'd reiterated on the Monday after their kiss. Even so, her attraction to him had only grown now that he wasn't interested.

"I dunno. It worked out for me and Joanne. Sorry, Nahla."

"It's nothing." *So, why did she still feel let down?*

"I need to go to the washroom. I'll do a sweep of the hallways while I'm at it."

Nahla continued to scan the hall. When she heard yelling on the opposite side, she hurried over, pushing through the growing semicircle of onlookers.

"You lying bitch!" Ashley charged at Leesa.

"Sore loser!" Leesa pushed back, and they collided in a livid slow dance.

Gerry got there before her and wedged himself between the girls, quelling the fight. The record stopped. He took Leesa by the elbow and gestured to Nahla to do the same with Ashley. Nahla marched her out the doors, into the hallway.

"What was that all about?" Nahla demanded. Irene Cara's upbeat rhythms pulsated from the hall. Perhaps Gerry was attempting to distract the students and shift the mood.

"She . . . she told everyone that I was cheating on Rodney . . . it's not true! I think she set me up somehow and . . . and he believed it. And now he's with her!" Angry tears streamed down Ashley's flushed face.

"Okay, okay, breathe." Nahla made eye contact with Maeve, who'd returned from the bathroom.

"He was *my* boyfriend. I can't believe she — and those other lying bitches — did this to me! They've had it out for me all year." Sobbing now, she turned away and covered her face with her hands.

"Listen, Ashley." Nahla touched the girl's forearm. "You can't get into physical fights with her, understand?"

"She started it!" Ashley wailed.

"Enough." Nahla was using her teacher voice, but she felt bad for Ashley — she was clearly on the losing side of this fight.

"You okay, Ashley?" Two girls waited nearby.

"You two take her back to the residence and take care of her," Nahla instructed.

"But we'll miss the last slow dance," one of the girls protested.

"Do it anyway! Be a good friend," Maeve said. They complied and walked away with Ashley.

"Poor girl," Nahla whispered.

"Like I said, draaaamaaaaa." They went back inside, and Nahla looked up at the stage, where Gerry and Leesa appeared to be deep in conversation. Something about their body language, the way he sat too close to her, looked strange.

"Maeve, could you go talk to Leesa, maybe let Gerry focus on the DJing?"

"Do I have to? Oh, wait — look! The fought-over boy is taking over." Maeve pointed to where Rodney Davidson, hand in pockets, headed up the stage stairs.

Leesa

Leesa took Rodney's hands and guided them to her hips. Although he'd been the one to ask her to the dance — at his buddies' urging, Leesa knew — he'd been distracted all night. She'd told Mallory and Jessica this wouldn't work! But they'd insisted, going into full gear, right after she told them things were done with Jason.

"Listen, Rodney, I know you and Ashley just broke up a few days ago. Are you okay to stay here?" Should she abort the mission or press on?

"Yeah, it's fine . . . she . . . it's best we both move on, you know?" His eyes roved past her, and Leesa knew he was tracking Ashley around the hall. Again.

"Do you want to talk about it? I mean, I've heard bits and pieces, but . . ." Leesa tightened her grip on his shoulders. Right after the French exam, Jessica had dictated the fake letters, and Mallory had penned them, trying to make her handwriting "boyish." Then they'd delivered them to their boyfriends, affecting sadness and outrage, and urging them to take action to protect their friend's honour.

"She . . . she turned out to be someone I didn't know. I had no idea she was cheating on me, but Jessica and Mallory had proof so . . ." His jaw tightened, and so did his clasp around her waist.

"They mentioned that." Mallory, a few feet away, gave her a "thumbs-up" sign.

"There were love letters from a guy, going back months and months." His eyes looked sad, and so she drew closer, pushing her breasts into his chest.

"Oh, I'm so sorry, Rodney. That must be really hard." She rested her head on his shoulder.

The song ended, and she went to get punch. Mallory and Jessica sidled up to her.

"Having fun?" Jessica smiled.

"Yeah, but he's really hung up on her. I think this was all too fast."

"Bitch had it coming." Mallory gave Jessica and Leesa a sly look. Leesa smiled in commiseration, even though she hadn't a clue what Mallory was talking about.

"Oh. My. God. She's coming this way and she doesn't look happy." Jessica tugged at Leesa's arm.

Before she knew it, Ashley was in her face, her eyes blazing fury. A confusing set of doubts and defences flew through Leesa's mind: she'd let things go too far; maybe she was the sort of woman her mother called a "homewrecker"; Ashley was causing a scene — how dare she; maybe she did deserve it.

Then Ashley's moist palms were on her bare chest and so she shoved back. Ashley smacked her in the face, and she reacted with a jab, striking something soft — *belly? Boob?* And before she knew it, she was being pulled away, then up on the stage, looking like the innocent victim, and Ashley, the monster, was being dragged out of the hall.

Gerry had been sweet — sweeter than she expected. After one whole song — not a good sign — Rodney finally showed up and walked her off the stage.

"I'm so sorry, I had no idea she'd react like this. I . . . I really don't recognize her anymore. Are you okay?" Rodney asked.

"I'm fine. Just a little shaken up." She sighed and put on a brave smile. Yes, she'd press on.

"I hope she doesn't try anything like that again. She's just taking it all out on you, and that's not fair."

"I can see her side of things. It must be hard to see us, you know . . . dancing . . . so soon after you two broke up." *Was that the right thing to say?*

"Wow, you're awesome, Leesa."

"I think you're awesome, Rodney Davidson. Do you want to get out of here?"

Winter Term,
January 1985

Little by little,
she is beginning to hear me,
but will she listen?

Zahabiya

The driver pulled my suitcase from the bus's damp undercarriage, and I lugged it to the front of Belltown's station. I pushed play on my Walkman, this year's Christmas/birthday gift from Tara and my dad.

While Simon Le Bon sang about trying to find a mountain hideaway, I considered how to traverse the final eleven blocks to the residence. Option one: the twice-hourly local bus that stopped two blocks from the manor. Option two: use the ten bucks my dad gave me for a cab. Option three: an uphill walk through a fresh foot of snow. A voice broke through Duran Duran, and in the distance, the shapes of a guy and a dog appeared. I smiled, pulled off my headphones, and waited for them. The last time I'd seen Jason was at the dance and I hadn't stopped thinking about him since.

"Aren't you a day early?" Jason's words transformed into vapour clouds. He seemed to be avoiding eye contact. *Was he nervous?*

"Dad is on call tomorrow, so the plan was to take Zahra to the bus station today and then drive me here. But this morning I said I'd take the bus, too, to save him the trip." The truth was that I knew a two-hour drive with my father would be pockmarked with sad and uncomfortable silences, the way it had been ever since my mom's death. A while back, Zahra had explained that, with my long face, straight hair, and almond-shaped eyes, I most took after our mother. My presence made him sad. And that made me sad, and I didn't want to feel like that anymore.

"So, did you have a good break?" Jason asked, still not looking at me. He was nervous, and the feeling was contagious.

"Quiet. We put up a plastic tree and did gifts, you know, the Muslim version of Christmas." I laughed. I didn't mention that on the twenty-seventh, we had a dinner for my sixteenth birthday, low key, the way I preferred it; I didn't like being the centre of attention.

"How about you?" I bent to scratch Toby's ears. He wagged his tail and rubbed his slobbery face against my Cougar boots. Stroking his back helped me chill out a bit.

"We did pretty much the same thing, except with a real tree. But I missed all of you boarders these past couple of weeks." He pulled his toque down over his red ears.

"Yeah, me, too." I straightened.

"You walking up? I'm going in that direction." I nodded, decision now made, and picked up my suitcase.

"Seen anyone else around town yet?"

"Just a few, mostly day students."

"So, no Lavinia yet? Cyril? Mei? Marie?" He shook his head. "Leesa?" I slipped on a patch of ice, steadied myself, and put my suitcase down to rest. Jason traded me the leash for the bag's handle. I shook out my throbbing arm.

"Not even my stalker who stopped being my stalker!" He laughed. "That was wild at the dance, eh? Ashley starting that fight with her?"

"I get why she did — even if Leesa wasn't the cause of the breakup, it was a jerk move to go to the dance with Rodney so soon after."

"And for Rodney to ask her to go."

"Exactly."

Our arms bumped, and even through the puffiness of our winter coats' sleeves, I was acutely aware of the space between us. I regretted rushing off right after the dance and wanted to tell him, but it was like the words were stuck in my throat. This was new territory for me. *Was it the same for him?* I opted to change the subject instead.

"So, the news this week was pretty intense, eh?" We talked about the recent nuclear weapons testing by the US, China, and the USSR and whether this meant the threat of nuclear war was a bigger possibility. When that got too depressing, we discussed the upcoming ski trip, which was pricey for us both. Meanwhile, Toby pulled me up the hill, more like a malamute than a beagle.

"Well, here we are," I said when we reached the residence.

"Look at the snowflakes coming down," Jason said. "They're perfect."

I raised my face to the delicate flakes. I closed my eyes and felt the wet melt on my warm forehead and cheeks. And then Jason leaned down and kissed me.

Nahla

Nahla boiled water in a rakwe and added the Arabic coffee her mother had mailed her. She'd sent her a birthday card in November, with a request to visit over the holidays, but her mother's written reply was: *Amahlek, Habibti.* Slow down. Her father still couldn't accept her decision and his only response was shunning. And her brother, the same age as her students, had become his enforcer each time she phoned home.

The silver lining was that her mother's discouraging message had arrived with a box filled with zaatar, coffee, and halwa, staples that she'd almost depleted.

And there was a golden lining: since then, she and her mother had become pen pals, chronicling daily activities, meals eaten, family news, and their weekly correspondence, and while a poor substitute for phone calls and visits, it was a consolation. She hoped neither her father nor her brother would discover and stop the mail.

In mid-December, her mother's letter carried a subversive plan: a secret Christmas Eve meet-up in Ottawa, the halfway point between their homes. Nahla arrived at the Lebanese restaurant to be embraced by her mother and two sisters, the table full of food and love that she'd been so sorely missing. It was almost like the days before she'd accepted the Thornton job. On the return bus to Belltown, her heart had been simultaneously full and broken.

She spent the rest of the vacation alone in the echoey residence. Well, that wasn't quite true. Sylvie had been a more consistent companion over the two quiet weeks. While this was somewhat discomfiting, she'd come to accept Sylvie's presence.

That morning, Nahla awoke from a dream in which she'd had a meandering conversation with the older woman, who'd offered brief, but wise, responses to Nahla's queries about the grade 10 class, which had two failing students. Then they dream-chatted about Michael, and Sylvie had advised her to let him go. Nahla agreed with her.

And yet, she couldn't let him go. It didn't help that even after he set the friends-only boundary, he continued to flirt with her in the teachers' lounge and had even dropped by her classroom occasionally, her body like a lit charcoal each time he was within a few feet of her. Which just left her feeling silly and confused.

As she sipped her coffee, she chided herself for mooning over him. After all, there was no point. A non-Muslim romance was doomed to fail, and she didn't have time to waste on trifles. But despite herself, her mind wandered, and her lips remembered his warmth. And then her imagination reeled itself forward, a fishing line hooking dreams of dating, falling in love, and the ultimate romantic flourish: his conversion to Islam, so her family could accept him.

She shook her head to clear the fog of fantasy. *What might she do to fill the day's remaining hours?* At least the students would return tomorrow, and classes would resume Monday. *It would be good to get busy again, wouldn't it?* As though in reply, an acidic dread pooled in Nahla's belly.

Her cup emptied, she turned it over in its saucer, leaving the dredge to drip its patterns. She walked the hallways with no one to monitor. She headed to the new wing, Margo's jurisdiction, but of course it, too, was deserted. On her way back to the old wing, she heard footsteps.

"Marhaba," she called out, then, "bonjour, hello?" She hadn't spoken to another living soul in too many days.

"Bonjour." Zahabiya's cheeks were flushed from the cold.

"You're the first one back."

"I figured." She opened her door, pushed her bag inside, and shrugged off her coat. Nahla recalled the girl's family situation and wondered if that's why she'd returned early. And yet she didn't seem unhappy; she almost vibrated with excitement.

"Come by after you've settled in. I have some Lebanese sweets you must try."

"Thanks, Miss Naim."

"Listen, while it's just the two of us here, call me Nahla."

"Okay."

Nahla continued down the hall to her flat, the tread of Sylvie's well-worn leather loafers plodding behind her. She turned over her cup to reveal the peaks and valleys the coffee had traced on the porcelain. She wasn't very good at reading grounds, but she thought she saw a woman flying through the air. And also, a man embracing a woman. She squinted at the cup. *Was she the woman? Was Michael the man?* She shook the thought away. This was all wishful thinking brought on by too much loneliness.

She looked at the grounds again, focusing on the flying woman. *What could that mean?*

Nahla frowned, her attention drawn to Sylvie's grey cahier, which now sat on the coffee table. *When had she taken it out of her bookbag?* She flipped it open to the two pages of Sylvie's spying.

04/18/84   ?   *quelques semaines ont passé déjà??*

"How many weeks have already gone by. But why, Sylvie?"

And then there was a knock at the door, and a girl, like her, who needed some company.

Leesa

Leesa arrived at the Sheraton on Saturday afternoon. Arranging two nights in Toronto had been a cinch; all she'd had to do was tell her mother that she wanted to bookend her Paris trip with seeing Lyndee Johnson, her childhood best friend. There hadn't been any argument about the hotel stays when Leesa clarified that the Johnsons were in the midst of renovations, and so she couldn't stay with them.

Leesa had supplied her mother a fake phone number for the Johnsons (she hadn't talked to Lyndee since the divorce) and a real one for the hotel, knowing it would be unlikely that her mother would call, especially if Leesa pre-empted any passing parental worry by calling collect from the airport and announcing her safe arrival to the housekeeper.

Room 412 was an exact replica of 618, and even with its repetition, romantic. They'd spent December 21 in the king-sized bed, only rousing to shower and order room service. They'd even eaten fettuccini alfredo and drank red wine in bed. And they'd talked for hours, like they used to. He'd listened when she told him about not wanting to spend time with her embittered mother, or worse, her father's happy new family.

On December 22, he'd left early in the morning, saying that he had commitments at home. She didn't ask what lies he'd told to explain his absence.

Now, she unzipped her suitcase and found the new pink teddy she'd bought for him. Doubting whether she was good in bed, she'd studied the *Joy of Sex*, half-hidden behind her mother's old business school texts in her study. While some of the illustrations made her gag (*Why was the woman so* hairy?), she realized they'd tried only a couple of moves depicted in the book and hoped they'd go beyond the five-minute missionary that seemed to be his favourite position, whether in the back seat of his car or in a spacious bed.

She unwrapped the lingerie from its tissue paper, recalling the store clerk's comment: "Your boyfriend is a very lucky guy." *Would she have been scandalized, impressed, or disgusted that he was older?* Leesa hated the idea that people would think less of him (or her!) if they knew. She couldn't wait until next year.

Of course, they'd construct a better story for how they'd met: they'd barely noticed each other while she was at Thornton. A few months after graduation, they'd randomly bumped into each other in Toronto and fell madly in love.

She planned to study at Queen's, prestigious enough and only an hour from Belltown. She'd take poli-sci — a good bet in case she decided to switch to journalism or go to law school later. They'd have a normal, non-clandestine relationship, she'd get her BA, and together they'd move to a big city far from Thornton, where they'd begin new, more interesting lives.

Two hours later, Leesa heard the click of a lock as he entered. She turned off the television, ripped off her bathrobe, and posed like a Playboy bunny, aware that her new teddy barely covered her breasts and butt.

"Wow, Babe, you look great!" He came over to the bed, kissed her, smelling of cigarettes and crisp winter air.

"You like it?" she asked coyly.

"Yeah, of course. And sorry I'm late. I got caught up with things at home. I didn't even have time for lunch. Let's have dinner first, okay?" He let go of her and went to the desk, where he combed through the menu.

"Sure, we can get room service," she said sulkily. "But how about a snack for now? Then we can go someplace fancy, have a real date? Remember? I have my parents' credit card. They never look at their statements, and anyway, I can tell them Lyndee wanted to go somewhere—"

"You know it's not safe for us to be seen out in public."

"If someone sees us, we could just say we ran into each other . . ." Yes! It could work with her fake origin story, only this first dinner would be . . .

"We can't, Leesa. Anyway, I'm not dressed for fancy." He pointed to his jeans.

"Fine," she whined. *Why couldn't he be more courageous? More romantic? Better dressed?* "I just feel like you could put more effort into our relationship." She heard her voice tail off into a simper. She hated when she did that. Her eyes welled up.

"I came all the way here, didn't I? Our relationship is important. You're important," he said gently, now at her side, rubbing her back.

"You don't care about me." She scampered off the bed and put on her bathrobe. She was too naked, and he'd brought in a chill from the hallway.

"Not everyone grows up rich, Leesa. Some of us have to earn a living, you know? Some of us have adult responsibilities."

"I'm sorry. I'm just being insecure." She pulled the robe around her and tied the sash tightly, then went to stand by the window.

He stood behind her and wrapped his arms around her waist. "Remember, you just have another year and half at Thornton. Not long. And we can have weekends like these once in a while to break it up. Let's not spoil the precious time we have together, okay?"

"Okay." She sniffed and turned to face him.

"And anyway, aren't I the one who should be insecure? I mean, you have a boyfriend now, don't you? Rodney Davidson? That guy you were with at the dance ?" His lips curled downward.

"C'mon, I told you. He's just a decoy. I have to tell Mallory and Jessica something when I go out to see you."

"You haven't done anything with him, have you?"

"Of course not." She kissed his cheek.

He fingered her robe's sash open, loosened it.

"Didn't you say you needed to eat first?"

"You can be my first course."

Zahabiya

I showed up for Wednesday's mail call, hopeful. Over the holidays, I'd complained to Zahra about my lack of mail at Thornton, and she'd rolled her eyes, grumbling about how old-fashioned I was (*"Who writes letters anymore?"*). Still, in front of me, and probably for dramatic effect, she'd slid open the kitchen drawer where Mom used to keep her special stationery. She wrote on a pale-green page, passing the matching envelope to me to self-address. I tried to sneak a look at it, but Zahra had ordered me away, laughing as she scribbled.

Sonia rolled up with the cart and distributed parcels and letters by first name in alphabetical order. As I'd done every week since the fall, I made myself comfortable on a nearby bench and watched the mail-sort chaos. Sometimes Lavinia or Marie joined me, but Mei never bothered. Still, I always listened for her name, just in case.

Sonia was a quarter-way through when Marie joined me on the bench and leaned into me heavily in greeting. Her shoulder was soft and warm, and I relaxed into the pressure.

"Waiting for a love letter?" she teased. I'd told the girls about the kiss on Saturday, but I'd left out the bit about it being my first kiss.

I knew for sure now — what Lavinia and Marie had known all along — that Jason liked me. But things weren't proceeding the way I'd imagined. He'd returned to his usual friendly, dorky demeanour, which was probably my fault. After the kiss, I'd smiled and thanked him for walking me home. *Did he think I hadn't liked it?* And since then, I hadn't been able to figure out how to return the romantic gesture. *What was wrong with me?* Maybe it was better to stay friends than risk my messing things up.

"Anything for me?" Lavinia asked, plopping herself down on the bench beside Marie.

Sonia called out Leesa's name, who held up a purple envelope and exclaimed, "Oh, a Christmas card from my friend in Toronto!"

"Sorry, nothing today," I answered.

"No huge box of chocolate this time?" Marie heckled Leesa.

"Well, it takes three weeks for mail to arrive from Paris," Leesa turned and glared at Marie.

"Make sure to save me some."

"You don't need any chocolate, trust me," Leesa sneered and walked away.

"She's so mean." I patted Marie's arm.

"Don't listen to her," Lavinia counselled.

"I don't let Barbies like her get to me." Marie crossed her arms over her chest, but I knew the comment stung.

"Zahabiya Dholkawala!" Sonia called out and then handed me two letters.

"It's a frickin' miracle!" Marie said.

"You got *two*? Hallelujah!"

"Yeah." I lowered to the bench and studied the two matching envelopes. Each had distinct handwriting. "I know this one is from Zahra, because I addressed it myself, but this one . . ."

I tore open the unfamiliar one first.

Dear Zahabiya,

I hope your first few days at Thornton are going well. I thought I'd write you a letter because sometimes it feels hard to talk when we are at home. And I heard you wanted mail!

I want you to know that I've missed you this year. I know we don't know each other well, and that it's still strange for you that I'm married to your father. I'm hoping in time that we will get to know each other better and become good friends. I admire you a great deal, and I know the last couple of years have not been easy on you.

It's not easy to lose a mother. As you might remember, mine died last year, which is not the same thing, I know. My mom was already seventy-four while your mom died much too young. Anyway, I want you to know that I understand some of your pain. And I also understand why you might have wanted to get away from this house, the memories. But I am here if you ever want to talk about these things or just if you want to do regular things as well. Feel free to call or write back if you'd like.

Love,
Tara

My eyes grew wet, and the page went blurry.

"Everything okay?" Lavinia asked. I felt Marie's hand on my elbow.

"Yeah." I inhaled and stood, the action helping me to suck the tears back into their ducts. "Just a dumb note from my dad's wife. I wonder what my sister sent me?"

I unsealed the second envelope, which contained two knock-knock jokes and a caricature of me reading a book. I passed this letter to

Marie, who read the jokes out loud to Lavinia. As I watched my friends laugh, the tightness in my chest eased a little.

Later, after study hall that night, I put on my coat and sat on the deserted front steps of the residence to reread Tara's letter. The concrete's chill seeped through my parka, but here I was sure to not be disturbed. I remembered back to last year, when Tara's mother died, about a month after the wedding. I'd expressed wooden condolences and then maintained a wide berth, as though Tara had contracted an infectious illness.

But I had to admit, this was how I'd behaved around Tara ever since Dad first introduced us to the mystery woman he'd been spending all his Tuesday and Saturday evenings with, returning home after each of these dates humming Beatles songs and smiling in a way he hadn't in a long time. We'd ordered pizza that night, and I could barely make eye contact with Tara when I'd passed her the chili flakes. I snuck glances at her curly black bob and the green eye shadow that complemented her light-brown skin. She was different from Mom, who although from the same community and generation, hadn't liked makeup and wore her hair in a long braid down her back. I still couldn't admit that I admired Tara's style.

I never asked how Tara's mother died, but it must have been sudden because she'd seemed fine at the wedding. In fact, she'd exuberantly called me her new granddaughter, enfolding me in a perfumey hug that I'd squirmed out of. At the time, I'd thought, meanly: *you're not my grandmother; I have two grandmothers already, and Tara isn't even biologically related.*

I'd treated Tara like a friendly stranger who occupied my house, rearranged the cabinets, and bought a new couch, replacing the more comfortable one I'd spent my entire childhood watching TV on. And in September, I'd conceded the house by leaving. It was the only way I knew to make the situation tolerable.

I stared at the manor's dark front lawn and spotted movement in the barren bushes, a twitch of a grey-brown head. A rabbit.

116

I wiped a tear, glad to not be alone. We shared a companionable silence for a minute or two. I knew I wasn't accepting Tara because I still couldn't accept my mother's death. I guess I hadn't actually made it through all the stages of grief yet.

"Yeah, I'm a jerk." The rabbit didn't move.

"Who are you talking to?" Leesa asked, coming up the walk. Her pink coat was almost neon when lit by the walkway's lamps. Her expression was bored, glassy. I wiped my wet face with my scarf.

"Myself."

The rabbit hopped away.

"You all right?" The question was polite, perfunctory.

"Just family stuff." And I didn't know why, but I added, "Got a letter from my stepmother."

"I hate my stepmother. Who doesn't hate their stepmother, right?"

"It's just not fair . . ." I sniffed, stopped myself. Leesa was definitely not a person to spill to.

"Life isn't fair. I learned that a long time ago." Leesa continued up the steps. I wasn't surprised by her admission. Here, at Thornton, students spoke of step-parents casually, while the concept was an oddity back at my old school, where, just as I'd been the only East Indian kid, I was also the only one with a dead mother and a stepmother. But Thornton seemed to be a magnet for broken families.

Only my family wasn't broken. It was like an ankle that stayed weak after a bad sprain. And I didn't want to hate Tara, but I wasn't ready to love her, either.

"Are you coming inside? You're going to freeze out here," Leesa said, her tone now uncharacteristically sincere.

"Yeah." I shoved the letter into my coat pocket and followed her in.

Nahla

"So, back to the grind." Maeve popped her head into The Attic Friday afternoon, interrupting Nahla, who'd been reviewing the January quiz. She'd followed Michael's suggestion to have the students mark one another's papers, but was perplexed that so many weaker students were scoring remarkably high. Now she'd have to audit all their tests and confront the cheats, tasks more time-consuming than marking everything herself.

"I don't mind being back to work. I got bored over the holidays."

"Nahla, I really wish you'd told us you were going to be like Rapunzel in her castle for two weeks." With three long strides from the door, Maeve towered above Nahla's desk, her blue eyes pools of concern.

"It wasn't as though I was locked in! And . . . I did take a trip to Ottawa to visit family." Nahla leaned away from Maeve's intense gaze and minty breath.

"You could've joined us when we got back from Florida! Why didn't you come to our New Year's Eve party, at least?"

"Well . . ."

"It's Michael, isn't it?" Maeve shook her head and pushed a pile of quizzes to the side and sat, her butt flattening against Nahla's wooden desk.

"It's kind of uncomfortable and confusing . . ." Admitting these feelings out loud was like freeing buzzing wasps trapped in a wall.

"Confusing?"

"Well, he still seems extra . . . friendly. Maybe flirty." Heat travelled up Nahla's neck to her face, settling around her cheeks.

"Mixed signals, eh?" Maeve's eyebrows stretched up her face.

"Maybe. I don't know." Nahla shook her head.

"He's not prejudiced, do you think? The type who only dates someone Caucasian? I mean, he doesn't seem that way, but . . ." Maeve squinted, silently assessing the evidence.

"I hadn't considered that." Of course she had.

"Or maybe there's someone else? He's never mentioned it, but he's a good-looking guy, right? With a job. Ha!" She clapped her hands. "That's a huge deal in this town."

"I guess so." *Maybe he was a womanizer, was playing with her emotions?*

"Want me to talk to him? Gather some intel for you?"

"No, no! Don't say anything. I don't want him to know that I'm even thinking about this! About him. Please promise not to say anything about me!"

"I'll very subtly ask him if he's seeing anyone. Cross my heart and hope to die. Pinky promise." Maeve placed her right hand on her chest and then linked her left pinky with Nahla's. The ridiculousness of the phrases and gestures made Nahla feel a sisterliness toward Maeve.

"Thanks. You're sweet."

"Ha! It'll be fun." Maeve batted away the compliment and opened Nahla's curriculum binder. "I should make something like this, so that I don't have to go searching for things each year. This is so organized. She even made separate sections for tests."

"You know, there was something else she left behind in her drawer."

"Oh, yeah? What?" Maeve continued leafing through the binder.

"An odd notebook." Nahla wrapped her sweater around her, for the room had grown suddenly cool. By now she'd learned this was Sylvie. "It was mostly empty. With just a couple of pages of coded notes about the comings and goings of a student."

"Really? Someone she had to discipline?"

"No, that's the thing. It records someone leaving the residence, then coming back in time for bedcheck. Following the rules, really. The first initial of the student is . . ." Just then she broke out into a coughing fit. Maeve thumped her on the back and passed Nahla her tepid cup of tea.

"Are you getting sick? It's really cold in this classroom."

"I . . . I don't think I'm getting sick." Nahla caught her breath.

"You should get Gerry to check on the heating. He's a helpful guy."

"Don't you find him a bit . . . too helpful? I always get the sense he's coming on to me."

"Gerry? It's just how he is. Come to think of it, both he and Michael have flirty personalities. So that might be what you're picking up? I just ignore it, and they know I'm unavailable, but with you I can see how you'd question it. But believe me, they are both good guys."

"You might be right." Maeve *had* known them for years.

"Anyway, what were you saying about the student's initials?"

"I think . . . Sylvie was watching Leesa Allen." She felt her throat get scratchy again. "But it could have been any girl with the initial *L* with two friends *J* and *M*."

"*J* and *M*?"

"I suspect that refers to her two best friends, Jessica and Mallory." She gulped back cold peppermint tea. "They share a room at the residence. Always walk around as a threesome. I get the feeling they intimidate the other girls."

"Girls can be meaner than boys, especially to girls who are different in some way." Maeve's shoulders slumped, and Nahla guessed she had first-hand knowledge of such treatment.

"But it's strange that Sylvie was watching her, right? I've been trying to make sense of it. I've even started keeping an eye out, noticing that—" Just then, Nahla's chest tightened, and Maeve backed up a foot to stay out of her cough's wind. And then Sylvie's whisper poked through, "Non. Non."

Nahla caught her breath. *Did Sylvie want this kept a secret from Maeve? But why?* Maeve could possibly help her decode the notes.

"Sorry, sorry. I think it's passing now. Probably just the chalk dust."

"Maybe you should go home and rest up. There is a cold going around. Our students are germ factories," Maeve said, already out the door.

Leesa

Belltown had one second-run cinema and being the only entertainment in town, it was a popular Saturday night venue for Thornton students. *Birdy* was turning out to be pretty good, more art house and complex than Leesa had expected. She checked her watch in the film's grey glow; it was more than half over already. Rodney passed her the popcorn in the dark. It was coated in buttery topping, so Leesa declined and sipped her diet soda instead.

Rodney had casually stretched his arm across her back almost an hour ago, and now she guided his left hand to rest on her breast. His breathing quickened. She hoped that Mallory, seated beside her, would see the naughty move. Both she and Jessica thought she was taking a prude's pace with Rodney. Well, perhaps she'd step it up to cock-tease.

While they'd been officially an item since the dance in mid-December, this was only their second real date since the New Year.

She'd intimated that she'd moved too fast in a previous relationship and needed to go slow, and he'd agreed, saying that he needed a little time to get his head straight after Ashley's betrayal. They'd held hands in the hallways between classes, hugged hello, and there'd been quick kisses. *But how long could she could maintain the ruse?* Her aloof innocence would only keep him wanting. *Cosmopolitan* had taught her this much about men.

Rodney kissed her right temple and took her hand, resting it on his knee. Her real boyfriend would have rested it on his lap, a hint for her to slide her fingers toward his crotch. But she liked Rodney's warm hand around hers, the solidity of his knee.

Onscreen, Birdy told his best friend, Al, that he wished he could die and be reborn as a bird. Sure, that was weird, but she understood. As the camera swooped over Birdy and Al's neighbourhood's crowded streets and their makeshift ballpark, Leesa sensed his desire for freedom.

Could she keep Rodney stalled at second or third base? These terms, so meaningful years ago, now sounded infantile; after all, she was a woman with a lover. *"Lover"* — *was that the right word?* Yes, she liked how that sounded. And one day, she'd call him her "fiancé," her "husband."

As though sensing her distraction, Rodney squeezed her hand, and she reciprocated. He pulled her closer, enveloping her in his warmth and Old Spice. She nestled into the cleft between his shoulder and chest and felt his hard pecs under her cheekbone. Her lover's chest was slightly fleshier than Rodney's, more comfortable. But she stayed put because Rodney seemed happy.

Realizing the movie was reaching its climax, she pulled her hand off Rodney's knee and sat up abruptly. *Even if she was two-timing, it didn't feel right to be sexy with Rodney and then half an hour later with her lover, right?* She was not a slut.

The film's light illuminated Rodney's blonde crewcut, the fine stubble on his jaw. His facial features were soft, boyish, his masculinity covered by a thin layer of baby fat yet to be shed. She imagined what his face might look like twelve years from now.

"You all right?" Rodney whispered.

"Yeah, just a headache." This was her preplanned excuse for ending their date immediately after the movie's end. She rubbed her temples. They both turned their gazes back to the screen.

Finally, the credits rolled, accompanied by "La Bamba." Jessica and Mallory stepped out of their row and danced up the aisle, boyfriends in tow. Leesa and Rodney followed.

"That was crazy shit," Thomas said when they reached the lobby.

"Crazy homo shit," Evan agreed. Jessica and Mallory giggled, their standard affirmative response to their Thornton boyfriends.

"Yeah, but deep, right? A huge statement about the impact of war," Rodney said, and Leesa nodded smugly. Her Thornton boyfriend was obviously the smartest of the three.

"Nerd." Mallory laughed. She and Jessica, underdressed for the cold, began a half-canter to the parking lot.

"You guys want a ride?" Evan asked. "I'm gonna go drop Thomas and Jessica at the guys' residence and then go park with Mallory." Thomas had a room beside the back door and would sneak in Jessica. Evan and Rodney's rooms, on the other hand, bookended the teacher monitor's flat.

"Hey, it's only nine. We have two hours until curfew. Want to go somewhere?" Rodney asked Leesa.

"I'm really sorry, but my head is killing me. Must have been the MSG from dinner. I'll just walk home, clear my head."

"I'll walk with you."

"No, you go with them, get a ride. I'll walk on my own. The quiet and cold air will be good for my head. Really, *go.*" She instantly regretted her emphatic tone. She hadn't counted on him wanting to walk eight blocks through slush. "Besides, you don't have your boots on. You'll wreck your loafers."

He lowered his gaze to his shoes, perhaps inspecting the penny he'd inserted into the top strap's slot, Thornton's latest trend.

"You coming or not?" Evan yelled from his car, revving the engine. Rodney shrugged, his lips stretched into a slight pout. He gave her a quick peck on the mouth and ran to catch up with the others.

Leesa exhaled a cloud of relief into the minus-fifteen air. She hurried up the street, spotted the red tail lights of his car, then scanned back to make sure the others couldn't see her. She jogged twenty yards and smelled Marlboro smoke wafting out of the cracked window. She opened the passenger side and slid inside the almost hot-boxed interior.

"Let's wait a minute, okay? The others are in the cinema's parking lot. They likely won't come this way, but . . ."

He leaned over, kissed Leesa hard on the mouth, then recoiled. "*Ugh*. You smell like bad cologne. Did you make out with that pimply teenager during the movie?"

"No, I did not!" She pulled him close. He kissed her again, this time even harder. His jealousy — or maybe it was the beer she smelled on his breath — made him more ardent. She ventured, "But, you know, in order to maintain an alibi guy, I do have to string him along a little, otherwise he'll lose interest."

"Let him." He kissed her neck now, tenderly, but drew back, as though smelling rotting garbage.

"Don't be like that . . ." This was getting complicated. Maybe she could ask her roommates about their summer and Thornton boy-friends, glean some advice about how to manage two guys. Probably she shouldn't have tried to see them both on the same night, within minutes of each other. And she should've gifted Rodney a bottle of Polo aftershave, so at least their scents matched.

"I don't like the idea of you 'stringing him along.' Wait, what does that mean? Are you having sex with him?"

"No. No. I've got a whole 'taking-it-slow' thing going on with him."

"Dump him. I mean, I like that you're being careful, but there's gotta be a better way."

"Mallory and Jessica now just assume I'm out with Rodney when I'm with you. If I don't have him, they're going to start asking questions again." She could have added — but didn't, because she knew he wouldn't understand — that Rodney guaranteed her a secure position in their crowd.

He turned away and glowered into the steering wheel, a mirror without reflection.

"Come on, he's a child. He barely knows how to kiss." She hoped he wouldn't sense her lie; so far, Rodney was a terrific kisser. He and that cow Ashley must have practised a lot.

"Listen, I don't like this." He started the car and drove up the hill, too quickly, skidding.

"What are you doing? Where are we going?"

"I'm taking you home."

"Why? We have until curfew," she protested, but he stopped near the side of the residence and killed the engine.

"Just get out. I don't think this is going to work." His jaw was set, rigid like stone.

"I don't understand!" She waited for him to reply. "Please, talk to me!"

"I said, get out."

Reflexively, she wiped around the edges of her mouth to tidy her lipstick, before opening the car door. Rodney called out to her from half a block away. Heart racing, her brain scavenged for something useful, and she called out, "Thanks for the lift!"

The car's tires spun out before it sped away.

"Hey . . . I got halfway up the hill and, um, he . . . was driving by. It was colder than I thought," she explained to Rodney.

"Who?" He peered after the car. Clearly, he hadn't seen anything.

"Oh, um, that was just . . . Mr. Wolfe." Leesa's pulse quickened.

"Our geography teacher?"

"Yeah, but what are you doing here?"

"They dropped me at the residence." He pointed down the street and across the soccer field. "But I didn't feel right leaving you alone when you're not feeling good."

"That's sweet." At the centre of a see-saw between one guy being mean, and another kind, Leesa wasn't sure what to feel.

She looked into his brown eyes. He was handsome in his own way. "Okay, c'mon in. Guys are allowed to sit near the front."

They pulled off their snowy shoes and coats and sat on a couch in the deserted lobby alcove. She realized she'd never hung out with a guy like this, in plain sight. A few girls came through the doors, frigid air gusting them.

"I thought staff aren't allowed to offer students rides." Rodney's expression was neutral, but Leesa's back stiffened. She shoved down her annoyance and the gnawing fear that lay just below. *What had just happened?* She'd clearly lost control of this situation. *Should she even be sitting here with Rodney? Or should she be downstairs, on the phone, sorting out things?*

"I'm pretty sure it is breaking the rules, but let's keep it between us? I wouldn't want anyone to get in trouble." The words stuck in her throat like a popcorn kernel's husk. She didn't care that her secret relationship was prohibited, had always believed their love, their relationship, was above any stupid rule. But now, spoken aloud, the notion was somehow . . . well, strange.

"Cool," he said, scooting closer to her on the couch. "How's your head?"

"Oh, much better." She relaxed, allowing herself to feel his warm lips, his hand roving down her arms. Here they were, kissing under the florescent bulbs of the front lobby. More girls swung through the front doors, and Leesa ignored them, reminding herself that what they were doing was normal. She breathed in his cheap, adolescent cologne and didn't mind it a bit.

Zahabiya

"That was intense." Lavinia heaved a sigh as the credits rolled.

"*Uh-huh.*" I was still stunned by the ending.

"Yeah, war sucks," Marie declared. We all nodded earnestly.

The screen went black, and we gathered our coats.

"Our entire school was here tonight," Marie said, as we filed out of the theatre and into the empty lobby.

"Except for the nerd boys," Lavinia said. Cyril and Jason had opted for the school's Saturday Dungeons & Dragons gathering instead of the movie, which was disappointing.

"Don't knock D&D. It's a lot of fun, although the female characters are nearly always scantily clad." Marie pushed open the cinema's doors, and we braced against the frigid wind.

"Like I said, nerd boys. The only way they'll encounter girls is through those characters. Well, maybe not Jason." Lavinia looked at me, but I remained silent. Marie sputtered a laugh.

"Ahem. Girl, that was a cue for you to spill," Lavinia persisted as we started up the hill.

"Well . . ." I began, trying to summarize my disorganized thoughts, but Marie interrupted me.

"Guys, look!" She pointed up the street. We watched as a girl got into a car. "Is that Leesa Allen?"

"That looks like her pink coat," I said.

"Why do we care?" Lavinia asked.

"I don't know yet, but I need to get a few photos." Marie pulled us back against the wall with one arm while rummaging in her bag for the camera she always carried. She clicked. "Don't know if there's enough light. Crap, there isn't."

While Marie clicked, and Lavinia muttered under her breath, I squinted, seeing two dark figures in the car. The shadows merged into one, then pulled away.

"They're making out." The car continued to idle for a minute, then swerved as the driver pulled away from the curb.

"Is this for an art project or something?" Lavinia stared after the vehicle, now almost out of sight.

"Something like that." Marie blew a plume of white vapour into the frosty air. We trudged up the hill, Marie two steps ahead of us. Lavinia and I shared a look of confusion. Why was Marie acting so strange?

"Anyway, so what about Jason?" Lavinia asked.

"No news since the kiss two weeks ago." I bent down to straighten my leg warmers. "I mean, we're still friends and hang out, but—"

"He hasn't made another move?" Lavinia asked. "That's weird. I don't get it."

"We've hardly been alone, and when we have been, he just gets really shy, and I guess I do, too? I think there's something wrong with me; it's like everyone else but me got the memo on how to flirt."

"What do you think?" Lavinia asked Marie, who'd been quiet.

"For God's sake, stop being such a coward. If you want to date him, ask him out." Marie turned and continued to walk a step ahead of us. "Just ask him out."

Marie's harsh tone silenced me.

"I agree, be direct. It's the only way you're going to know." Lavinia wrapped her arm around my shoulders. I appreciated her gentler tone.

"I know, you're right. It's just that in the moment, I can't find the words. I dunno why."

We walked up the manor's steps and as we passed the lobby's alcove, Marie stopped short, mouth agape.

"Let's go." Lavinia pulled Marie by the arm.

"Is this the *Twilight Zone* or what?" Marie asked.

"What do you mean?" Lavinia frowned.

"She got into that car, and now is necking with Rodney!" Marie peeked around the corner at the lovebirds.

"So . . . ? She must have been with him in the car, and now they're here," Lavinia said.

"I guess *they're* not cowards." I continued down the hallway.

"Sorry. I shouldn't have said it that way. I'm just a little preoccupied. Zahabiya, I'm sorry."

"It's fine." I exhaled and mentally shook off the hurt.

"Listen, let's dump our stuff and meet back in my room. I want to show you something. It's important." Marie strode ahead of us. Lavinia headed toward her wing, and I followed Marie, a few steps back, into ours.

I opened my door, relieved to have the room to myself for a bit. Mei was probably out with her own friends, the small clique of Thornton punk kids she'd connected with recently. She'd started to wear face powder a shade lighter than her pigment, in addition to ringing her eyes in black pencil and shadow. When not in uniform, she only wore black. When I'd asked about the transformation, Mei had shrugged and said that she'd finally found a crowd she fit in with. "We all like the same music." I hardly saw her these days, except when we had to be in our room.

After hanging my coat and changing into slippers, I went to the window and stared out into the dark. I thought about Marie's words. I had to admit that she was right — I was scared. I was scared of being rejected by Jason, or worse, getting close and then losing him. Like I'd lost my mom. I hated that lately all my choices — coming to Thornton, being cold to Tara, being super shy with Jason — seemed to be about that.

I slid open the window and let in the frigid wind. While she wasn't a fan of winter, my mom used to say that a burst of icy air was good for the brain. I breathed it in for a minute, then shut my window. Yeah, I needed to get it together. I needed to face my fears. I just wasn't sure how.

I walked across to Marie's, where she was poring over some loose photographs that she'd spread across her bed. I stood by her side and scanned her display.

"You're doing a project about cars?" I was confused; these were nowhere as artistic as her other photography projects.

"Kind of."

"All right, so what's this all about?" Lavinia joined us by the bed.

"Wait," Marie said, gathering up everything. "We'd better move. Barb might be back soon, and we don't want her blabbing." Barb was one of the more popular girls who hung around Leesa.

"Zahabiya's room, then. My roommate is in the same category," Lavinia said. "Carrie's a nice girl. I can't believe she's in with that crowd."

"Yeah, they're two-faced. Nice in private, but barely acknowledge me otherwise."

We crossed the hall and congregated around my bed. Marie closed the door behind us.

"Remember when I overheard that lover's argument with Leesa way back in November?" Lavinia and I both nodded. "So, here's the photo of that car. You can't read the licence plate. I wasn't at the right angle, but it's definitely a blue hatchback."

"Okaaaay . . . and?" Lavinia asked.

"A few days later, I passed by that car — or one that looks just like it — in the *staff* end of the parking lot."

"And the car from tonight looked like that, too," I said. "But there might be a lot of blue hatchbacks out there."

"I saw the first three numbers of the licence plate tonight. *LNO*, something, something, something," Marie said. "We should write that down."

I offered her a pen, and Marie wrote the digits on the manila folder.

"Crap, I wish I'd gotten closer that day in the parking lot so we could compare the plates." Marie squinted at the photo and shook her head.

"Wait, do you think one of the staff is taking advantage of Leesa?" Lavinia asked.

"I think so." Marie exhaled and squinted at us, gauging our reactions.

"Who?" My mind travelled to a TV show I'd watched last year, about a soccer coach who'd abused a fifteen-year-old girl on his team. At first, I'd thought the girl was partly responsible for getting involved with him, but by the end I could see that he'd taken advantage of his authority and her age. I didn't like Leesa, but I wouldn't ever want to see that happen to her.

"I don't know. Because this photo," she pointed to the one from November, "isn't that good, I haven't been able to confirm."

"That's serious, if it's true."

"But something about this doesn't make sense. If Leesa was in Rodney's car tonight, then maybe that was also Rodney's car back in November? He could have parked it on the staff side." I sensed that Marie wasn't telling us everything.

"They have different permits. I've passed by it a few more times. Crap, I should have written down the licence plate."

"I agree with Zahabiya; this is confusing." Lavinia nodded.

"Listen, if you guys don't believe me, that's fine," she said, her face going red. She wound her camera and popped out the roll. "I'll go develop these. And on Monday, I'll go take some photos in the school parking lot, get his licence plate. And we can compare all the photos. Then you'll see I'm right."

"No, Marie, we believe you, but—" Before I could finish my thought, she'd gathered up all the photos and slammed the door behind her.

I took a step toward the door, but Lavinia said, "Leave her. She'll come around. I've learned when she's in a mood, it's best to leave her be."

Nahla

"So, I got the goods for you." Maeve's eyes were bright as she scanned the menu. A week had passed since she'd offered to gather information about Michael's love life.

"And . . . what did you find out?" The waiter arrived, and they hurried to give him their order.

"He's single!" Maeve singsonged with jazz hands accompaniment, then shoulder-checked to ensure no one had overheard her performance. The restaurant was packed with a buttoned-up after-church crowd.

"I see." So, he just wasn't interested in her, then.

"He says he's busy with his art and helping out his mother. Did you know his father died five years ago?" Maeve lowered her voice. "His mother had some kind of nervous breakdown after that, so he lives with her. I can't imagine living in my parents' house."

"He's a good son, it sounds like." All week, Nahla had been judging him as a Casanova to fend off her longing. Now this image popped like a soap bubble, replaced with a picture of an admirable man.

"There's more . . ."

"What?" Maeve's expression was cunning. Nahla felt a stone drop in her stomach.

"Well, I needed to find a way to find out if he was interested in you . . ."

"Oh, no, Maeve. You said you wouldn't bring my name into it!"

"I didn't do it directly!" Maeve held up her hands in self-defence. "Just listen, okay?"

"Okay, sorry. Go on."

"I started talking about how I was making my own curriculum binder, just like Sylvie's, and I told him that you'd mentioned that you'd found that mysterious book with notes about one of the popular girls. Anyway, when I talked about you, his eyes lit up, so I commented on *that*. I said, 'Michael, your face is giving you away! You like Nahla!'"

"Oh, God, Maeve!" Nahla held her head, mortified. She wasn't sure she wanted to hear his reply.

"And, you know what? He said, yes, he likes you a lot. Apparently, he got scared off because he dated a co-worker in the past and it ended badly."

"So, he was telling the truth." The waiter slid their plates onto the table. Nahla said a silent prayer over her noodles, but really it was for herself and Michael. She leaned in, hoping that there would be a happy ending to Maeve's long-winded report.

"So, I told him to stop being such a dodo and ask you out," Maeve said, midchew. "And you know what? He said he would! You're welcome! I just solved the Michael-Nahla problem!" Maeve stabbed a chicken ball with her fork and held it up in victory.

"Are you sure he didn't think I put you up to it?" Nahla's dish tasted undercooked, the sticky sauce over the noodles congealing as it cooled.

"No, the conversation was really organic. I promise. We were just two colleagues gabbing. He didn't suspect a thing." She shovelled forkfuls of rice into her mouth like a woman who hadn't eaten in years.

"Well, thanks, Cupid."

She had her doubts that Maeve's efforts would lead to anything, but when Michael dropped by her classroom on Monday afternoon — his expression bashful or perhaps sheepish — she understood that they had. They made stilted small talk about their weekends and the weather before Michael steeled himself and said what he came to say.

"Listen, I know I said that we shouldn't date because we're colleagues, but I realize now, after getting to know you, that that was silly. We're both sensible people. Maybe we should at least give it a try, maybe go out, get to know each other better?"

"I'd like that. And yes, of course, we'll be sensible. If it doesn't work out, we'll go back to being . . . respected co-workers." *Is that what they were to each other?*

"Or friends at the very least."

"Yes, of course, friends at the very least." Chills of excitement raced up her back, scurrying to her throat, spilling out into a smile that matched his.

Leesa

Leesa zipped up her coat and slid on her boots. A bell rang, signalling study period's end. Like most Wednesday evenings, the hour before going out had felt interminable, but tonight, instead of anticipation, there was worry. She had to fix things.

"Someone's in a hurry to get some nookie!" Mallory commented, stretching in her chair.

"Wait, I thought the guys had some special house meeting tonight," Jessica said.

"Oh, really? Rodney didn't mention it. Maybe he's cutting."

"I don't think they're allowed," Jessica called as Leesa rushed from the room. She really needed to pay more attention to Rodney's schedule. Oh, well, she'd have to concoct an excuse of waiting for him, then going for a walk on her own or something.

She stepped around the back of the building, taking care not to slip on the ice crust the salt hadn't yet slushed. She saw a hatchback parked a block away, farther away than usual. But no, it was slightly larger and maybe a different shade of blue.

Except in passing hallway glances at school, they hadn't interacted since their argument on Saturday night. Their normal phone call just before study hall had been a small relief, blanketing over her anxiety like a threadbare quilt.

But where was he now?

She was about to turn around, but an arm poked out of the driver's side and waved like a flag.

She pulled on the unfamiliar door handle, slid in. Her back slammed against the seat with the car's abrupt acceleration.

"Sorry, not yet used to the peppy gas pedal." He steered them in the direction of their usual spot. She exhaled.

"Whose car is this?"

"Remember I mentioned my aunt getting rid of her old car? This is it. Sold it to me cheap. It's an '82. A Firenza, a nice upgrade."

"It's definitely bigger than the old one." She eyed the *Oldsmobile* logo near the dash. Fitting name.

"Yup, which I sold. Got a few hundred for it."

"That's great." Her father had given her a 1984 Fiat in June when she turned seventeen, but she'd barely driven it. She'd love to be able to give it to him.

He still hadn't looked at her, his gaze on the road ahead.

"So, how are you?" she broached.

"Good, fine." She wished she could shine a flashlight on his face, properly scrutinize his expression, and more so, magically view his inner thoughts and feelings.

"You're . . . you're not still upset about Rodney are you?" She shooed away her mild guilt about the daily make-out sessions in the library's book stacks. Since the weekend, she'd decided she liked Rodney. And now she was part of a group of six and one of the most popular couples at school. She rationalized that she'd stay with Rodney for the year, and maybe even next year if that made sense, and when they graduated, they'd part amicably. High school romances weren't expected to last; everyone knew that.

"Look, I get you're trying to keep us a secret by using him. But I don't wanna hear about, don't wanna know about, it."

"All right." He was right; the only way she could juggle them both was to keep things separate. He turned a corner too quickly, and the car veered out into the middle of the road. An oncoming car's headlights blinded her, and she thought for sure they'd crash. But both drivers braked in time, and Michael navigated the car back to their side of the road.

"Fuck." Visibly shaken, he drove more slowly.

"But thank God you have quick reflexes."

To shift the mood, Leesa considered telling him about Jessica and Thomas almost getting caught half-naked by the residence monitor, but then couldn't because the anecdote involved Rodney creating a distraction. She tried to think up another funny story.

He pulled over, and she realized she'd spaced out for most of the drive. The farmer's field was blanketed in thick snow that reflected the nearly full moon's illumination.

"Hey, I thought maybe I could tell everyone I'm going to visit Lyndee Saturday night and then you and I can go back to the hotel. Do you think you can get away?" She squeezed his bicep, strong and more substantial than Rodney's. She felt the muscle relax.

"Sorry, I've got plans Saturday night." He stroked her thigh. Leesa stiffened. "It's just a boring work thing. Lowery is hosting. I have to make an appearance once in a while, right?"

"I guess . . ."

"Listen, but I have something important to talk to you about." His eyes darted to her face and then through the windshield.

"Okay." She rubbed his hand to soothe herself.

"That bitch Leblanc kept a notebook."

"A notebook?"

"It had information about us. Details about your comings and goings. It doesn't have our names, apparently, just your initials. And Nahla — Miss Naim — has it with her."

"About my comings and goings?" She already knew about Leblanc's spying and she was so over it. What made her pay attention was the mention of Miss Naim.

"See, Babe? I told you Sylvie was dangerous."

"How did you find out about this?"

"Meddler Maeve — Miss McKinney — was blabbing about it in the staff room. I think everyone might know about it by now. Pretty soon Headmaster Lowery is going to ask to see it."

"So, it's a kook's diary." She relaxed. "And you said with just initials, right? And nothing about you? Just calm down."

Here he was, talking about Leblanc again. A dead person, someone who wasn't even a threat to them anymore. *Was he going paranoid again?* She helped herself to his cigarette pack and lit a smoke. She took the first drag, passed it to him, and checked the glove compartment for the flask he carried. She untwisted the cap, took a swig, grimaced at the bitterness, then passed it over to him.

"I have to get it from Nahla. I have to see if there is anything that could implicate me."

"Has Miss Naim ever said anything to let on that she knows about us? She hasn't talked to me about it."

He shook his head in reply, rolled down the window, and blew smoke out into the night air.

"Well, then? What's the problem?" *Why was he being so illogical?*

"I have to know for sure."

"I think it's better if you stay out of it." She pressed her lips together to contain her true feelings: she wanted him to stay away from Miss Naim. Despite his denials, a tiny and probably irrational part of her still didn't believe him about that cool night last fall when Miss Naim came home with smeared lipstick and smelling a little like Polo. And anyway, any attractive woman, and especially one closer in age, whom he saw so regularly, could be a threat.

"I'll just try to talk to her about it at the staff thing. And then we can see each other on Sunday afternoon instead. We can rent a motel room over in Olmstead, so we don't have to drive all the way to Toronto."

"I can't on Sunday. Um . . . Jessica bought concert tickets, and I said I'd go." It was Rodney who'd bought tickets to see The Spoons.

"Well, we'd better make good use of our time now, then. We only have half an hour before we have to get you back." He leaned over and kissed her. He unzipped her coat, slid a cold hand under her blouse. She exhaled, choosing to let go of her irritation with him. She focused instead on his hand on the back of her head, his laboured breathing. All signs that they were okay.

Zahabiya

I followed Lavinia's advice and waited for Marie to cool off, which was hard. I worried that she was so pissed off, she wouldn't want to be friends anymore. It was a relief when she knocked on my door on Wednesday night.

"So, I was going to develop the roll from my shots on Monday, but there wasn't one." Marie's shoulders slumped. "Stupid me, I forgot to load the camera."

"Sorry, Marie." I'd gone over the weird conversation about the blue hatchback many times in my mind, wondering if I'd said something wrong. I resolved to tread more carefully around the subject.

"But I still have the roll from Saturday night to develop. And I just bought a new roll." She passed me the camera, its weight forcing me to grab hold with both hands. "You have a spare tomorrow morning, right? Can you pass by the parking lot and get the photos? I've got classes back-to-back all day."

"Do you really think . . ." I wanted to say no, but Marie's expression was pained. I made my tone gentler. " . . . this will prove anything?"

"We have to try. If something is going on, don't we have to find out?" Marie shook her head, as though disagreeing with her own thoughts.

I wondered why this couldn't wait until Friday, or another day when she had a spare. But then, my mind travelled back to that show and to the girl who was being abused by her coach.

"So, how do I use this thing?"

———

I walked through the parking lot, Marie's camera in hand, freezing in my kilt and blazer. She was certain our focus was a blue hatchback, but had given me instructions to photograph every smallish blueish car.

I spotted and snapped seven vehicles' backsides. Some were too big, but I only wanted to do this dubious exercise once, so I was thorough.

"Whatcha doing?" Gerry opened his car door. I hadn't noticed him sitting in the last blue car I photographed. He stepped out and locked the vehicle. A blue jay landed on the grey Beetle parked next to it, her bright plumage catching my eye.

"Oh, well . . ." The blue jay cheeped loudly, distracting Gerry and giving me a second to think. I remembered Marie's excuse for pulling out her camera after the movie.

"It's . . . for an art project . . . Mr. . . . Gerry." Although I'd seen him around school, I'd never really spoken to him, and like the other maintenance staff at Thornton, I didn't know his surname.

"Well, if you think she's art-worthy, go ahead. Here, take another one, with me in it this time." He posed for me, chest proud, hands on hips, pelvis cocked forward. I adjusted the focus and considered that Gerry's car was an exact copy of the one we'd spied after *Birdy*. It also matched Marie's photo from the day she witnessed Leesa arguing with a man in this same parking lot. Through the viewfinder, I studied Gerry's letchy pose and flirty gaze. Holy crap. *Was this the staff person Marie thought was the abuser?*

143

I told myself not to judge, to keep an open mind. But the longer I looked at Gerry, the more creeped out I felt.

The bell rang, and I hurried inside, Gerry jabbering on behind me about having just gotten rid of his old clunker.

I took my seat at the back, just as Mr. Stephenson was starting class.

Jason waved at me from the next seat over; I mouthed a "hello." He pointed to the camera and mimed a question with his palms open.

"All right, ladies and gentlemen, no art for the first half of class today. We have the obligatory monthly quiz," Mr. Stephenson announced, and we all groaned. He opened his desk drawer, pulled out a pile of sheets, and started distributing them.

"It's Marie's," I said. Mr. Stephenson glanced our way, and I lowered my voice. "I was borrowing it."

Maria, Lavinia, and I had agreed to keep this "project" among ourselves for now. I put the camera back in its case and stuffed it into my bookbag.

"Can I ask you something?" His frown told me this wasn't about the camera.

"Sure," I said, bracing myself.

"Do I need to separate the two of you?" Mr. Stephenson had materialized beside Jason. He tossed us each a test paper.

"No, sir."

"No, sir."

"Don't look so serious. I was just joking," Mr. Stephenson said, before returning to the front of the room. "Okay, everyone begin."

I glanced at Jason, but he was now focused on the test. The fifteen multiple-choice questions about Impressionist art were easy. I checked my work, then looked up to see that Jason was scribbling fretfully. He tore a page from his notebook, and when Mr. Stephenson's back was turned, slid it across to me.

I'm not sure if you feel the same way about me, but I really like you. Do you feel that way, too?

144

His worried expression, so open and vulnerable, made my heart crack open. I wrote,

Yes, I do really like you . . . I wasn't sure if you did!

He took the note and scrutinized it a moment, then passed the page back to me with a new note:

I know, I'm bad at this kind of thing.

Me, too.

Okay, so, we'll be bad at this together?

Works for me.

He read my words, then gazed up at me in a manner that made my skin prickle in a good way. Since the weekend, I'd been rehearsing the words for a version of this conversation in my mind, but I hadn't found a moment to talk with him alone. Finally, we were having it. There was so much more I wanted to say.

Mr. Stephenson grabbed the note out of Jason's hand. I gasped.

"Maybe I do need to separate the two of you. Frankly I'm sur-prised—" He read the note, stifled a laugh, and returned it to Jason.

"My mistake. Okay everyone, time's up. Pass your test to the person in front of you for marking, and we'll go through the answers together."

Jason and I spent the rest of the class trying not to crack up.

Nahla

On Saturday, Michael suggested they meet at Headmaster Lowery's staff gathering, then slip away for an 8:30 p.m. reservation at Stella's, a restaurant in the next town over, where they'd be less likely to be gawked at by students. The candlelit ambiance reminded Nahla of her favourite Montreal haunts. She confessed she hadn't been home since September.

"Not even for holidays?" He refilled her wine glass from the bottle on the table. She waved her hand to slow his pour.

"Well, my father is upset with me for taking a job so far away, for moving out."

"But you're an adult. What's his problem?"

"True, twenty-four is an adult, but only if a girl — or I should say, 'a woman' — is married. I don't know a single unmarried woman from my community who lives on her own. It just isn't done. To him, the problem is . . . that I bring shame." She took a sip of wine to wash down the acidity in her words.

"Wow, really traditional." He shook his head, which left her wondering if she'd portrayed her family and culture as backward. She knew that most white Canadians saw Lebanese and Muslim people this way and she didn't want to perpetuate a stereotype.

"The real problem is sexism, and that's in every culture. But anyway . . . just imagine if my father could see me now, drinking wine and on a date with a handsome non-Muslim man." She blushed at her babbling. "Oh, boy. Le vin desserre la langue."

"What's that mean? Sorry, it's been a while since I took French in school."

"Wine loosens the tongue." She was enjoying her lightheaded courage. It was 1985, after all, and women were allowed to be forward, right?

"So, you think I'm handsome, eh?" He winked at her. "*You* look lovely tonight." She blushed at the compliment, glad her efforts had been noticed. She'd washed her hair that afternoon, coaxing it into perfect corkscrew curls. She'd also used blue eyeliner, like she'd seen some of the girls do, and wore a new bright-red lipstick. She sat taller in her chair to highlight her cleavage.

"Tell me something about you. What's your family like?"

"It's just me and my mom. Dad passed five years ago." He swatted his mouth with his napkin, as though wiping away his admission.

"Sorry."

"When I left for university, I never thought I'd come back — it wasn't a happy home. Dad was a mean drunk. But right after I got my degree, he got sick, and my mother asked me to come home. I got this job a week after he died. Then I just stayed because my mother needed company . . . I guess the wine's loosening my tongue, too." His smile looked forced.

"We sometimes make hard sacrifices for our families." But she was tired of sacrifices; she was enjoying the freedom of this night.

"At least I have my art studio in the basement. But I've gotta move out soon, even though it will upset my mom. I'm saving up money, so I can quit and focus on my art. Then I'll move somewhere that has an art scene . . . maybe Montreal, who knows." Even though she knew he was just being flirtatious, her heart swelled.

———

"Can you drop me at the back? I'd like to avoid a potential audience," Nahla asked. They were still a few blocks from the residence.

"I was thinking the same thing. I know how fast news spreads around here. Hey, that reminds me. Maeve is telling everyone you found a secret diary?"

"I can't believe she did that! But yeah, it's Sylvie's. It's cryptic, probably meaningless. But I'll show it to you sometime, if you'd like."

"Yeah, sure. I like a mystery. Is this a good spot?" He pulled up across the street from the back entrance and cut the engine. The street was deserted.

"Perfect. But if it's okay, I'll give it a couple of minutes before going in." She scanned the street behind them.

"No worries. I have a cute story for you." He told her about intercepting his students' love note on Thursday.

"Oh, that is cute! Zahabiya and Jason are a good match."

"It was kinda hilarious — and so innocent! When I was a kid, teachers would have read a note like that aloud and embarrassed you."

"I'm sure they appreciated your discretion."

"Ah, young love." He smiled at her.

Two generous pours of wine had anaesthetized the nervousness that, earlier in the night, had run through her like a twitchy mouse. Now, when he leaned in for a kiss, it felt easy, natural, her body warm, relaxed, open.

"It's getting cold. Can I come up for a bit? Is there a way to slip in the back?" He kissed her again. She considered his suggestion, charmed. *He really did like her. But would he expect sex? Were Canadians that fast?*

"Maybe next time, Michael. I've had a terrific night. But now I'm ten minutes late for bedcheck."

"I won't stay long . . . I always wondered what teacher suites were like."

While tempted, she recognized his fib.

"I'll ask Margo to cover bedcheck for me next Saturday — how's that?"

"I'll take it." When they kissed again, she kept one hand on the cold door handle, so she wouldn't lose her resolve.

"Goodnight, Michael."

"Goodnight." He started the engine and waited until she'd unlocked the back door before driving off.

With her coat still on, she began the first-floor bedcheck. The girls were asleep or ready to tuck in. When she arrived at the last door, Mei and Zahabiya were reclining in bed, talking quietly, the way she and her sisters used to do. She walked on, wishing she had someone she could confide in tonight. Perhaps she'd call Maeve in the morning.

When she came around to the lobby, she found Leesa Allen sitting near the front doors, alone.

"Hey, Leesa, you should be in your room by now."

"Yeah, I'm going." Leesa turned and marched down the hallway toward the stairwell. Nahla counted to twenty before doing the same.

She climbed the stairs and with a tight chest, peeked past the first door. The three girls were in the midst of a conversation that they concluded when they saw her.

"Girls. Lights out." She deepened her voice, so it sounded authoritative.

"Yes, Miss Naim," Jessica said. Leesa looked out the window, and Mallory rolled her eyes. Nahla carried on down the hallway. Everyone was accounted for. She could say that she'd done her job.

She was glad to reach the end of the hallway and her flat. She shut her door and closed her eyes, dwelling on the last few minutes in the car with Michael. The wine's swimmy feeling lingered, and she called up the body memory of making out with him.

She opened the window and lit a bedtime cigarette. She exhaled into the dark but turned around when she felt the familiar, chilly vibe of Sylvie's presence. She recalled her teta telling her that sometimes she could catch a glimpse of spirits in their home if they chose to be seen. Nahla, now emboldened by the last caresses of alcohol and nicotine, wished that Sylvie would make herself visible.

"Allez, Sylvie. Parle avec moi."

She filled her water glass at the sink and spied Sylvie's notebook on her kitchen counter. All week, she'd meant to return it to Sylvie's family, especially after hearing Maeve tell everyone about it in the staff lounge. But she'd kept forgetting, as though multiple temporary amnesias had intercepted her intention.

"What do you think of my handsome date, Sylvie?" Nahla said aloud.

"Regardez encore." Look again.

As she'd done many times before, she flipped to the two pages filled with Sylvie's handwriting.

As she read, it dawned on her that Sylvie's notes could be about illegal activities. *Why was Leesa standing by the front doors tonight, appearing to be keeping watch?* Margo once mentioned that she thought someone in the residence was selling marijuana at the school. *Had Nahla interrupted something tonight?*

"Ma chérie, Leesa n'est pas une criminelle."

"No?" *Then what had she been doing?* She waited.

"Sylvie?" Silence, again. Maybe her mind was playing tricks on her.

Nahla closed the notebook in frustration. It was a waste of her time. Sylvie's lingering likely had nothing to do with it or with her. Maybe Nahla needed to light some bakhoor, say some prayers, and evict the spirit for good.

She resolved to ask Mrs. Reeves for Sylvie's family's mailing address on Monday.

Leesa

On Sunday afternoon, they were back at their usual spot beside the farmer's field. The horse grazed. The countryside's silence enveloped them, like itchy wool stuffed in ears.

"How was your staff party?" She rolled her window down a crack.

"Dull."

"Did you see Miss Naim there? Did you ask her about the notebook?"

"No, I couldn't get there until late, and she apparently was there, but left early. I'll try to talk to her this week."

"That's funny."

"What?"

"She came home late last night." At least this time, when she got near her, she didn't smell like him.

"Really?"

"Whatever, who cares about that bitch."

He fished in the glove box for his flask and offered it to her. She took a sip of the bitter drink and passed it back to him. She watched as he took several gulps, emptying the flask, like a man dying of thirst.

When he didn't reach for her immediately after, a thought, maggoty, wiggled through Leesa's mind, and not for the first time: *Was he losing interest in her?* But then he stroked her thigh and said, "This is nice, right? We don't often get the whole afternoon to ourselves."

"Yeah, it's nice."

"Why don't you just blow off your concert tonight, so we have more time? We can go for a drive, get something to eat."

She could have been sweet and agreed, or told him a lie about why she couldn't, but now he was annoying her. She'd organized her whole schedule around him and his ridiculous paranoia.

"No, that would be rude. I can't just cancel at the last minute and keep moving things around all the time. And, by the way, Mallory and Jessica are going to see a movie next Saturday, and so probably Rodney will ask me, too, and it will be weird if I don't go, so I think I'm busy next Saturday night."

"Hey, hey, don't get all worked up about it. And I told you not to mention that dumbass's name. Go to your movie, then next week we can have the whole Sunday to ourselves. Okay?"

"Okay. Sorry, I'm just a little stressed right now."

"Let's see if we can make it better." He opened his door and got into the back seat, then gestured to her to join him.

Zahabiya

"How was your first date?" Lavinia asked. We were walking across the frozen sports field after Sunday night dinner. The yellow street lamps illuminated the hardened ridges of frigid mud that made our steps uneven.

"Sweet. We made pizza, then hung out in his basement."

"Were his parents home?" Marie asked.

"Yeah for a few minutes, but they mostly left us alone."

"And . . . ?" Lavinia nudged me.

"We watched TV, and you'll both be proud of me: I was direct. I made the first move and said, 'Wanna make out?'" I was proud of myself. Ever since we passed notes in art class, I'd resolved to hold back less, to take more chances, and not wait until I had the words just right before saying them.

"Girl, you might be a late bloomer, but you sure are a fast learner." Lavinia laughed.

"Good job," Marie said. But I could tell her mind was elsewhere; she'd been subdued for most of the evening. I knew she'd picked up her developed rolls that afternoon and wanted to show them to us.

We entered the manor, the warmth from the lobby's old radiators thawing me. We agreed to meet up in my room. I was uneasy about what the photos would reveal, especially after that photo shoot with Gerry.

Five minutes later, Marie laid seven photos across my bedspread, as though setting up a game of solitaire.

"Here are all the blue cars that Zahabiya photographed." Marie then pulled another two photos from her folder. "Here's the one I took from November, when I overheard the argument in the parking lot." She turned it over and showed us its label in purple marker: *Argument*.

"And here's the car we saw Leesa getting into after the movie." On its back was *MOVIE* in green block letters. Both older photos were taken from a distance, one slightly over-exposed and the other dimly lit. Still, we agreed that Argument and MOVIE looked like identical cars.

We turned our attention to the row of seven cars I'd photographed.

"These are way too big," I pulled away two station wagons from the lineup. I was pleased to see that I'd managed the lens; all the photos were in focus, the licence plates readable.

"And those two sedans can go, right?" Lavinia discarded them. Now, only three hatchbacks remained. Lavinia placed them under Argument and MOVIE. One was longer and flatter, so we took it out, too.

"And this one on the bottom left has a small dent in the back. Do those?" Marie asked, scrutinizing the earlier photos. She shook her head. "Too hard to tell."

"I spot a difference! This hatchback," I pointed. "See? This one has a teeny-tiny little sticker on the back window, but our earlier ones don't, right?"

We stared at the photos, our focus broken when Mei walked into the room.

I caught a whiff of stale cigarette smoke; Mei had adopted the habit recently.

"Mei, c'mere. Have a look at these four photos. Which one doesn't belong?" I invited her into our semicircle. Marie filled her in on our mission.

After a moment of scanning the images, Mei picked out the car with the sticker.

"We have our winning car," Lavinia said, looking at the triad of images that remained in the lineup. "But, what does it mean?"

"It belongs to Gerry," Marie said, sliding out one more photo from her envelope. It was the one with Gerry posing with his car.

"That was the photo I told you all about! Why'd you hold that one back, Marie?" I asked.

"But it couldn't be Gerry with Leesa that night! I've been here the longest, you guys." Lavinia pursed her lips at the photos. "I mean, okay, he's kinda goofy sometimes, and this photo is . . . *eww*. But he's got a good heart. There's got to be another explanation."

"Yeah. I held it back because it confused me. His licence plate doesn't start with *LNO*. And I swear that night I saw an *LNO*." Marie turned over her manila folder where she'd written the letters.

"Gerry did say that he'd just bought the car. Could he have gotten a new licence plate, too?" I studied Gerry's *MZY 65R* licence plate.

"We need sustenance." Mei plucked a bag of gummy worms from her desk drawer and passed it around.

Lavinia declined the candy bag, but picked up MOVIE. "I still think Rodney was in the car with her that night. How else do you explain what we saw?"

Marie kept her gaze on the photos, her expression inscrutable.

I chomped on a green worm, letting it melt on my tongue. Our collective gears seemed stuck.

Outside, a dog barked. Then barked again and started howling. He was all I could hear. I tried to block him out, so I could think, but it was impossible. I went to the window. Outside, a small woman was being pulled down the sidewalk by a beefy German shepherd. When he saw me through the glass pane, he wagged his tail and barked again. His owner yanked at him, regaining control, and he finally followed her away, glancing over his shoulder at me. With the quiet, my mind cleared.

"Geez! Finally, that noise stopped!" Lavinia said.

"I have an idea. When I can't solve a math problem, I start over, from the beginning. Bring back all the other photos?" I wasn't sure what I was looking for, but Marie nodded and placed all the blue car photos in a line.

"Look! Here's an *LNO!*" Mei slapped the bedspread, and the photos sprung up in unison. It was the long, flat hatchback we'd earlier discarded.

"Crap, how did I miss that?" Marie picked up the photo, looked at it closely.

"Whose car is that? Staff or student?" Lavinia asked.

"I'm pretty sure staff, but unless we see the owner—" I said.

"We can't know for sure." Lavinia folded her arms into a tight knot over her chest.

No one said a word. We stared down at the photos in a confusing, silent standoff with them.

"No. No. I have a strong feeling about all this. A strong feeling. But why is the *LNO* on this car?" Marie frowned. "It's like they switched licence plates. And who did Gerry buy his car from?"

"He didn't say," I replied.

"I have to ask: Why are you so obsessed with this? I mean, we know you don't care about Leesa Allen." Lavinia studied Marie.

"I'm not obsessed . . . I just . . . I know what I saw." Marie looked hurt.

"If it's not Gerry, who do you think it is?" I ran through the other men on staff: Mr. Wolfe. *Maybe?* But he seemed nice. Mr. Thompson was all business, so it was hard to get a read on him. Mr. Patel was like a kindly uncle type, the only teacher who pronounced my name correctly. *Mr. Stephenson?* Unlikely, he was so cool about things. *Headmaster Lowery?* I'd only really talked to him during my interview.

"Until I have definitive proof, I don't want to say. Not yet." She stood and paced the small room.

"I think . . . I think we have to take Marie seriously." Mei made extended eye contact with Lavinia and me. "What if she's right? I mean, I don't really care about Leesa either, but still, she might be a victim, and there might be others."

"But if you could tell us who you think it might be, we could narrow it down at least," Lavinia said. Marie shook her head.

"I know," I said with a resigned sigh, "on Monday before classes, I'll go give this gross photo to Gerry — his office is in the basement, right? Then I'll find a way to casually ask him who he bought the car from. Does that work?"

"I'll come with you," Lavinia said, reaching for the candy bag. "Maybe just one."

"Okay, that's good," Marie said. "We have a plan."

Marie exhaled and sat down on the bed. I had no clue what we were going to find out, but I did know Marie needed us to do this for her.

———

A few times that week, Lavinia and I tried to find Gerry, but another custodian said he was off sick. We updated Marie every couple of days and each time we had no news, she grew more withdrawn. She redid my photo shoot on Wednesday, and on Thursday I saw her lingering by the parking lot like a lonely paparazzo. On Friday, Marie came down with a bad cold that was going around and called her father to pick her up.

I wasn't sure what to think. I was worried for Marie and also relieved that we were taking a break from this blue car project. And yet, I continued to make mental lists of teachers and staff, deliberating about their qualities and the possibility that one of them was the person Marie refused to name.

Nahla

Nahla buttoned her coat while Michael paid the bill. That Saturday, they'd gone for drinks and dessert. She'd suggested a late date, so that, if things went well, she could bring him back to her place after curfew. But would he still want to come up? She'd tidied in preparation, had even put fresh sheets on her bed.

And what did *she* want? It had taken her and Baashir two years to get to sex; they'd both been young and religiously guilt-ridden. She knew that this wasn't how it worked for most people, and anyway, she'd known Michael five months already. That was enough time. She was no longer young and refused to be religiously guilt-ridden.

This time, they parked around the side of the residence when they saw a couple of girls rushing in through the back; curfew was in a few minutes.

"Let's give it ten minutes to be safe?" she asked. He nodded, lit a cigarette for them both, and he chatted about the weather. *Was he uncomfortable?* It seemed to her that Canadians talked about precipitation and temperatures a lot, especially when they felt awkward.

"Any updates on the Zahabiya and Jason romance?"

"I think they might have moved their desks a couple of inches closer this week." He scoffed.

"Naughty!" She checked her watch: 11:12 p.m. "I think we're good, but if we run into anyone, just say you're picking up an art book from me?"

"Got it," he smirked.

They started up the utility stairwell. At the top, she entered the hallway, paused, and held up her hand for him to wait until she found the right key and unlocked her flat. Then she beckoned him across the hallway and shut the door quickly behind them.

"We made it! Undetected!" He said, laughing.

"*Shhhh!* Better lower your voice." She hung her coat on the single hook by the door and then layered his on top. "It's funny, Sylvie never had the need for more than one hook in all her years here?"

"She probably died a lonely old maid," Michael muttered.

"That would be so sad." *What if she'd never had the opportunity to go on a date, to feel as carefree as Nahla did right then?*

He placed his hand over the small of her back and pulled her close. His lips were warm, needy, his hands roving across her hips.

"Coffee?" She pulled out of his embrace and swayed slightly as she filled her rakwe with water. She hoped the hot drink would clear her head. Once again, she'd drunk more wine than she'd intended at dinner.

"Sounds good."

She boiled water, stirred in the coffee, turned off the heat, and filled two tiny cups.

"Too bad we don't have whiskey. We could turn these into Irish-Arabic coffees. A mix of both our heritages, right?"

"Maybe next time," she laughed.

"So, do you like living here?" Michael took a few steps away from her, covering the entire length of the main room, then peeked into the bedroom. She took a seat in her reading chair and gestured to its identical companion.

"It suits me. Though, I can't imagine living here for as long as Sylvie did." Nahla shivered, sensing Sylvie's presence. She poured more ahwe and wrapped her hands around her cup's warmth."

"She was odd. And that notebook she kept? People are still talking about it."

"I know. Just before Friday's staff meeting, Margo and Frederick asked me a hundred questions about it. Maybe it's because Sylvie was such a mystery and then her sudden death just added to the mysteriousness."

"Maybe."

"There are only initials, but I am pretty sure I know who she was watching." The lights flickered, and Nahla silently acknowledged Sylvie; she'd been playing with her bedside lamp for weeks now.

Michael peered up at the lights, frowning.

"I have a theory! Margo said she thinks someone was bringing marijuana into the residence last year. I think Leesa Allen — you know that girl you and I talked about before?" He nodded. "I think she and her friends might be dealing drugs."

"Really?"

"But I cannot figure out why rich girls would want to deal drugs." One of her fellow students at university had sold pot, but he'd used his earnings to pay tuition.

"Now, when I think of it, Sylvie did raise the issue once at a staff meeting. She asked if any of us had noticed drug problems among students." He stroked his jaw pensively.

"Well, Sylvie's surveillance might have had an impact, because it looks like the pattern of activity she was monitoring stopped in the spring. But I think it might have resumed this fall."

"Do you still have the notebook? After all the hype, I'd love to have a look."

"Yes, I've been meaning to send it to Sylvie's family, but I still have it."

Nahla headed to her bedroom to retrieve it. She turned, surprised to see Michael a step behind her. He sat on the bed. She passed him the notebook.

"It's empty." He opened the book to the middle.

"It's just the first two pages." She flipped the pages back to the beginning and sat next to him.

"My French is terrible. Translate for me?"

She sidled up to him, his body warm at her side. Together, they went line by line:

04/18/84   ?   *quelques semaines ont passé déjà??*

"She's wondering how many weeks have already passed. Perhaps she'd been noticing something, but only started taking notes that day," Nahla explained.

"Right, mid-April. She might have raised the issue at the staff meeting shortly after that," Michael said.

04/25/84   9h02   *L marche vers le nord*

"The following week, walking north at 9:02."

04/25/84   9h57   *de retour*

"Returning just before ten."

"The girls are allowed to go out between study period and bed-check, right? I wonder why Sylvie got so suspicious?"

"Perhaps she noticed that there's a Wednesday night pattern. There's something regular that this *L* is doing every week."

05/02/84   9h03   *vers le nord, mais rentre dans un char bleu*

"Once again, a week later, and walking north, but returning in a blue car. But it looks from the next entry it was a pretty quick outing. Wonder whose car it was? Maybe the dealer's?"

161

"*Hmm,* maybe," Michael said.

05/02/84   *observe L dans l'espace commun à 9h15*

"He could have come to her this time? Just twelve minutes later she's in the common area. A lot of girls congregate there between the end of study period and bedcheck. Margo thought it would be a good time to sell whatever she'd picked up."

"That does make sense." Michael bounced, shaking the bed. "I think you've cracked the mystery."

05/09/84   9h03   *march vers le nord*
05/09/84   9h58   *de retour, visiblement perturber*

"The old pattern again, but this week, she comes back looking upset."

"What's this say?" Michael pointed to the next lines.

05/16/84   5h00   *rencontre avec L, l'interroge sur ses plans.*
                        Pas prévu.
05/16/84   10h00   *de retour pour le bedcheck*

"Sylvie asked her if she had any plans that night. *L* said she had none, but in fact again she sees her coming in at 10 p.m. for bedcheck."

"Okay . . . what's next?" Michael sighed, making Nahla wonder if he'd grown bored of the conversation.

05/23/84   9h02   *demeure dans l'espace commun jusqu'au*
                        bedcheck

"That week, she's hanging out in the common area until bedcheck. So, she didn't go out."

05/30/84   9h02   *dehors avec M & J aux tables pique-nique*

"Same for the next week. Except, she's with her friends in the backyard."

"Well, it looks like whatever was going on stopped. Maybe Sylvie confronted her?"

"Here's the thing. I have seen her go out many times in the same pattern. I guess I'll just try to keep my eye out. Margo says she will, too. What more can we do, right?"

"Well, thanks for showing me. But as usual, Thornton drama turns out to be a lot of nothing."

"I guess you're right." Of course, he was. She felt a little silly now.

Michael checked his watch and rose to his feet. She tugged on his sleeve.

"You don't have to go so soon, do you?" They locked eyes, the energy between them like an electrical charge. She reached up, touched his shoulder, and pulled him closer. She closed her eyes, kissed him, the dark under her lids like the bottom of the ocean. Her limbs relaxed. Her thoughts slowed, then disappeared as she allowed her body to take over. She was glad she'd changed her sheets.

The next morning, head aching, Michael long gone, her bed cold, she questioned herself. She took a long shower and after, while drying off, was pulled by a ritual she'd avoided for some time. She turned on the faucet, washed her right hand with her left three times, and repeated the process on the other side. Then, she cupped her hand to her mouth three times, inhaled the stream into her nostrils. She washed her face and arms, and passed water over her already-wet hair and feet. Then she dressed, covered her head, and pulled out her long-ignored sajdeh from the closet.

She unrolled it, orienting herself eastward.

After performing her prayers, she remained on the mat. She apologized to God for drinking too much. For being hasty with her lust. But she made no promises to stop.

The morning was quiet, still too early for most girls to be awake on a Sunday. She studied the sajdeh's swirling patterns, red and gold and black, and knew that Sylvie was near.

"I like him." She said aloud. "Is that so bad?"

She felt a maternal hand on her back, steady, cool. But it also held a lack of agreement, a sentiment she shrugged off.

Leesa

Leesa tromped three blocks, damp seeping through her suede boots. He'd been cryptic when she'd phoned him earlier that Sunday, instructing her to meet him farther away than usual.

When she arrived at the specified corner, he wasn't there. She frowned and checked her Swatch: 12:15 p.m. on the dot. *Had he ever been late?* She filed this fact in the mental folder, already quite full, that she'd labelled *Worrisome boyfriend behaviour.* A few minutes later, his car came barrelling around the corner, skidding and splashing her. She brushed off her jeans, breathed deeply, and opened the car's door.

"Sorry I'm late." He pulled away from the curb as she buckled her seat belt. She didn't detect anything unusual in his expression.

"Hey, we have more time today. Why don't we drive to Olmstead and check into a motel?" She tried to make her tone as sweet as honey.

"I dunno, Leesa. I know I suggested it last week, but we need to be cautious. Olmstead might be too close. And, by the way, we need to switch our Wednesdays to Tuesdays." He sneezed into his hand, the steering wheel twitching slightly to the right.

"Why?" She swallowed hard, forcing down her irritation.

"Because I found out that Leblanc was documenting all the Wednesdays that you came and went from the residence last spring. Now Nahla and Margo — Miss Naim and Miss Jones — think you might be a drug dealer doing deals on Wednesdays, so they're both keeping an eye on you those nights." He accelerated as they headed out of town toward their spot.

"What?" Her brain cramped as she took in the information: *Mademoiselle Leblanc; Wednesdays; Nahla and Miss Jones; drugs?*

"But at least no one seems to suspect we are together." He fished a tissue out of his pocket and wiped his nose.

"But wait..." She exhaled when she registered the word "together."
"But how did you find all this out? Did you see the notebook?"

"No . . . she talked about it with a couple of us in the staffroom on Friday, and I tried to casually get all the details. And can you believe she and Margo think you're a pot dealer?" He smirked and circled his finger over his right ear.

"I hardly ever smoke pot. Since Lorrilee Manning graduated last year, none of us can even get any." Leesa frowned.

"*She* was dealing?" He blew his nose, long, loud.

"Duh, everyone knew about Lorrilee." Leesa looked out at the snowy farms on her right, trying to process everything.

"Well, I'll tell her that. But just to keep her off our scent, let's change our day to Tuesdays. Crap, I usually watch *Bizarre* on Tuesdays." He drove past the farmer's field and pulled over a hundred metres from their usual spot. "In case anyone at this farm is watching us, too."

"Are you serious? Take a chill pill. You just said she doesn't know we're together." Leesa turned up the heat, warmed her hands in front of the vent.

"We can't be too careful. There's a lot at stake, Leesa. My career, my reputation." He turned down the heat, unzipped his coat.

166

"Fine." Clearly, he was scared, the way he was scared last spring before he'd called things off. She would have to be calm for them both.

"And for the next few weeks, just confuse her a bit. Find a way to make her think you have a boyfriend or something." He flinched at the word "boyfriend," a small tremor travelling through his jaw.

"Okay, if that will make you feel better."

"And you know what? I'll keep tabs on Margo and Nahla. I've been trying to run into them a lot more in the staff room and stuff."

Leesa peered at him, her mental worry file folder popping open again. He brushed her cheek with his index finger, then pulled away to sneeze again. He honked into a tissue, and while she found all the mucous gross, she didn't allow it to deter her. Time with him was precious. Leesa knew to take advantage of every single minute she could get with him.

On Tuesday night, when Leesa called him before study hall, he told her he couldn't get out of bed.

"Hey, you passed it on, you know. I have a sore throat today."

"Sorry." He sneezed into the phone. It was ear-splitting. She held the receiver away from her head while he sneezed a second time, then a third.

"*Ugh*, maybe I'll get a day off school if I'm lucky." Sick students spent the day in the infirmary, doted on by kind Mrs. Matthews, who brought tomato soup and cheese sandwiches on a tray.

"But listen, go out tonight anyway. Be really obvious about it. See if you can get Miss Naim or Miss Jones to notice."

"And do what? It's frickin' freezing outside!"

"Just go for a quick walk, Babe. Just to break up the pattern. Like we talked about. Maybe we can see each other in a couple of days. Saturday, for sure."

After they hung up, she called the boys' residence. Two hours later, after study period's end, she and Rodney sat in the lobby's alcove, his lips and cheeks pink from his jog over. He kissed her and whispered in her ear, "Hey, wanna go somewhere on Saturday afternoon? Maybe get a room somewhere? I can get a car." When she hesitated, he added, "I mean, if it isn't moving too fast for you?"

"Let me think about it, okay?" She noted that the front of his khakis was stretched taut.

Miss Naim strolled down the hallway, and remembering her mission, she entwined her legs through Rodney's.

"Hey, you two, keep it decent, okay?" Miss Naim called out with uncharacteristic cheer, not the usual scolding tone. Then, as she walked away, her sneeze echoed like a bullhorn through the hallway. "Oh, excusez moi! This winter cold!"

Leesa recoiled when the teacher sneezed a second time, then a third.

"Gesundheit!" Rodney, always with good manners, yelled after her.

"You know what, Rodney, I think it's a great idea. Book us a room. If you want, we can use my parents' credit card."

Zahabiya

Saturday night, I nibbled popcorn in the dark theatre, sandwiched between Jason and Lavinia, who were flanked by Cyril and Marie. Jason and I were on a date, but the others had tagged along.

Jason's warm right hand had rendered my left clammy. *Micki & Maude* was fun, but I couldn't help wondering what Jason was thinking each time a sex scene began, and there were many — the movie was about cheating and bigamy. We'd made out a lot, but always clothed, with a silent agreement about how far things should go. I knew it would be up to me to raise the issue and take us a step further, but I wasn't sure if we were ready for that yet. Or maybe I was the one who wasn't ready.

In one of the scenes, Maude and Rob pretended to be dinosaurs, roaring and swiping at each other in some kind of rabid foreplay. It seemed ridiculous, but Jason laughed out loud and squeezed my hand.

Later, Rob interviewed a group of nude models whose only attire were gun holsters. Lavinia exclaimed, "Wow!" and I snickered. *Was she reacting to their handgun enthusiasm or their naked butts?* Probably both.

As the credits rolled, Marie muttered, "So much for the vow between Micki and Maude," referring to the wronged women's deal to shun philandering Rob. "I swear, if women don't stick together against evil men, nothing is ever going to change."

"Well, he lied a lot, but he wasn't evil, was he? He really wanted to be a father." Jason shrugged on his coat. My hand, finally untethered, needled back to life. I agreed with Jason's sentiment, but the bigger question in my mind was why the women were drawn to Rob at all. They were so much more interesting and powerful than he was. But that wasn't what Marie was protesting.

"Figures a guy would say that." Marie strode ahead of the group, up the aisle and toward the doors.

"What's up with her?" Cyril asked.

"It's Tom, her ex-boyfriend. When she was home this week, she found out he started seeing someone else," Lavinia whispered. "Be nice to her."

"Yeah, she's really upset he moved on," I said.

When we reached the lobby, Jason touched Marie's shoulder and said, "Hey, sorry to hear about Tom."

Marie shook him off. "I'm over it. I mean, we really haven't been together since my father drove us apart. He can do whatever he wants with his stupid life."

"Still, it's gotta hurt," Lavinia said.

"Let's talk about something else. Distract me, people, distract me!" Marie joke-ordered, cutting through the tension.

The door opened, cool wind brushing my face. It was Gerry, exiting the theatre.

"Hey, look who it is." Our campaign had stalled because he'd been off sick and then Marie was away. "I still have the photo in my purse."

"Go! Go ask him about the car before he gets away!" Marie prodded me.

"What are you talking about?" Cyril asked. I rushed out.

"Sir? Sir? Gerry?" I called. He looked at me, startled. "Remember me? From school?"

"Oh, the photographer! Want another photo?" He laughed and struck a red-carpet pose.

"No, actually I wanted to give you this." I passed him the photo.

"Cool. It's not bad! Thanks."

"I was just wondering . . . I um . . . I just got my licence this year? And I'm thinking about buying a used car. But I don't really know how that works? And I wondered if you bought your car through a dealer around here or . . . ?" I clumsily parroted the line the girls had scripted for me the previous weekend.

"Oh, no, never trust a dealer. I bought this from one of the teachers, Michael. Mr. Stephenson. I like to buy from someone I know. Better chance the seller isn't gonna pass off a lemon, you know?"

I registered his words, pressed on.

"And one more question: Do you get a new licence plate when you buy a car or do you take your old one with you?" Mei had researched this, so we already knew the answer, but I thought I'd double-check.

"No, you take your old one with you. But you'll have to apply for a new one because it'll be your first car."

"Oh, okay. Thanks." I turned back to the group, now huddled by the theatre doors.

"We filled the guys in," Lavinia said.

"So? What'd he say? What'd he say?"

"Gerry bought it from Mr. Stephenson, and he transferred his new licence plate over," I said, still processing the information.

"I knew it. I knew it!" Marie raised her arms in a cheerless cheer. "It's Mr. Stephenson."

"That's a lot to digest," Jason said, taking my hand.

171

"Yeah." Was this who Marie had suspected all along? When I went through the list of staff and teachers, my mind had wanted to skip over Mr. Stephenson.

"He must own the flat, long hatchback with the *LNO* licence plate. We have to confirm that." Marie nodded.

"And confirm that what you suspect is really happening," Lavinia reminded her.

"Does this really add up to Mr. Stephenson being a pedophile? I mean if something is happening between him and Leesa Allen, she's, like, seventeen," Cyril said.

"It's an abuse of power," Marie said. "And I think it's been going on for years."

"He's in a position of authority, and she's a student," I added, picturing the two of them together. I understood Cyril's point, though; Leesa seemed mature and strong-willed. Even if it was a mask, it was a convincing one.

"I dunno, guys," Cyril shook his head.

"If it's true, how did we all miss it? I've always thought he was a good teacher." Lavinia looked up at the sky. I followed her gaze. The moon was a sliver, and stars pinpricked through the dark.

"He's a great teacher. It'd be shitty if it's true," Jason said. I nodded. My brain grappled with the contradiction: the teacher who was so cool that he didn't bust us for passing notes. The teacher who might be abusing a student.

"Listen. The evidence says it all. Plus . . . I know . . . personally . . . that he's a letch." Marie turned and walked away from us.

"Wait. Marie? What do you mean you know *personally*?" Lavinia caught up to Marie and grabbed hold of her sleeve. They shared a silent, tense look. Lavinia's face fell.

Nahla

Despite having a cold and sleeping fitfully all week, Nahla had never been more energized. She awoke at dawn in time for fajr prayers, then folded her mat and caught up on lesson planning and marking. When unoccupied, she fantasized about Michael.

And now, out for a late dinner together with him once again, their banter was easier than ever, perhaps because of their new intimacy. He brought along a portfolio filled with photos of his paintings, and she marvelled at his talent.

While he went to use the bathroom, she looked out the window, the blanket of snow rendering the road bright and spotless. She thought about the previous Saturday and how she'd enticed him to stay after they'd studied Sylvie's notebook. He'd hesitated at first, affecting shyness, but that didn't last long.

The memory continued to unspool: he'd undressed her with an almost manic energy and was on top of her in what seemed like an instant. It reminded her of her first time with Baashir, his inexperience, neediness making him unable to take his time. *Was Michael inexperienced or had he just been nervous their first time together?*

He returned to the table as their desserts arrived.

"Can I ask you something?" She picked up her fork, looked Michael in the eye.

"Sure, anything." He smiled uncomfortably, as though readying himself for something difficult.

"Have you had . . . very many . . . girlfriends?" She averted her gaze, took a small bite of her dessert.

"A few over the years. Nothing serious. I've been mostly single for about five years now. I've had a lot going on at home, after my father died . . ." He trailed off.

"Yes, of course."

"And how about you? Have you had many relationships?"

"Just one boyfriend. Ended a year ago."

"I sort of got that feeling. You have an . . . unjaded, almost demure air about you." He looked her up and down, his gaze disarming.

"Well, it all felt very risqué at the time. He was my teaching assistant in third year . . ." A heaviness settled over her stomach, and she put down her fork, the tiramisu too rich.

"Was that complicated? Because he was your TA?" He pulled back in his chair slightly, as though viewing her from another angle.

"We had to keep it a secret, both because of his position and because neither of us wanted our parents to find out." She rubbed her stomach, coaxing it to settle.

"Secrecy can add to the excitement."

"It created so much unnecessary stress!" She rolled her eyes.

He laughed, and the conversation's thread dropped. He wolfed down his cake while she picked at hers. She hoped that he would want to come over again. *Did she project inexperience?* She'd felt sophisticated and brazen after last week.

As she got into his car, she spied something shiny wedged into the seat. She pulled it out — a silver hair scrunchie — and handed it to him.

"Oh! That must be my cousin's. She's always wearing those things. I bought the car from my aunt." He stuffed it into his jacket pocket.

"She's on trend, your cousin."

"Yup. A huge Madonna fan."

The snowploughs had left high banks around the residence, and Michael had to park closer to the new wing.

"Nahla, I think I should have an early night. I'm still not 100 percent." He cocked his head to one side and hesitated.

"Oh." She hadn't expected this and wasn't ready for the night to be over. "Maybe a quick coffee? I promise I won't keep you late."

Was that pushy?

"Sure." His tone was neutral, so she let go of her uncertainty and led him along the unshovelled sidewalk and then around the back of the building. Most of the windows were dark.

"The girls should be in their beds by now, but let's be careful." She unlocked the back door, and they climbed the stairs, listening for activity. She snuck him into her suite quietly.

He sat in one of her club chairs. She put water to boil.

"You know, it was helpful to talk about the notebook last week. I realized I can't be a spy like Sylvie was — it'll ruin my peace. It motivated me to finally get around to mailing the thing off to Sylvie's brother. I really shouldn't have kept it so long anyway."

"Good."

The pot boiled, and she stirred in the Arabic coffee. He was quieter and didn't seem as flirtatious as the week before. Perhaps he was tired.

"I really do feel like I was making a big deal out of nothing now. Leesa is a pretty, popular girl. She must have been seeing a boyfriend on Wednesday nights, maybe the same guy I saw her kissing in the lobby a couple of times this week."

"Oh?"

"Yeah, they were all *over* each other," she laughed, stroking his arm. "I checked with Margo to find out if I was supposed to do something about it, but she said to leave them be."

"Who's the guy?" He pulled a flask from his pocket and poured some in his coffee cup. He didn't offer her any, but she was okay with that. She'd been successful at keeping to her self-imposed limit of one glass of wine at dinner.

"I think his name is Rodney? He's not in my classes. He must have opted out of French this year."

"I thought boys weren't allowed in the residence."

"They can sit by the front doors, but not any farther. Like up those back stairs and into a girl's room." She sat on the arm of his chair and leaned into him suggestively. He grabbed her tightly and pulled her down onto his lap. She tasted a mix of booze and ahwe, and felt his incisors cutting into her lips.

Leesa

"Maybe you can go in the back and dodge the monitor?" Rodney asked when they pulled up in front of the residence at twelve minutes after midnight.

"The back door will be locked by now." She gazed back at him, his eyes appearing grey in the dark of the car. She didn't want to step out into the cold just yet.

"Sorry, we'll probably both get detentions."

"Well it's too late to worry about it now. Anyway, it was worth it."

It really had been. After they'd checked into the motel, and while she was in the bathroom, Rodney had surprised her Harlequin-style with champagne and candles and scattered rose petals on the bedspread, items he'd hidden in a duffle bag. While he wasn't very confident, there was a sweetness and attentiveness to their lovemaking she hadn't experienced before.

"Yeah, it sure was." He smiled, then looked past her. He pointed to the silhouette of a person standing in the front doorway. "Someone's waiting for you."

"Probably Miss Naim." She hurried up the steps. Miss Jones greeted her with a theatrical yawn and a disapproving look.

"So sorry! We went for a country drive, but got stuck in a snowbank. We had to get a few guys to help us out, then we ended up being a bit late." Leesa hoped the story sounded credible; it had been snowing all night.

"*Seventy-five* minutes late now." Miss Jones held up her wristwatch. "Detention Monday."

Leesa was too happy to bother arguing; a high school punishment couldn't shake her high. Not only had Rodney been romantic, but also she'd had her first orgasm, that is, her first with a lover. Orgasms had always been elusive, and she'd assumed that she was just one of those girls *Cosmopolitan* said didn't climax easily with a man.

But no. Now she was a woman with two lovers. Truly cosmopolitan, sexy, desired.

On her way to the stairs, a group of pyjamaed girls ahead of her rushed toward the new wing, whispering excitedly. Nerds. She'd be so glad to graduate from this dressed-up nursery school next year.

She stared after them, recognizing Zahabiya and Mei. With them was Fat Marie (who insisted she was rich, but had to be here on scholarship). And in the front, leading them, was Whatshername, that Jamaican girl from biology. Lavinia.

Despite herself, she was curious, and she followed them from a distance to the new wing.

"Is that it?" Lavinia raised her chin to the window.

"Ohmigod, Lav, you're right. You're right," Marie said.

"What are we looking at?" Leesa came up behind them and peered out into the darkness.

"Well . . ." Zahabiya seemed to stammer. *What was wrong with her?*

"Oh, it's not a big deal," Lavinia said, but her sideways glance gave her away.

178

Leesa looked out and then she spotted it, parked thirty feet away. She stiffened.

"We were just thinking that that looks like Mr. Stephenson's car." Marie's gaze was steady.

"Is it? So what?" Leesa turned to walk away. "I'm going to bed."

Was it his car? And if so, why was it parked there, and at 12:17 a.m.?

"It looks like the art teacher is screwing the French teacher." Mei's tone sounded like a taunt.

"Oh, grow up. That's what adults do," Leesa paused and called over her shoulder. "What do you think I was doing tonight?"

She crossed the residence, adrenaline buzzing through her. In her bedroom, she changed into her pyjamas in the glow of a nightlight. She couldn't get Mei's words out of her head: *The art teacher is screwing the French teacher.*

She wished she could wake her roommates. There was so much she needed to process with them, but of course she couldn't. In the dark, she silently went over it: the nerds scoping that car that looked like Michael's. *And was he here with Miss Naim?* There had to be another explanation.

Michael loved her, was devoted to her.

She scrunchied her hair into a golden Madonna-esque waterfall, grabbed her toiletry kit, and opened the door. Just as she stepped into the hallway, she spied Michael ducking into the back stairwell. Miss Naim's doorway was ajar, as was her bathrobe. Leesa registered the teacher's startled look just before she shut her door. Tears stung her eyes. She wanted to run outside into the frigid night in her flannels, but, of course, she couldn't.

Zahabiya

"It's the flat hatchback," I said, after Leesa had left us, leaving behind a wet trail from her boots.

"I'm going out there to get the licence plate. Why didn't I bring my camera?" Marie scampered down the hallway and out the new wing's side door. She goose-stepped through the knee-high snow in her bedroom slippers.

"Shit." Mei placed her palm against the cool glass. "Girl's got balls."

Marie got within a few feet of the car, paused, then ran back in.

"*LNO 322*. You remember the *LNO*," She pointed at me. And you remember the *322*," she said to Lavinia.

"*LNO*," I repeated.

"*322*," Lavinia echoed.

"We've got him." Marie smiled without any joy. She stamped her feet and shook off the snow stuck to her pyjama bottoms.

"But Leesa just said she was out on a date," I said.

"Isn't it a coincidence that Leesa got home at the same time you saw his car?" Marie demanded.

"That car's been here a while. Look how much snow is piled on top of it," Lavinia said. "And if Leesa barely batted an eye when you said Mr. Stephenson was with Miss Naim, then—"

"Then maybe we're wrong," I completed the sentence.

"Or he's lost interest in Leesa," Marie said.

"Speak of the devil." Mei pointed out the window at Mr. Stephenson, who was hurrying to his car. He dug into his pocket for his key, but then, perhaps sensing our presence, squinted in our direction. Illuminated by the hallway light, we had to be visible to him. None of us moved. He got into the car, revved the engine, and drove away without brushing the snow off his windshield.

"Okay," Lavinia said softly to Marie. "Please talk to us? What did he do to you?"

Back in our room, Marie sat on Mei's bed, her chest puffing out as she inhaled. Then she let out all the air and said, "It was my first year at Thornton. Grade 9. It was really shitty. I was the only Native kid here . . . still am . . ." She paused while we nodded in sympathy. "And everyone was really snobby. I had no friends. I'm so glad you got here for grade 10, Lav." She glanced Lavinia's way.

"You were my first friend here, too, girl."

"So . . . in grade 9, art was all I had. I'd always drawn and stuff, but Mr. Stephenson introduced us to all these other mediums. He told me I had talent and offered to let me use the art room after class and he basically took me on as a special project."

My stomach clenched. The TV show about the abusive coach flashed in my mind. All this time I'd pictured Leesa in the victim's role, which was bad enough, but with Marie it was horrible.

"This doesn't sound like it's gonna end well." Mei rose from her bed, grabbed a bag of wine gums, and emptied them out into two piles, one on her bed, where she and Marie sat, and one on mine, for Lavinia and me.

"Yup." Marie popped a red wine gum in her mouth. "But I didn't really get it. Not until this year, when I started seeing him and Leesa. It's like the penny only dropped a few weeks ago."

"So . . . we'd do art stuff, but talked about personal things, too. Spent hours alone together. He'd give me these really long hugs that I thought were so great at the time. I crushed hard on him. Now I know it was creepy, but at the time it felt good . . . like I had a kind of friend." Her eyes darted toward each of us. "I know, it's stupid. How can a teacher be a friend to a fourteen-year-old?"

"Not stupid," Lavinia murmured, reaching across the space between the beds to pat Marie's arm. "Not at all."

"And not your fault, Marie," I added.

"My counsellor from my old school would call that grooming," Mei said, quietly, shoulders slumping.

"Grooming?" I asked.

"It's what that pedo was doing to Marie, making 'friends' with her, getting her to open up to him. Touching her inappropriately," Mei said.

I recalled Mr. Stephenson's compliments on my art projects, and the way he often patted my shoulder when he passed my desk. I'd thought he was being nice, but he was just a sleazebag.

"There's more, isn't there, Marie?" Mei asked.

"He invited me to come to his home studio, and I was so excited about it I told my dad. I thought he'd be proud I was getting this 'special invitation.' I was so naive."

"I hope your dad tore a strip off that asshole." Lavinia balled her fist.

"I know he met with him. I don't know what was said, or, more accurately, knowing my dad, what was threatened. At the time, I thought he was overreacting and I refused to talk him for months." She shook her head and stared at her hands.

"Your father stopped it before it went from inappropriate to way worse," Mei said, eyebrows raised.

"Yeah. After that talk with my father, it all stopped. He never mentioned his home studio again. He stopped talking to me after class. I was embarrassed. I felt bad for him. I missed him."

"And soon after, he started paying a lot of attention to Leesa — who is shitty at art, by the way — and because I didn't understand, I felt like she'd taken something from me. When I saw her yelling in the parking lot, that feeling came back. Once I guessed it was him in the car, my first reaction was that I wanted to expose them out of spite. But then, I started to realize what might be happening."

"He moved on from you to Leesa. And that's been going on now for what? Almost three years?" Mei shook her head.

"Probably? You know I almost didn't come back to Thornton the next year. But that summer I met Tom, and so my father sent me back here to keep me away from him. For a year, he questioned me about Mr. Stephenson *and* Tom!" She reached for another wine gum.

"Wow." I didn't know how to console Marie. I was still in shock that she'd been abused and that this whole blue car project had been as much about her as it was about Leesa. That she knew all along but couldn't tell us. That she'd been dealing with this all alone.

"And now Tom is with someone else." Marie turned away, and the room hushed as we gave her a moment to collect herself. Mei passed her a tissue.

"Girl, why didn't you say anything about all of this?" Lavinia leaned forward and took her hand.

"You know me — I have to figure things out on my own first."

"I wish I'd known. I could have been there for you. And I feel bad that I wasn't more . . . on board these last couple of months." Lavinia looked like she was going to cry.

"Me, too. I wish I could have done more," I said.

"It's okay."

"At least your father found out. And did something," Lavinia said quietly.

"Well, he stopped the douchebag from targeting Marie, but it wasn't enough, because—"

"Because the douchebag moved on to another girl." I finished Mei's thought.

"Yup." Mei opened the window, lit a cigarette. Lavinia squinted in her direction. Marie didn't seem to notice.

"This is all so messed up. This place is so messed up. I'm glad that at least I've got you weirdos. We're like a Benetton ad, but more real." Marie rubbed her face.

"We just need a white girl for our magazine spread," Lavinia joked, but I knew she was sad, as we all were. I looked over at Mei. It was getting cold with the window open.

"Hey, are you okay?" Marie asked Mei, only then registering the smoking.

"Just needed a smoke."

"So . . ." I said, pulling at the collective, loose thread in our conversation. "Do you think it's over between Leesa and Mr. Stephenson?" I yawned and glanced at my clock radio: 12:35 a.m.

"Maybe. But we have to tell someone regardless," Lavinia said. "Maybe your dad, Marie?"

I imagined Marie's dad getting the headmaster involved. And possibly all the parents finding out. How would my dad react to this? Would this be an easy excuse to not allow me to come back next year?

"I feel like we should talk to Leesa first, but what if she thinks it's normal the way I thought it was?" Marie said, disagreeing with herself.

"A teacher, then?" Lavinia reasoned.

"If Mademoiselle Leblanc was still around, she would have helped. She was so level-headed," Marie said. "Miss Naim might have been my second choice, but—"

"God, I always thought she was cool. Why is she seeing that loser?" Mei grimaced.

"We don't know that for sure," I protested.

"Who else was he visiting so late at night?" Mei countered.

"We need to confirm that." Marie looked at me, and I knew what she was going to ask next. "You're pretty close to her, right Zahabiya?"

"Right." I sighed.

After Lavinia and Marie had gone to bed, Mei opened the window again and lit another smoke. I wanted to yell about the cold, and cancer, but I was too tired. Outside the window was the faint, familiar song of a pair of mourning doves. I closed my eyes and let their chorus be a lullaby.

Nahla

Michael got out of bed and stood, embarrassed-looking and pantless. He searched for his clothing.

"Sorry about that. I'm not usually so . . . I must have had too much to drink—"

"That's okay, it happens. Listen, you don't have to leave right away." She held out her arms.

"I guess I just have a lot on my mind, and I'm still getting over this cold," he continued his ashamed apology, and she felt bad for him, wanted to comfort, but didn't know what ailed him.

"Come back to bed, we can talk a while," she repeated, but he'd found his trousers and was zipping up. She searched for her skirt, but he was already in the living room, so she grabbed her robe and shrugged it over her still fully buttoned blouse. As she followed him to the door she thought: *Maybe this was a mistake. Maybe he doesn't really like me that way or at least not enough.*

He pulled on his coat, and there was a second round of apologies. *Was he sorry for the bad sex? For not staying? Or for being there in the first place?*

He glanced back at her before disappearing through the back stairwell door. And in that briefest of moments, she sensed movement down the hall, a witness, the girl she'd come to dislike and had probably misjudged. Nahla registered this as a sign of something, a bad omen. The girl stared, and Nahla's throat was too dry for words, so she clutched her robe and pressed her hand against the door.

By breakfast, everyone would learn of her indiscretions, for Leesa would certainly tell her friends, and the whispers would move through the student body like a chill wind. And then the teachers would come to know and perhaps, even, Headmaster Lowery. She'd have to seek advice from Maeve. *Perhaps she should call Michael and warn him, too?*

Nahla tossed and turned, flopping like a fish on a dry dock. The newish mattress chafed the old bedframe, and she troubled over whether the earlier sounds of lovemaking might have travelled to the girls next door.

But then, it had all finished so quickly. Too quickly to rouse anyone and barely herself. By the time they'd unwedged themselves from the reading chair, stumbled into the bedroom where Michael had pressed himself into her, she'd had a few seconds to enjoy herself.

She adjusted her pillow. A dull ache in her neck niggled at her, and she rolled onto her back. She reached into the empty space beside her, but it wasn't vacant. Sylvie beckoned. She shifted a few inches closer, so their fingers could meet and intertwine.

She closed her eyes, tried to slow her restless mind. Images flashed behind her eyelids: Michael's apologetic expression, the slope of his shoulder as he disappeared into the stairwell, the sparkle of a silver scrunchie high atop Leesa's head.

"Miss Naim, could I talk to you?" Zahabiya stood at her door at 10:05 a.m., her weight shifting from one foot to the other.

"Of course." Zahabiya had come to chat a few times that term, and Nahla liked her. And she was glad for the distraction, already exhausted by her own perseveration about Michael and Leesa seeing them. She'd tried to reach him an hour earlier and had left a message with his mother.

She scrutinized the girl's serious expression. *Were there problems at home?* Then she wondered: *Had she heard anything about Michael being there last night?*

"It's a situation that's happening to a friend, and I'm wondering what to do." Zahabiya frowned, as though formulating the right words.

"Oh, yes, your friend?" Nahla smiled wanly. Quite a few Thornton girls who'd sought her counsel had used this familiar ruse.

"Yeah. From my hometown. From my old high school." Zahabiya blinked, then blinked again.

"Yalla, allez, go ahead."

"Okay, so I think my friend might be in an inappropriate relationship with a teacher. I think he might have been, um, taking advantage of her."

"Taking advantage?" Nahla leaned in. "You mean, sexually?"

"I'm not positive, but I think so." Zahabiya sucked in her lips and frowned.

"Have you asked your friend directly what's going on?"

"No . . . I think she'd deny it."

"Then, you might need to go to her parents. Or the headmaster or principal?"

"Yeah, okay." But she didn't sound convinced.

"Zahabiya, this sounds very serious."

"I should try to talk to my friend first."

"Okay, but don't sit on this too long. Why don't you come back tomorrow and update me?"

"Okay."

Nahla checked the time. *Why hadn't Michael called back yet?*

"Hey, Miss Naim, are you okay? You look a bit . . . not like yourself."

Nahla smoothed down her hair. Zahabiya's manner was earnest and brought to mind her younger sister, Hoda.

"I'm all right. I just had a bad sleep . . . but . . . maybe . . . I could ask you a question." Nahla paused, chose her words carefully. "Teacher monitors here don't have a lot of privacy, and that sometimes . . . is challenging . . . Would you tell me if there was any gossip spreading about my personal life?"

"Oh! No, I haven't heard anything." The girl shook her head. But her expression shifted. *Did she seem disappointed? Deflated?* "I'm sorry. Perhaps that question made you uncomfortable."

"No, it's okay, Miss Naim. Really."

"Well . . . promise me you'll update me after you talk with your friend?"

"Yes. I promise."

Zahabiya left, and Nahla sunk into her chair. So far, no gossip. Or maybe it just hadn't reached Zahabiya yet. *Had it been wrong to ask her the question?*

And one of Zahabiya's friends was being abused by a teacher. She mentally replayed the conversation. It did seem like the question was about a friend, and not Zahabiya. She couldn't quite put her finger on it, but something about the situation didn't feel right.

Leesa

Leesa walked through the quiet neighbourhood, broody thoughts playing in a repetitive loop: *Was this her fault?* If she hadn't been so dismissive about the notebook, if she hadn't postponed their date, if she hadn't gone to the motel with Rodney, if she hadn't started seeing Rodney in the first place . . . *Was this her fault?*

Leesa recognized his two-bedroom bungalow from last year, when he'd forgotten his wallet and had driven home to retrieve it while she'd waited in the driveway, slunk low in the passenger seat, invisible.

She knew he wouldn't like the pop-in, but unlatched the picket fence and went around to the back of the house anyway, leaving fresh footprints in last night's snow. She didn't know what else to do. She'd tried calling at 8 a.m., hanging up as soon as his mother answered. She'd waited by the phones, but he didn't call her back.

On the second attempt, at 9:30 a.m., Leesa tried a different tack, put on a French accent, and asked to speak with him. His mother said,

"I'm sorry, Nahla, he's still not up," which made Leesa fret for another half hour. Then, getting more creative on the third call, she impersonated a cashier from the local art supply store. The old bag insisted on taking a message rather than getting him. Leesa made up a lie about some stupid paintbrush being in stock.

She peered into a basement window well. He was sprawled on a pull-out couch, blue light dancing across his stubbly face. She knocked lightly on the glass. He hurried to the back door and rushed her downstairs.

"What are you doing here?" He whispered over the roadrunner's bleeping. His eyes were puffy, bugged out.

"I was walking by and wanted to see you. I tried calling."

"*Shhh.* My mom's still home. She won't leave for another—" he checked the wall clock, "few minutes."

They sat stiffly on the stale-smelling sofa bed, passing a cigarette between them, the television volume turned low, so that they could monitor his mother's church-leaving preparations through the moody floorboards. Leesa scanned his art studio. Weak sunshine slanted into the low-ceilinged room from small casement windows, illuminating dust motes. In a corner was an abandoned easel surrounded by blank canvases and closed tubes of paint. A few paintings hung on the walls; she recognized these pieces from back in grade 9 when he'd shown her his portfolio. An avocado fridge and matching washer and dryer set squatted along one wall beside the television, where the coyote failed at his quest to trap the roadrunner for the umpteenth time.

"Bye, Michael," Mrs. Stephenson called from upstairs. "I'm going now. There are messages for you by the phone. And please don't forget to shovel the walk."

"Okay," Michael called back, his voice strained. He stubbed out the cigarette, now just a butt. The door banged shut. He got a can of beer from the fridge, cracked it open, and offered her one. She hadn't ever drank in the morning, but accepted it.

"So, there's a rumour going around that you were at the manor last night." She hadn't meant to blurt her insecurities, not right away, but she'd been strangling them for hours already.

"Oh, that's why you're here." He looked at her carefully. Leesa kept her expression neutral. "I dropped off Nahla. A bunch of us got together over at Maeve and Joanne's — Miss McKinney and Miss Robertson's place. I wasn't planning to go, but you had to reschedule."

"You dropped her off?"

"Yup." He stretched his arm across her shoulders, pulled her in tightly, his fingers insistent. "Why haven't we done this before? My mother is never at home at this time. As long as no one saw you — you were careful, right?"

She nodded, trying to put her conflicting thoughts in order: *He's lying and probably having sex with Miss Naim. He wants me here, isn't mad that I came over. And I'm lying and having sex with Rodney, but that's meaningless. Is Miss Naim meaningless, too?*

"And good news: she mailed that notebook back to Leblanc's brother, which means she's no longer watching you." He cooed this into her ear while stroking her back, as though she were a skittish cat.

Then he straightened, sat up, pulled away. "She also told me she saw you necking with Rodney last week."

"You told me to be obvious about it, so when she walked by, I put on a show." Guilt rippled through her for a second, but she held her breath, shooed it away. *Stay on task.*

"I heard that you were seen leaving the manor. Not just dropping her off."

"Sure, I walked her up. She insisted I see her place because I'd been talking about getting out of here, maybe being a monitor in the boys' residence. She asked me to stay for a drink, but I got the three-minute tour and left." He cupped her face. "Hey, what's wrong?"

"Nothing." She processed his lie, inspecting it as she might a zit on her own face: *Leave it alone, cover it up, pop it?* She understood men were weak and ruled by their genitals, but still, the deceit signalled danger.

"Babe? You know you're my girl, right?" He gazed at her, and when she didn't reply, he kissed her neck. She turned toward him, tasted cigarettes, beer, morning, on his tongue.

"Promise you won't go to her place again?" It came out as a whine, and she hated herself for it.

"Promise." He held up his fingers like a boy scout. "Why would I go back there?"

"Okay."

"Maybe it's time you dropped Rodney before things go too far with him."

"Okay. I'll do it right after the Valentine's Dance." She *had* let things go too far with Rodney. She'd let herself enjoy it too much, hadn't thought before she'd acted.

"Thanks, Babe. Since you're here, let's take advantage of church." He pushed her down against the mattress, the force of it a reassurance; even if he was with Miss Naim last night, she was the one he loved. The one he'd chosen.

Later, she slipped out the back door, but stopped when she heard the clomp of boots on the front stoop, followed by a knock on the front door. She flattened herself against the clapboard at the side of the house.

The screen door squeaked open.

"Oh, hey, Gerry!" Michael said, his voice too chipper. He was probably scanning the street right now, worrying that Gerry had seen her leave.

"Hey, I thought I'd drop off this pack of cigarettes. I found it just under the seat. I'm on day two of quitting, so thought I'd better get rid of it before I fall off the wagon. New Year's resolution. Now February resolution." He laughed.

"Oh, thanks. And good luck with that. How's the car driving?"

"It's in good shape for its age. One of your students even took a photo of me with it last week!"

"One of my students?"

"Yeah, that little East Indian girl. Said it was for an assignment. She had a real fancy camera, with a long lens?"

Leesa frowned. *Were they talking about Zahabiya?* She recalled the posse from last night, Zahabiya among them.

193

"Weird. I haven't assigned anything new. I won't until after March break. Just means more marking."

"Dunno. Ah, well. Kids. I'll let you go, get your Sunday rest."

Leesa waited a minute, then re-entered through the back door, and went up the steps to where Michael stood in the living room, still staring out the half-open door. Impulsively, she pocketed the note by the phone.

"Don't worry, I heard him coming before I got to the front of the house." Leesa scanned the cramped living room with it floral-printed couch and shelf with ceramic figurines. Tacky.

"Good. That was a close call."

She stepped into the hall, glanced into a room with a sewing machine, treadmill, and bookshelf. "Where's your room?"

"She converted it to a sewing room when I went to university. I took over the basement . . ." He trailed off, his mind elsewhere.

"I wonder why Zahabiya was taking photos of your old car?"

"I have no idea." He paused, giving the question a second glance. "You know, it was weird, but I think I saw her last night when I left the manor. She was with a few others. Lavinia, a girl I didn't recognize. And . . ."

"Marie."

"Marie Hill? You know her?" He frowned.

"Of course, we're in the same year."

"Are you friends with her?"

"Why would we be friends?" She grimaced. "We're in . . . different crowds."

He looked distracted, as though trying to catch hold of an important detail just outside his reach. His mother pushed open the front gate, and Leesa hurried out the back door.

As she walked home, she thought about her brief encounter with the four girls last night. She couldn't recall if Marie had had her camera slung around her neck, the one she always seemed to have with her. The kind of camera, with the long lens, that Gerry would describe as "fancy."

194

She pulled the note she'd pocketed and read the messages written in cursive:

Call Nahla: 968-5727
Quinte Art Supply has your brush.
Call Aunt June — her neighbour has that one-bedroom for rent.

Zahabiya

Marie, Lavinia, Mei, and I contemplated our next steps. We'd been at it almost an hour already.

"You thought we should we talk to Leesa first." Lavinia turned to Marie. "She might listen to you."

"I feel like it's the kindest thing, but I'm not sure anymore. She hates me." Marie shook her head.

"Could someone else do it?" I asked, but hastened to add, "But I'm not volunteering. I've already done more than my fair share of reconnaissance work."

"It's true, Nancy Drew," Mei said, poker-faced. "I agree, it's kind to talk to her first, but she's mean."

"I'm supposed to go back to Miss Naim tomorrow. Maybe she can talk to Leesa."

"But she's dating him. Her question about gossip has to be about him being there last night. Has to be," Marie said.

"You can't trust someone with divided loyalties." Mei sighed.

There was a knock on our door.

"Come in," I called.

Leesa stepped in and closed the door behind her. I held my breath. *We'd kept our voices low, but had she overheard us?*

"So, juicy gossip, right?" She said with fake exuberance.

"What do you mean?" I tried to make sense of her sunny veneer.

"About the teachers last night? I would have thought you four would have told *everyone* about Miss Naim and Mr. Stephenson. I asked my roommates if they'd heard anything, but they were clueless."

"That would be kind of an asshole move," Mei countered. "And anyway, we didn't see them together."

"So, why exactly were you spying on Mr. Stephenson?"

"We weren't spying. We just happened to see his car," Marie said.

I turned to Marie. She and I shared a long look, then she sighed and nodded. "Yeah, okay. Let's get this over with."

Mei got up and offered Leesa her chair. "Sit."

"What's going on?" Leesa asked. She perched on the edge of Mei's chair.

"There's something important we need to talk with you about," Lavinia began and looked at Marie to continue.

"Back in grade 9, I was in Mr. Stephenson's art class," Marie's began, her voice soft.

"Yeah, so?"

"He paid a lot of attention to me, after class." She continued on with her story, and hearing it a second time made me understand more deeply than before that Leesa was in a bad situation. *And were there others?* Mr. Stephenson was a favourite among the students, and I often saw him talking to girls alone before and after classes.

Marie's face had gone pale. Leesa's jaw twitched. She looked like she was going to get up and leave.

"The thing is, Leesa," Lavinia joined in, "we are concerned that Mr. Stephenson is being inappropriate with you, too."

"And just so you know, we haven't told anyone about this, Leesa. We're not into gossip," Mei added.

I wondered if we should show her our photos, explain how we arrived at our suspicions, but before I could suggest it, Leesa stood and stepped toward the door.

"You think Mr. Stephenson is *abusing* me? You're crazy. You all have overactive imaginations. We're just friendly. And unlike you dweebs, I have a boyfriend." Hand on doorknob, she added. "And, Marie? You're delusional if you think he was interested in you. Even back in grade 9 you were a fat, ugly pig!"

And then she was gone, her words a windstorm whipping up sand that stung Marie's eyes and clouded my vision. Even Mei was quiet.

In the minute it took us to recover, Miss Naim appeared at the door like a piece of debris blown in with the squall.

"Zahabiya, could you come to my flat? I'd like to talk with you."

The four of us looked to one another, silently calculating. I turned to Marie for direction. She shook her head slightly. I didn't know what to do.

I took a breath and followed Miss Naim out.

Nahla

On Monday evening, Nahla and Maeve sat in a back corner at Wong's, waiting for their dinners to arrive.

"I don't know what to make of it," Nahla said in a low, conspiratorial voice. "I mean, on Sunday morning, she practically told me that a teacher was abusing her friend. Then by the afternoon, she was backpedalling and saying it was all a misunderstanding!"

"Do you think she got cold feet?"

"I don't know. But what can I do? The friend is at her old school. I don't even know her name."

"Unfortunately, this kind of thing is too common and often swept under the rug." Maeve shook her head.

They paused their conversation as the server plonked their plates onto the table.

"Well, I don't want to be part of sweeping something like that under the rug. If there's something I can do."

"Just leave it alone for now. Maybe check in with her in a few days."

"Yeah, okay." Nahla inhaled the steam rising from her chicken.

"And I should tell you, the rumours you were worried about finally reached me today. I overheard two students talking just before class. I shut them down and gave them a lecture about slander. Scared the bejesus out of them."

"See? I knew that awful girl would tell everyone. What was the exact wording?"

"That Michael was seen leaving your suite at 2 a.m. this weekend. Something like, 'The art teacher and the French teacher are sleeping with each other.'"

"It was around midnight, not 2 a.m.! Oh, what should I do, Maeve? What if Headmaster Lowery finds out?" Nahla put down her fork. She imagined being called into his office, questioned about Michael, losing her job, returning to Montreal in shame.

"Leave it alone. Gosh, that seems to be my motto today!" Maeve chortled, a half-eaten sweet-and-sour chicken ball threatening to bounce. "But seriously, it will pass. And if Lowery questions you, deny it."

"Right. Right. It's not like she has proof." Nahla exhaled and pushed a piece of broccoli around her plate. Maybe she could skirt this.

"Exactly. Acknowledge that you've been dating and deny the rest. And on the upside, sounds like things with Michael are going well if he was your late-night caller? And this Thursday is Val-en-tine's," she singsonged.

"I'm not sure. He's being odd. We didn't talk at all last week, but he was away sick. And since our date, he hasn't returned my calls. I looked for him today, but he wasn't in the lounge at his usual time or in the dining hall. And Maeve . . . on Saturday night, at my place . . . it was pretty bad."

"Bad . . . sex?" Maeve mouthed the words.

"Yes." Nahla exhaled. "And after, he couldn't leave fast enough. I'm pretty sure it's over."

"I'm so sorry, Nahla."

"It's okay, I'll survive. It's only been three dates." And months of longing.

"You will . . . okay, so this is not the best moment to ask you this, then." Maeve flashed an uncomfortable smile. "Joanne is supposed to chaperone the dance. Could you take her shift? Valentine's Day is actually our anniversary."

"Of course, Maeve. It was fun last time . . . kind of."

"Remember that brawl between those girls!" Maeve laughed.

"More than ever, I can see why Ashley wanted to fight Leesa." She pierced a piece of chicken with her fork.

———

The phone was ringing when Nahla slipped her key into her door's lock. She ran in, hoping it was Michael. It was Fatmi, her sister.

"What's wrong?"

"Nothing is wrong. I'm home alone, so I thought I'd try you."

"But when Baba checks the bill, he'll be angry."

"It's been six months already. Let him be angry!" Nahla smiled; Fatmi was developing a strong backbone. Her own, in contrast, felt porous.

"So, what's new?"

"I got offered a translator job in Quebec City. I start after graduation. One of my professors helped me get it."

"Fatmi, wow, mabrouk. But how are you going to manage this adventure?"

"I have you as a role model, single and living on your own . . ."

"Well . . . yes, I suppose I probably am single." She spilled about her dates with Michael and her worries about his recent distance. It was a relief to share, even if Fatmi had almost no experience with men.

"Don't you think it might be better to date someone more . . . promising? Someone Arab? I mean, Baashir broke your heart. You don't want to go through all that again."

"I guess I got caught up. I wanted it to be promising. But maybe it could still work. I mean, he could convert . . ." When she said the words aloud, she heard how ridiculous they sounded.

"Baba will disown you if you marry a white guy."

"I feel disowned already." Nahla slumped in her chair.

"No, no, this is only Baba in shock. You know, the other day, I overheard him boasting to a friend that you had a good job. He said you're living in a women's residence run by nuns — to make it sound more halal, ha ha!"

"Well, there are no nuns, but his version is not that far from the truth." She massaged her jaw with her free hand.

Before they ended the call, Fatmi promised to campaign for Nahla's visit during March break. The possibility of going home in a couple of weeks was like sunshine breaking through an overcast sky. She was probably losing Michael, but perhaps she might get her family back.

Leesa

Leesa sat at a picnic table near the library and lit a cigarette. The final class bell had just rung. Warm for February 12: students were out enjoying the day, parkas unzipped.

Her first pull of the tobacco was a consolation. She watched students pass by, talking, laughing, and her already-grey mood shifted melancholic; she was one of the most popular girls in school, yet she was an island among all this activity, a barren rock in a rushing river. *Who were her real friends anyway? Jessica and Mallory? Rodney?* No, none of them would understand. All of them would use it against her.

Across the parking lot, she spied Michael. She was about to signal to him, but that bitch, Miss Naim, called out. He waited as she caught up to him. She looked agitated, and they talked for a minute, his hand on her shoulder. Reassuring. Intimate. Then he got in his car and drove away, and Miss Naim went back inside.

What was that about? Well, she'd find out later tonight. She'd ask him about Marie, too. She was nuts if she thought her father broke up a budding romance — there was just no way! Leesa and Marie were polar opposites: *How could Michael like them both?*

She remembered grade 9, a lifetime ago. She'd had a huge crush on Michael, but Marie was the teacher's pet, grabbing all his attention. Then at some point, she stopped being his favourite.

That was the only thing about the story that made sense. Michael would have had to be aloof with Marie if her father had unfairly accused him of being inappropriate. That would be the smart thing to do.

And then, Michael finally noticed *her.* *They* were kindred spirits, soulmates. What *they* had was special. She tapped an inch-long ash from her cigarette.

The library door slammed. Damn. Just thinking about Marie had made her appear. Surrounding her were those stupid girls, the ones who knew. Who *thought* they knew about her relationship. Until Saturday night, she'd barely registered them; they'd existed on the periphery of her world. Now, she'd need to keep tabs on them. *Would they tell anyone?* She'd need to find a way to dissuade them from doing that.

Lavinia nodded at her, while Marie pretended she was invisible. Mei gave her a long look. *Did that bitch think she was better than her?* Even though the truth stung, there was an almost-perverse pleasure in repeating her words to Mallory and Jessica: *The art teacher is screwing the French teacher.* A perfect rumour to discredit the nerds if they did talk.

Last out the door was Zahabiya, holding hands with Jason. *Were they together now?* Leesa tamped down a flare of jealousy as quickly as it rose in her chest.

Zahabiya raised her hand, like a limp white flag. Leesa flicked her cigarette into the melting snowbank.

On the way to the farmer's field that night, Leesa readied herself.

She only half-listened to his complaining about being assigned to chaperone the Valentine's Dance. She was preparing her own rant.

"I can't wait to get out of this job. It's like I'm a glorified babysitter sometimes. And you're gonna be at the dance with that asshole date of yours." He pulled over by the side of the road.

She stared coolly at the moon, mostly clouded over, the farmer's field without its nightlight.

"Cut the bull," she said, turning to him. He narrowed his eyes. "I know you've been lying to me."

She paused, momentarily distracted by the déjà vu that crowded into the car with them. Hadn't she overheard her mother confronting her father with these exact words?

"What are you talking about?" His eyes turned doleful. No. She wouldn't allow that to confuse her.

"About Miss Naim. I saw your car parked outside the manor Saturday night. It was after midnight."

"Right. I told you I was there." He reached for her, tried to pull her close. She resisted.

"And I saw you leaving her flat. And I saw you talking to her this afternoon."

"Oh. She mentioned that she thought you'd seen us. Babe, don't misunderstand the situation — I told you I came up for a few minutes. She's really hung up on me. This afternoon I was explaining that I didn't feel the same way about her." He bent his head, tried to meet her eyes.

"I didn't just see you. I saw her, half-naked. Here's what you need to know. If I ever, and I mean ever, see you being close with her in any kind of way — touching her, spending non-work time with her, and even worse, lying to me about it — I will tell everyone about us."

"What? Nothing really happened. Leesa, what are you saying?"

"I'm saying that I will broadcast to the world that I was fourteen when you first kissed me, that we were making out when I was fifteen, that we had sex for the first time when I was sixteen." Leesa felt her cheeks grow hot, but resisted touching them with her cold fingers. She needed to stay strong, look strong.

"Why are you flipping out? Is this about your father?" He squeezed her arm.

205

"No." Leesa felt the gut punch, but steeled herself. "I'm saying no more lying. No more Miss Naim. Or else I blow everything up. Your career, our relationship, everything. I can do that, you know."

"Leesa, you're being hysterical. Just calm down. I don't like Nahla. I'm not even attracted to her." His eyes darted left and right.

"Is that what you told Marie's father when he confronted you about her?"

He hesitated, and — in the three-second delay before he vehemently sputtered out a "What?" — she was able to discern the truth. Guilt masked as shock couldn't disarm her; she'd witnessed her father enact it with her mother too many times.

She wished he hadn't hesitated, wished she could paper over this part of the confrontation. *What did it mean that he could be attracted to both Marie and her?* All they had in common was their age. Their age. She pushed away the thought.

"How did you hear that nonsense? Listen, people at this school love to spread lies. Right now, there's one circulating about me and Miss Naim."

"I started that. I thought it might help if anyone found out about us."

She studied his face, wondering if she should tell him about the girls and their suspicions. No, not now. That wasn't the most important thing, and anyway, it would just scare him off. She refocused.

"Let me repeat myself, so it's clear. I am not exaggerating." No longer able to hold back tears, she sniffled through her threat. "I will tell everyone about us — Headmaster Lowery . . . my parents . . . your mother — everyone — if you ever see Miss Naim again or lie to me again. Now, take me home."

On the drive back to the manor, he was quiet, and she wondered if she'd been too harsh. All she wanted was to keep him. She wiped her tears and took his hand.

"I know we have a future together. This is just a bump in the road. You've been under so much stress worrying about that stupid notebook. And you got tempted by Miss Naim. It happens."

"I'm sorry if you got the wrong idea, Leesa," he said, with what sounded like a tremble in his voice. It wasn't exactly what she wanted to hear, but it was enough.

Zahabiya

"It's pretty in here," I said, trying to cheer up my friends. It had been a rough few days.

"It would be better without the aroma of Salisbury steak, though," Lavinia said. Paul Jeffrey had turned her down when she asked him to the dance, telling her he'd started dating someone from home over the Christmas holidays.

"Yeah, there's definitely eau de mashed potato in the air," Marie said glumly. She wasn't ready to talk to her father or the headmaster yet, and we were giving her a little space. What had begun so urgently seemed to need a pause now. I could respect Marie's pace, but I didn't like it; sitting on a secret as big as this made me uncomfortable.

I scanned the room for Jason, who was meeting me there. The dining hall had been transformed into a convincing ballroom. Helium hearts bobbed from the rafters, a disco ball littered sparkles across the floor, and Wham!'s "Careless Whisper" played over the sound system.

"There's Mei." Marie pointed to the dance floor, where she was dancing with Kwame. She'd insisted that they were just friends, but their grip on each other was pretty tight.

"And there's our favourite project over there." Lavinia looked to the back of the room, where Leesa and her crew were gathered.

"Wanna dance?" Jason came up from behind us and slipped his hand into mine. "Or I should say, 'Come Dancing.'" I smiled at his punny reference to The Kinks song that had just started. I swayed to the upbeat rhythm while mouthing the nostalgic lyrics. Jason was a bit like a Ken doll, handsome, but all stiff arms and legs.

When the song ended, the DJ turned on Lionel Richie's "Hello," and the dance floor emptied and reconfigured into boy-girl pairings. Jason stepped closer to me, and I felt his light touch on my waist. I rested my forehead against his shoulder. He smelled of Irish Spring soap. I synchronized my movements to the music, guiding Jason to slow his steps.

"You look nice tonight," he said, breathing into my ear.

"Thanks, you, too." He'd recently got a haircut and had started using Dippity Do to make it spiky on top.

"This colour is really nice on you. Is this new?" He fingered my blouse's sleeve.

"It was my mom's. But it's the first time I've worn it." Over Christmas break I'd rummaged through the basement closet where Dad had moved Mom's dressy clothes after Tara moved in. He told Zahra and me that he was saving them for us, but I suspected he just couldn't dispose of them; shifting them down two flights of stairs had taken him more than two years.

I liked opening that basement closet, running my fingers over the fabrics, and imagining Mom's scent still on them. The robin's-egg-blue silk blouse, with its ruffled yoke and shoulder pads, was her favourite for "Canadian parties." It was the first of her garments I'd claimed for myself.

"It suits you," he said, not a single note of pity in his voice.

Out of the corner of my eye, I glanced at Miss Naim standing near the stage. I did a double take; she was eyeing me. Guilt roiled my stomach; I didn't like misleading her and knew my clumsy story had made her worry.

I led us into a half-turn, so that my back was to Miss Naim.

"Hey . . . is . . . Miss Naim . . . staring at us?"

"I think so," I whispered. I told him about lying to her. "Is she still looking this way?"

"Yes. No. Mr. Stephenson just joined her . . . now she's talking to him."

"Good . . ." I sighed and concentrated on Lionel Richie's angst. Jason's body was warm, and I wanted to take off his wool jacket, so I could feel his body through the thinner cotton of his shirt.

"Hey, tell me something: Do they look like a couple to you?" I asked.

"Maybe? They're standing close together . . . and talking . . . but it is loud in here."

"What else do you see?"

"She has her hand on his upper arm . . . sorta like this." He ran his hand up my bicep, squeezed lightly, sending tingles down my back that made me giggle involuntarily.

"Anything else?"

"No, just more talking. You guys think he's dating Miss Naim and also doing something weird with Leesa?"

"Yeah. That's why I couldn't tell her the whole truth, you know?"

"Right. Hey, he's shifted away from her a bit. They look tense now. He's walking away . . . and she's following him."

"Let's turn so I can see, too." Jason and I moved ninety degrees. Mr. Stephenson paused, said something, his hands raised in defence. Miss Naim's finger pointed an accusation at him.

"*Hmm*, seems there's trouble in paradise," Leesa said. She and Rodney had appeared out of nowhere and were dancing two feet from us.

"Wow, she looks really mad. Wonder what he did to deserve that," Rodney said.

"I bet he's breaking up with her. I mean, she's such a bitch. She's probably a nympho," Leesa said.

"Leesa, you know that's not true, " I said. She glared at me. I looked back at Miss Naim and Mr. Stephenson.

As though sensing they were being talked about, the teachers halted their argument and looked our way. I followed Mr. Stephenson's gaze as he locked on Leesa, who loosened her grip on Rodney and returned his gaze in response. "Hello? "Lionel Richie sang.

Miss Naim, too, was a spectator to the silent but obvious moment that Leesa and Mr. Stephenson were sharing. She frowned, studied Mr. Stephenson, then Leesa, then Mr. Stephenson again. Then, she fixed a confused gaze on me, and I froze. Mr. Stephenson walked away.

"Rodney, let's go get something to eat." Leesa grabbed Rodney's hand.

"That was . . . something," Jason whispered.

"Yeah . . . and add it to our list of circumstantial evidence we have no idea what to do with." I pulled his itchy jacket open just wide enough to rest my cheek against his shirt. I listened as his pulse quickened. That's all I wanted to focus on, all I wanted to know.

Nahla

Nahla waited for the last song, the impossibly long "Stairway to Heaven," to end. With Robert Plant's final "hea—van," she switched on the lights, causing a chorus of grumbling from the two dozen couples still clinging to one another on the dance floor. Gerry directed the dance committee to return the tables to their original positions, and she herded the stragglers out the doors, Jason and Zahabiya among them. The other staff, including Michael, had decamped minutes earlier.

She walked the long hallway to collect her coat and purse from the teacher's lounge. She couldn't wait to leave the building, have a cigarette, be alone with her thoughts. Just as she entered the lounge, Michael slammed his locker shut. They'd kept to their opposite corners of the hall, like two fighters avoiding the ring. But now, here they were, within striking distance, florescent lights like spotlights. He gave her a wide berth and wordlessly vacated the room.

Probably for the best; she didn't know what to say to him, what to ask, what to think. *Why did he stare so long at Leesa Allen? Could Zahabiya's story be about them?* She'd mulled over the possibility most of the evening. He was a cad, leading her on and then dropping her yesterday, and later refusing to talk about it, even during her attempt to confront him at the dance. *But he wasn't an abuser; he couldn't be abusing a girl if he was interested in her, an adult woman, right?*

But then, she remembered, hard stone in her belly, that he was no longer interested in her. Perhaps he'd never liked her as much as she'd liked him. What they had was . . . khalaas. Fini. Over. She had to accept it now.

And about the mystery girl who was "in an inappropriate relationship with a teacher": she'd have to talk to Zahabiya again, coax the truth — whatever it was — from her.

She pushed her arms into her coat and was about to turn off the lights when they flickered slightly, and she paused to look back. Sylvie? There, in her mail cubby, was a thick yellow package. The envelope was stamped: *RETURN TO SENDER: INSUFFICIENT POSTAGE*. Strange, she'd had the post office clerk weigh it and affix the correct number of stamps for her. So annoying!

She pushed the parcel into her small purse. As she walked out the back door, it bulged out and bounced against her hip, as though telegraphing Sylvie's scrawls: *char bleu, back before bedcheck, Wednesdays*. Now she imagined Sylvie by their window, watching Leesa go out the back door, walk toward a car, perhaps his blue car, every single Wednesday.

Her mind, disbelieving, wandering, slid to memories of being in the passenger seat of that car, kissing him. It had felt good to be desired and touched. *Surely some of that had been real?* But how quickly all that had crumbled. *Had she done something to turn him off, to make him change his mind and leave so suddenly that last time? Was it her comment about not wanting to drink too much? Had he perceived that as a judgment? When she'd insisted he use a condom, had he felt slighted?*

She stumbled on an icy patch, the yellow parcel falling to the snow. She had an urge to abandon it there, but she leaned over, brushed it off, stuffed it back into her bag.

They'd even had fun talking about Sylvie's notebook; it had been like foreplay for their first time together. But now she wondered if he'd been overly curious. While other staff — Maeve, Frederick, Margo, and Gerry — had asked her all about it, he'd been the only one who'd wanted to see it, read it.

She paused, exhaled, and looked up at the night sky, the waning crescent moon shining bright through a gap in the clouds. "Sylvie, what am I going to do?" She wiped her face, only just realizing that she'd been crying.

She butted out, climbed the residence steps, composing her expression into something teacherly, adult, appropriate.

"Miss Naim, there's a problem." The serious-looking girl who met her at the door was from the other wing.

"What's wrong? You're Lavinia, right?"

"Yeah. Something's wrong, all right. Come see." The girl walked briskly ahead, business-like, leading her to Mei and Zahabiya's room. They and Marie stood amid a hurricane wreckage scene of clothing, books, and toiletries. Lavinia closed the door, and the upturned room, with all five of them crowded inside, was claustrophobic.

"What happened here?" Nahla gasped.

"Well, obviously some asshole trashed our room." Mei transferred clothing from the floor back into a drawer.

"And . . . they took my money," Zahabiya said, crestfallen. "I'd been saving a bit from my allowance each week. For emergencies. I had twenty-seven dollars hidden in my desk drawer."

"Who would do this?" Nahla scooped a textbook from the floor.

"Someone who is clearly angry with us," Marie said, looking at the others.

"Abso-fucking-lutely." Mei snatched a hanger and rehung a skirt and jacket. Nahla was about to scold her for her crude language but couldn't summon the energy.

214

"I agree." Lavinia, too, made eye contact with the others, avoiding Nahla's gaze. The girls appeared to be communicating in code, in looks and shrugs and sighs.

"Zahabiya, does this have something to do with what we discussed over the weekend?" Nahla's eyes welled up as she asked the question, her mind travelling back to the dance, to Leesa and Michael, to her own heartbreak.

"We think so."

"Why don't you come with me to my suite, so we can speak privately." Nahla turned to go, but Zahabiya didn't budge.

"I think we should all be here for this," Marie said, sitting on one of the beds. Lavinia, Zahabiya, and Mei followed suit, a spontaneous sit-in. Zahabiya offered Nahla a chair. She remained standing, crossed her arms over her chest.

"This note was in my drawer." Zahabiya read it aloud: "*Don't say a word. I can make you and your friends' lives miserable. If you do what I say, you will be rewarded every week with what you lost.*"

"A threat and a bribe." Lavinia translated for Nahla.

"Tell me who you think did this." Of course, Nahla knew the answer. Again, the girls hesitated.

She sat in the offered chair. The parcel fell to the floor with a *thunk*. She collected it and was about to return it to her bag, but hesitated when she felt the sensation of a cool breeze against her cheek.

Why not? She needed the girls to talk.

"This belonged to Mademoiselle Leblanc. She kept some notes that you might be able to help me understand." She tore the envelope, opened the notebook to the front pages, and passed it to Zahabiya, who began reading, haltingly, out loud. Nahla translated the more complicated words. The girls didn't seem puzzled or surprised by the information.

"So, Mademoiselle Leblanc was suspicious, too." Lavinia shook her head.

"It's like we're finishing her work." Marie nodded.

"Suspicious of what?" Nahla asked. No one answered. Zahabiya

215

read out the last entry, turned the page, saw it was blank, and held it out for Nahla, the back cover flapping open.

"Wait. What was that?" Marie asked, grabbing the book from Zahabiya's hands.

"What?" Zahabiya asked, leaning over to see.

"O . . . mi . . . God . . . Here it is, on the back page. *LNO 32*. She was missing the last digit. But she knew. Mademoiselle Leblanc knew!" Marie held up the book for all to see.

Nahla had flipped through the cahier many times, but these letters and numbers were written so close to its spine she'd missed them. What did they mean?

The room went still as the girls resumed their Morse code of glances and exhalations and nods.

"What's *LNO 32*? What did she know?" Nahla demanded.

"Mr. Stephenson's char bleu," Mei murmured.

"His licence plate." Zahabiya's voice was soft, barely audible.

Nahla looked around the room, at the chaos, at each girl's face. Mei's expression was defiant, Marie's mournful, Lavinia's earnest, Zahabiya's pitying. All of them wise, wiser than she would ever be.

She listened as they laid it out. They showed her photographs of two cars. She remembered riding in them both. As she listened, clues lined up like a domino line in her mind, ready to topple: Leesa leaving on Wednesday nights; the silver scrunchie; Michael's interest in her only after Maeve told him about the notebook. Then Marie shared her experience. A sudden lightheadedness overtook Nahla, and she wanted nothing more than to escape the airless room.

"All right. Thank you for talking about all of this with me. And . . . I'm sorry this happened to you, Marie. It's late now, so you should all get to bed. We'll deal with this tomorrow." They made plans to meet early the next morning.

She then walked the old wing woodenly, ensuring all were in bed. When she glanced into Leesa's room, she was unobtrusive. There was so much she wanted to say to the girl, but knew she couldn't, not now.

She finished the upper floor and let herself into her suite. She opened the window wide, pulled a blanket around her shoulders, and sat there, smoking cigarette after cigarette, until the pack crumpled in her hand. She felt Sylvie's presence beside her and wished she could ignore it.

Leesa

Early the next morning there was a soft knock on the door. Miss Naim stood in the hallway, looking like hell, dark circles under her eyes, frizz piled atop her head in what was supposed to be a bun. Her dress was wrinkly and not in a fashionable way.

"Please come with me." Her tone had a bossy edge that annoyed Leesa, especially before her first cup of coffee.

"What's this about? I still have to do my makeup." Leesa turned to resume her morning routine.

"This won't take long." Miss Naim had the audacity to touch Leesa's elbow, but she shook it off and shared a look with Jessica and Mallory. They'd heard from Barb, Marie's roommate, that there had been some kind of closed-door meeting last night in Zahabiya and Mei's room. Earlier in the evening, Leesa had concocted a story about them — that Zahabiya and Mei had called her a "slut" — and had sent Lauren, Barb, and Carrie to toss the room while everyone was out at the dance. She'd inspected the damage herself and left her own personal touches. She was shocked the nerds had ratted her out.

Leesa followed Miss Naim down the hallway. She stared at the woman's shoulders, more delicate than her own, and wondered if Michael had found the quality attractive.

Marie and Zahabiya were waiting in Miss Naim's suite. A couple of chairs had been pulled in, and Miss Naim told Leesa to sit beside the other girls.

"Why are they here?" Leesa did her best to look puzzled, which was half real. *Shouldn't Mei have been present instead of Marie?* Her empty stomach roiled, realizing they had snitched on more than the prank.

"There's something we need you to see." Miss Naim passed Leesa a small, worn-looking notebook, explaining that Mademoiselle Leblanc had been its author. Leesa hadn't imagined it to be so shabby-looking; with all the attention Michael had given it, she'd pictured something leather-bound, perhaps with a gold clasp. *Also, didn't Michael say it had been returned to Leblanc's family?* Maybe that had been a lie, one of many he'd fabricated.

She fought to compose her facial muscles to appear blasé, but as she read through the entries, her eyes teared up. She recalled those Wednesdays last spring just before and after the abrupt breakup. To see them witnessed, documented, felt like the floor being knocked out from under her. Again.

She finished reading and looked up to see Marie gazing at her consolingly, as though they shared some sort of sisterly bond.

"Obviously, Leblanc was an odd and obsessive old woman. Everyone knows that."

"You were meeting Mr. Stephenson," Miss Naim said.

"No! Why would you say that? I told you two," she pointed at Marie and Zahabiya, "that you're imagining things. I just went for walks on my own, and I had a boyfriend last year. Okay, I don't like to talk about it, because he was a townie who had a girlfriend he was cheating on to be with me. He had a blue car." She smiled, admiring her own quick wit.

"That's not true, Leesa. We know." Zahabiya took off her thick glasses and cleaned them with the edge of her kilt.

Marie leaned over, took the notebook, and flipped all the pages until the back page was revealed. "This is Mr. Stephenson's licence plate number. Missing the last digit."

"What does that prove?" Leesa's heart raced. "You know, Leblanc was probably trying to frame Michael. They never got along. He told me."

"Listen, Leesa. I know you feel like you have to protect him because you care about him. I understand. I felt close to him, too. I thought we had something special, too. He asked me to call him by his first name, too," Marie said.

"I don't believe a single word that comes out of your mouth. There's something wrong with you. You're a compulsive liar or something." The closed room was stuffy. She turned to Miss Naim, "I'm telling you: I just went out for walks, and I had a boyfriend."

"Michael read it, too." Miss Naim looked at her with sad eyes. "He downplayed it, too."

"You showed it to him? He said that he'd never seen the book."

Miss Naim nodded.

"How long ago?"

"A couple of weeks back, but," Miss Naim paused, "why do you ask?"

Leesa's mouth grew dry, as though her saliva was turning to mud. She'd spoken too fast, almost lost control of the situation. She wanted to bolt from the room, but that would reveal too much. She had to pull herself together, she had to.

"Leesa. It's hard to think about, but there's something wrong with Michael. He's abusive." Marie's eyes brimmed with tears.

"Listen, I'm sorry if you think he did something to you." Leesa felt a hard pressure on her chest as she pushed against the kernel of truth in Marie's words. He'd tried to deny the thing with Marie, but she'd seen through him. *But maybe it wasn't actually that strange to be attracted to someone younger?* At fourteen, she was already mature. At fourteen she managed her bank account, flew alone across the Atlantic, and organized her own schedule. Fourteen felt like a decade ago.

"It's not your fault. That it happened," Zahabiya said to both Marie and Leesa.

"Or that you . . . love him and want to protect him," Miss Naim added.

"I don't love him! He and I are just friends. We talk sometimes, that's all."

"What sort of friends?" Miss Naim asked. Leesa didn't answer, internally chastising herself for once again saying too much.

"I think maybe he was attracted to me, to us, because our attention, our admiration made him feel more important," Marie ventured. Leesa watched as Miss Naim's eyes widened and her expression turned sad.

"Let's be honest, Miss Naim. Nahla. You're just doing this because you're mad at him. We all saw him dump you last night at the dance. It was so pathetic," Leesa spat. Miss Naim looked down at the floor. Zahabiya and Marie exchanged worried glances, and Leesa knew she was regaining lost ground.

"Okay, well, Leesa," Miss Naim said, rallying, "we asked you here because we wanted to talk to you first . . . to be sensitive to you, before we meet with Headmaster Lowery."

"We didn't want it to come as a surprise." Zahabiya nodded. Leesa wanted to slap the sympathetic expression off her face.

"Of course, you'll have your chance to tell him your side of things after. All of this will be dealt with confidentially to respect your privacy," Miss Naim added.

Leesa stared at them, intentionally mute now. How was she going to deal with the fallout? While Michael had been fearful all along about getting caught, she hadn't given it much thought herself. Even after Marie shared her embarrassing story last week, she'd only imagined having to fend off easily deniable whispers among the students. She didn't think they'd go to a teacher. Now she felt like a fool for not predicting, not preparing for this possibility. She inhaled, then rearranged her face into something that resembled sincerity.

"Listen, this is a big misunderstanding. I appreciate your concern for me, but you are making a huge mistake." Now she visualized the consequences and drama playing out in front of her: her parents finding out, her friends ditching her, Michael losing his job.

She stood as gracefully as she could, aware they were watching her. She closed the door behind her gently. What she wanted to do was light a match and burn the place down. She steadied her breathing on the walk back to her room.

———————

"Wow, you look upset. Did they accuse you of doing it?"

"Yeah, but I convinced them it couldn't be me. I told them we were at the diner downtown, and said I still had a receipt." She opened her purse and pulled out the slip. Nestled beside it were nine one-dollar bills, four twos, and two fives.

"Good."

Leesa considered that Miss Naim hadn't mentioned the room toss. She'd miscalculated, believing her threat would silence Zahabiya, Marie, Mei, and Lavinia. *How had she so badly misjudged them?*

After first period, she was called in to Headmaster Lowery's office. She hadn't been able to eat breakfast or concentrate in class. She rehearsed her lines all morning:

1. She knew Mr. Stephenson from grade 9, and they'd maintained a friendly teacher-student rapport ever since.
2. She was shocked to hear these rumours and also the ones involving Miss Naim having multiple boyfriends coming to her suite.
3. Did he hear that Miss Naim was in fact interested in Mr. Stephenson, who rejected her? Maybe this was her revenge against him?

4. She did recall that Mademoiselle Leblanc seemed to take an unnatural interest in her, and she always wondered why.
5. She felt bad for Marie. She'd heard that she was mentally unstable and had a tendency to lie.

Zahabiya

On Saturday afternoon, we waited in the library for Marie's father, Mr. Hill, to finish his meeting with Headmaster Lowery. Marie had phoned him the day before and asked him to back up our claims. Lavinia had asked her parents to contact the headmaster, too.

"My mom said she'd threaten to pull her contribution to the domed running track fund. Lowery's always bragging about that project." I knew Lavinia was trying to do all she could. While she hadn't started at Thornton until grade 10, she told me she'd felt bad for not noticing Marie's distress over the years. With hindsight, she could recognize the subtle clues in Marie's mood shifts around Mr. Stephenson.

"Good strategy," I said.

"Has your dad called yet?" Lavinia asked.

"I . . . I haven't been able to talk to him. He's been on call for the last couple of days." The truth was that I'd only reported positive things about Thornton, building an argument for why he should let me stay another year. A situation like this would only bolster his desire to pull me out. I wasn't going to tell him.

"Call him today," Lavinia said. She turned to Mei.

"Hey, don't look at me. My parents wouldn't believe me if I told them there was an army of pedophiles loose at the school."

"What do you mean?" Lavinia sat up straight. We all did.

"Nothing."

"Mei. It's not nothing." Marie rubbed Mei's shoulder. They shared a long look. Before all this, they'd only been friends through their link to me, but now they'd grown closer, had begun to go on walks together, excluding me and Lavinia. It had been making me kind of jealous.

"So, I had my own pedo. It was my grandfather, on my father's side. The pig died a couple of years ago. Probably rotting in hell." She drummed her fingers on the table, inhaled sharply, and looked down at the floor.

"That's awful, Mei." I tried to make eye contact, but she was carving her initials into the table with her fingernail.

"Oh, Mei, I'm sorry." Lavinia exhaled a long sigh.

"She told her parents after his funeral. They called her a liar," Marie told us.

"We already weren't a close family, but it was World War III after that, then I got shipped here." She finally looked up to notice our sad faces. She added, "Listen, he didn't *rape* me, if that's what you're thinking. It was mostly a lot of pervy touching where he wasn't supposed to be touching a granddaughter."

"Still wrong," Marie said. "I told her she should tell her grandparents on her mother's side. They're nicer. It's good to have support, Mei."

"I dunno. I talked to my school shrink. I think that's enough."

"We're here for you, girl. Is there anything we can do?"

"Yeah, Mei. You can lean on us," I said. But internally I was reeling. First Marie, then Leesa, and now Mei. I'd never known anyone who'd been abused, at least no one who'd talked openly about it. Now I wondered how many people around me had had to deal with sexual abuse.

"Thanks. But I'm all right."

Marie's father arrived, and we dropped the conversation. He gave Marie and Lavinia a hug, and Marie introduced Mei and me to him. He was a tall, solid guy, and his bear hug floated me off my feet for a second.

"Listen, girls, as I told Marie, besides talking to Mr. Stephenson back when Marie was in grade 9, I also went to Headmaster Ford, who retired a few years ago. He promised to reprimand and monitor Mr. Stephenson and to put my complaint in his file. But Lowery seemed surprised, didn't seem to have a record of that."

"Headmaster Lowery started the year after, when we were in grade 10," Lavinia told us.

"So, Headmaster Ford didn't do anything." Marie held her head.

"Well, Mr. Stephenson will be officially fired by the end of the day. Headmaster Lowery told the creep to go home yesterday morning, so he is taking it seriously." He put an arm around his daughter.

"Thanks, Mr. Hill." I was relieved that Mr. Stephenson was gone.

"Call me Donald!" He clapped my back with his free hand. "I mean it, call me Donald."

I smiled across him at Marie; she was a mini version of her father with her strong build and manner of speaking.

"So, do you think it's over, then?" Lavinia asked. "Will this stop him?"

"It feels . . . over for me. Like I got some kind of closure for myself. But who knows if he's still seeing Leesa."

"And there might be others, too." Mei shook her head.

"Leave that for Headmaster Lowery to sort out. You girls have done your part. And I know he already asked you to keep this confidential. That's going to be important in case of future legal action."

"Plus, it's better for Leesa if the whole school doesn't know her business. Are we united on this?" Marie put her hand forward, and the five of us, her father included, huddled together and stacked our hands, one atop the other.

Monday, after French, Lauren bumped me in the hallway.

"Stinky bitch," Barb sneered. "She really needs to wear roll-on." Lauren and Carrie scoffed. They walked away, and I went to the bathroom to sniff my damp armpits. I only detected the chemical residue of baby powder scent, but I was self-conscious all day.

After dinner, I told Mei what had happened.

"Me, too. They called me an 'ugly nerd' today. Child's play. I told them to go fuck themselves." Mei rolled her eyes and lit a cigarette.

"It worries me."

A stirring in the bushes by the road caught my attention. A grey-brown head with long ears popped out.

"Look." I stopped to watch him. "I see rabbits around here a lot. They must have a burrow close by."

"Cool." Mei paused, too.

"Animals always calm me down, maybe because my mom used to point them out, used to teach me about them." Oddly, I didn't feel like crying when talking about her this time.

"That's really cool."

I crouched down, held out my hand, but the rabbit darted away. "Leesa can't stay angry forever, right?"

"Who knows? But you can't let her get to you. She's the rabbit in this situation, but she's pretending to be a coyote. You gotta start seeing her as the rabbit."

I nodded. I knew this, but Leesa and her friends were convincing as coyotes.

———

At Thursday's assembly, Headmaster Lowery announced that Mr. Stephenson "had been let go." No further explanation was offered, and a wave of shock moved through the chapel's pews, the students like sailboats in a storm.

Mr. Stephenson was liked, maybe even loved, by most.

Jason squeezed my hand. All of us who knew the truth — Mei, Marie, Lavinia, Cyril, Jason, and I — had to pretend to be as stunned as everyone else. Which wasn't that hard for me, because while I'd helped to get him fired, a part of my brain was still making sense of it all. I'd liked him, too. And I believed Marie.

I looked around at my peers. Just a couple weeks ago, I'd been as clueless as they were. After Mei's disclosure, I went to the library and did a deep dive about sexual abuse. There were only three books on the subject, but I'd sat in the stacks and read them all, learning about how prevalent and invisible abuse was. I was still rattled, couldn't unsee it now that it had been made clear.

When we filed out for first period, Lauren hissed at me, "You stupid skank."

"Who's the skank?" Mei asked, grabbing hold of a handful of Lauren's hair before shoving her away. Lauren scuttled off and caught up with Leesa, Mallory, and Jessica. From down the hall, we heard her protest, "Omigod, she pulled my hair!"

"What the hell?" Lavinia asked.

"Me and Mei have been dealing with that for a few days," I said quietly.

"I know, and it's weird cuz, they aren't doing it to me or Lav," Marie said, "Which means that . . ."

"Whatever they think they're getting revenge for is not what they're really getting revenge for," Jason completed the thought and squeezed my hand.

"I thought that by telling Miss Naim to not report the wrecking of our room, it would be a kind of goodwill gesture, so Leesa would see we had good intentions. Hasn't worked," I said.

"Don't forget the robbery," Lavinia added.

"Why haven't you reported this to Headmaster Lowery? This school clearly has a problem. There's a culture of abuse here," Cyril said. After he'd heard Marie's story, he'd stopped being conflicted about the issue. I'd given him one of the library books I'd read, and it seemed like he'd absorbed its message.

"He's right. This has to stop," Lavinia said.

"I didn't want to make things worse. Maybe that's wrong."

"They're irrelevant." Mei leaned down, whispered to me, "Remember, she's the scared one."

"I think we should wait and reassess after March break. It's only another week," Marie said. "Maybe Leesa needs more time to come to terms with what happened with . . . him."

Marie rolled her shoulders, as though releasing years' old tension. My own throbbed.

Nahla

Nahla's finger hovered over her answering machine's *Delete* button. She hit *Save* instead and then pressed *Replay*:

> "I know you're ignoring me. And I know you reported
> me. This is my third call. Call me back."

His voice was steady and strong, followed by a long pause. Then, as he continued, his speech turning raspy, sinister sounding:

> "Go tell Lowery that you made it all up. If you don't,
> I'll make your life miserable."

While she knew his tone was likely affected, a bad imitation of a thriller's antagonist, she pulled her drapes closed.

When he first started calling a week and a half ago, his messages had been friendly ("Hey, I think there's some kind of misunderstanding, let's go for dinner and talk."), then they'd turned cooler and negotiating ("Listen, I know I'm not your favourite person, but would you at least listen to my side of things?"), and now this. *Could he make her life miserable?* Well, he was halfway there. But her anxious mind troubled all the possibilities beyond these messages, everything from minor mischief to major crimes. *And would he conscript Leesa?* She thanked Allah that the girl had mostly avoided her, and in a few days would be on a trans-Atlantic flight home. And today, Gerry had installed a second lock for her.

She dialled Headmaster Lowery's home number. As he'd requested, she reported the latest message's content.

"Thank you, Nahla. Listen, do you have somewhere to go over March break? I think it's best that you're not at the residence all alone."

"I'll try to make arrangements." Fatmi had managed to negotiate a weekend visit over the holiday. *But what would she do with the remainder of the time? Maybe Maeve and Joanne's place? How would she explain the threat when she had to keep it secret?* She had nowhere to go; her flat no longer felt safe, and her family's home was unwelcoming. Not since leaving Lebanon and coming to Canada had she felt so displaced.

"Good, continue to save all the messages. I'm going to contact our lawyers for advice on this latest one."

"Okay."

"While he was terminated for valid performance issues, our lawyers have said he could fight our claim. So, we need all the ammunition we can get."

"Could . . . could he come back to Thornton?"

"It's a possibility. Which would be a travesty. Keep this between us, but when I dug into his file, there were vague notes about him being coached around professionalism. I have a feeling Mr. Ford, my predecessor, dealt with him before, but ineffectively." He sighed into the receiver.

"Oh." Nahla's throat went dry. If Michael returned, she'd have to find a new job. *And what about Leesa and the rest of Thornton's girls? Who could ensure their safety?*

"But we're not there yet. Just keep doing what you're doing. The lawyers are going to reach out to Mr. Ford next week."

"All right, thanks." Once the line went dead, she grabbed her new rape whistle and unlocked the door. The floor creaked beside her, and together, she and Sylvie began the study period rounds.

Leesa

When she arrived in Paris, her parents, in the same room for the first time in ages, forced her into a "family dinner." Over lasagne, her favourite meal from five years ago (way too fattening now), they made small talk about her friends, her extracurricular activities, her grades, pantomiming normal parental concern. Then they asked her about Headmaster Lowery's report.

"Do we have to go over this again?" She'd talked to both of them on the phone two weeks earlier, when she'd gone into damage-control mode.

"Yes, we do." Her father sliced into his lasagne with his fork, the noodles resistant. He picked up his knife.

"It's all right, Leesa. I used to get infatuated with my teachers when I was your age, too," her mother commiserated.

Before she could answer, her father jumped in. "I'm glad the teacher was fired. I have a mind to call our lawyer and sue the man. You're only seventeen! When did this all start?"

"Nothing happened! Like I told you, I flirted with him a bit this year. We talked a lot. He remained professional. People made up stories about us. It's insane!" Leesa pushed her chair back from the table. *Did they really believe Lowery?*

"Leesa, I phoned Lyndee's mother. We know you lied about visiting her over the holidays." Her mother pointed at her with her fork, a piece of lettuce stuck within its tines.

"Oh, that! I was with my boyfriend, Rodney! I swear!" She performed a laugh and slapped the table to disarm them.

"Okay, then," Leesa's father challenged, "What's Rodney's phone number?"

"No! You'll embarrass me!" Rodney knew nothing about Michael, at least not yet, and from what she could tell, no one did.

"We also noticed a credit card charge for a Comfort Motel in February," he said.

"Again, with Rodney!"

"Even if you were going to hotels with 'this Rodney,'" he curled his fingers into air quotes, "It's concerning."

"This is all our fault." Leesa's mother rubbed her temples. "We haven't been checking in as much as we should."

"You're so independent and . . . grown up, I think we forget sometimes that you're still a teen," her father said.

"But it's also the school's fault. When I went to Thornton, there was no way something like this could happen."

"You don't believe me. My own parents don't believe me." Leesa rose from the table and stomped off.

The rest of March break was like house arrest, only with parental interest: a mani-pedi and shopping trips and lunches with her mother; dinners at her father's condo with his wife, Ginette, and her little brother, Liam.

While she mostly resented and resisted her parents' controlling —
this delayed correction to their self-absorption — a small part of her
liked the attention. They looked at her differently now, with curiosity,
as though she was an exotic bird who'd flown into their living rooms.
She was visible to them again. And Liam, he was actually kind of cute.

She hadn't seen Michael since the dance, agreeing by phone to lay
low. On the second Sunday afternoon when her mother finally left her
alone for a few hours, she dialled his number. She hoped she wasn't so
anal as to scrutinize every line of the phone bill. He picked up on the
third ring.

"How're you doing? I miss you so much!"

"Hey, Babe. You know what? Maeve just left a message saying
there were rumours that I'd been stealing my art supply money, and
that's why I got fired."

"Well, they gave no reason at all. So, people will make up reasons."
She held her breath, but couldn't stop herself, "So, do you miss me, too?"

"Yeah of course, Babe! You're all I think about."

Her heart swelled with love and relief. She wasn't sure how he'd
feel toward her after the threats she made before Valentine's. While he
knew it was Miss Naim, Marie, and the other girls who'd complained
to the headmaster, she worried he'd somehow blame her for the consequences that he alone faced, and she was helpless to influence. And
she felt responsible for attracting Marie's attention and arousing her
suspicions on the two occasions she photographed them together.

"My lawyer thinks I can sue for wrongful termination. If that
happens, I'll get a cash settlement, and we can start seeing each other
out in the open."

"But then Headmaster Lowery will know that Miss Naim and the
girls were telling the truth about us." But it wasn't the truth. This wasn't
abuse. It was love.

"We can make up a new story about how their rumours caused you
so much stress it brought us together and we only just started seeing
each other after I was fired. Sound plausible?"

"Maybe that could work." She pictured Jessica's and Mallory's reactions to this explanation. *Would they think she was cool or desperate?* She hadn't planned on being at Thornton, within their sights, when they finally went public.

"Well, let's just wait and see what pans out. Did you break up with Rodney? It was murder seeing you at the dance with him. I refuse to be in that situation again."

Leesa wanted to argue that the point was moot because he'd been fired, but she left it alone.

"Soon. I promise. Can we just see what the rumour mill is spinning when I'm back at Thornton?" If the nerd girls leaked the information, Rodney's presence would help.

"But—"

"Oh, crap, my mom is home. Gotta go. I love you." She hung up, flipped open a magazine, and greeted her mother with a bored look when she came in the door. But beneath the facade lay a new fear. Before, when their secret was theirs alone, sneaking around had been a thrill. Now it felt dangerous.

Her heart ached for him, an old fissure deep inside it threatening to crack open again. She knew its lonely depths too well, and Michael, the only person who'd truly been there for her these last few years, had been the one to heal it. *What if she lost him?* She wouldn't let that happen. She'd have to be brave to protect their love.

Spring Term, March 1985

> Oh, Marie.
> Who else did I not see?
> Who else did I fail?
> Again, the light beckons.
> I must stay.

Zahabiya

On the last day of March break, I rifled through the basement closet that stored my mother's clothes, looking for a dress for the spring formal. It was months away, but Jason had already asked me, and I wanted to find something good.

Having a boyfriend was different from how magazines and movies portrayed it. Jason wasn't a knight in shining armour or a romantic fool. He was a close friend, one I couldn't keep my hands off of. We'd travelled a far distance from our shy first dance, and now snuck off to make out almost every day — in his basement, in a corner of the library, at the edge of the soccer pitch.

To my surprise, Jason broached the topic of sex, and also to my surprise, I suggested we wait. I wasn't in any hurry. Mei, Marie, and Leesa's experiences made me realize I could trust myself to know when it was the right time. I no longer felt like I had to "catch up" with anyone else's schedule. And I knew Jason would never pressure me.

Zahra, always a know-it-all, said that Jason was a good starter boyfriend for me: someone kind and respectful to test things out with, and that was true in a way. But my relationship with him wasn't a practice romance, like my friendships with Marie, Lavinia, and Mei weren't practice friendships. They were just what they were: everyone was important.

I leaned into the basement closet and inhaled, but there wasn't much of my mom's scent left. And none of the dresses seemed right; they all were the wrong length or were too "old" to suit me. Zahra didn't have anything that fit me, and my meagre savings had been stolen. I cringed at the idea of asking my dad for money for clothes; he still grumbled about the cost of tuition.

Tara lugged a full basket of laundry down the stairs. "Find anything? Zahra said you're looking for something fancy."

"No," I snapped, irritated that Zahra, who had recently warmed to Tara, had shared my business.

"Check the top shelf — that box up there has more of your mother's things." Tara pointed, then carried on to the laundry room.

Grudgingly, I pulled down a large plastic bin. I opened the lid, and her perfume wafted out. Inside were six saris with matching blouses and petticoats that she used to wear to weddings and Indian parties. A sari wouldn't help me fit in with Thornton's popular crowd, but I'd long lost interest in those snobs. Instead, I imagined my friends oohing and aahing over the vision of me wrapped in yards of silk. Yes, it might just work.

I pulled out a midnight-blue sari with gold patterned trim and held it against my body. *But how would I put it on?* When I was younger, I used to sit on the end of my parents' bed, watching my mother undertake what seemed like a very involved process of folding and pinning.

"Put on the blouse and petticoat, and I'll show you how to wear it," Tara called, startling me. It was as though she was reading my mind from the laundry room.

"No, that's okay . . ." The washer door slammed shut, then Tara was at my side.

"I saw a photo of your mother in that one. She looked beautiful."

"Nah, it's too complicated."

Tara shook her head. "Zahabiya . . . just . . . could you just . . . give it a try? Come, give it to me. I'll iron out the creases."

I relented and carried the blouse and petticoat upstairs to my room. The blouse was slightly tight. I tried to recall the width of Mom's shoulders and the size of her biceps, but came up blank.

"Hey, it fits." Zahra settled herself onto the carpeted floor.

"Okay, let's get this over with," I scowled, all the while knowing I was probably being unreasonably negative.

"You need heels to get the length right," Tara said, coming into my room with the ironed sari in her arms. Zahra rose to grab pumps. Tara then showed me how to pleat. I held my breath as she encircled me in the blue silk, her fingers fumbling against my skin as she tucked the fabric around my waist.

It had been a long while since I'd been touched in this functional, maternal way, and it was the first time I'd permitted Tara to be that close. Perhaps Tara, too, felt uncomfortable, because she chattered the whole time about pleat width and the necessity of safety pins.

When the last adjustments were done and the pallu pinned to my shoulder, Tara stepped back, and the three of us studied me in the full-length mirror.

"Take off your glasses for a sec?" Zahra asked. When I handed them over, Zahra stared at me, mouth agape. "Wow."

"What?" Without glasses, my reflection was fuzzy.

"You look . . . just like her."

"You do," Tara whispered.

I squinted into the mirror, absorbing their words. Dad wandered in, and he, too, gazed at me.

"Doesn't she look nice in a sari?" Tara prodded.

"Yes. Yes, very nice," he said. Zahra passed me back my glasses, but I didn't put them on, didn't want to break the magic.

The next day, the four of us pulled into the manor's circular driveway, crammed with the cars of other returning students' families.

Dad popped the trunk, and a shriek rang out from a car behind us: "You didn't pack my pillow!"

"There wasn't room, Johanna, with your million other things," her mother shot back.

"You never listen to me," Johanna continued her yelling, oblivious to the dozen or so onlookers.

I led my family toward the entrance. Ahead, another girl stamped up the steps, her perplexed-looking parents trailing after her.

"Is there a full moon or something?" Zahra asked.

I held open the door, observing my family in a way I hadn't before: they all looked, and behaved, like normal people. Like a normal family.

In the lobby, we ran into Marie and Lavinia, who were saying goodbye to Mr. Hill. The girls had spent the first five days of break at Lavinia's place in the Bahamas and the final four at Marie's house. I'd been invited along for the trip and had mentioned it to Dad, not expecting, and not receiving, his approval.

Everyone introduced themselves. Mr. Hill was at least six inches taller and wider than my dad.

"Thank you for inviting Zahabiya to your places." My father looked to Lavinia, Marie, and Mr. Hill. "We just couldn't let her go this time — we get so little time together as a family these days."

"I know what you mean, I got ripped off myself! Ripped off!" Mr. Hill joked, a raucous sound booming from deep within his chest.

"He comes into town for work almost every week." Marie rolled her eyes at her father.

"Maybe during the summer holiday you all can travel to the Bahamas together," Dad offered, and I beamed at my friends.

"Sounds good to me," Mr. Hill said. "I'm proud of our girls and how mature they've been—"

"Well, we should head in and drop off my stuff. I know you all have a long drive home ahead of you," I said, wanting to cut short the conversation in case Mr. Hill planned to talk about Mr. Stephenson.

When they were leaving, Dad leaned out of the driver's side window and said, "Listen, I think it's best that you do grade 13 at home. It'll be your last year before university. It's better to save the tuition for that."

I pursed my lips and waved goodbye in response. *What could I really say that would make any difference?* He was in charge of this decision. I climbed the steps, now in a mood — I had friends here, a boyfriend. I had changed everything by coming here. *What if I lost all that?* Maybe I could convince him otherwise. I had to.

I returned to my room to unpack. I unzipped my duffle, then remembered that Zahra had handed me a plastic pharmacy bag when she'd hugged me goodbye.

I emptied the contents onto my bed. There were bottles of my brand of shampoo and conditioner, deodorant, toothpaste, maxi pads, cotton swabs, a bag of chips, and a chocolate bar. A care package.

I put the plastic bag aside. Outside, a bird chirped raucously. I closed my eyes and listened for a minute; I'd learned to identify bird-song this way with Mom when we went for hikes. I guessed it was a robin, perhaps a winter holdout or one returning with the near-spring weather. When I opened my eyes and looked out, I saw her on a nearby branch, fat, orange breasted.

I folded the plastic bag and noticed something stuck at the bottom, one of my mother's pale-green envelopes. Inside was a letter and two ten-dollar bills.

For a second, a magical thought — that my mother had left me money — fluttered past like a bird. I used to have these moments of forgetting — of denial and surreality — the first year after she died, present and past threading together.

I unfolded the note:

> *Hi Zahabiya,*
> *I hope the toiletries and cash come in handy.*
> *Love, Tara*

I refolded the note, revising, imagining that maybe Mom and Tara were somehow in cahoots.

I tucked the envelope into my desk drawer. *But where to hide the precious tens?* I'd learned that I needed to be smarter, to expect the worst from Leesa and her goons. They'd continued to stare and mutter "bitch," "stupid slut," "ugly nerds" at Mei and me every chance they could until we'd dispersed for March break.

I circled the room, trying to think like a spiteful, wealthy, mean girl. Or, as Mei had suggested, a hurt, scared, heartsick girl.

A bully and a victim. Thornton was teaching me that someone could be both, that were shades of grey in things I'd once thought were only black and white.

I stashed one bill in a shoe at the back of the closet. The other I stabbed with a safety pin and attached to the sari's petticoat. I hoped they'd be safe.

Nahla

"So, it's your last night here. Looking forward to going back?" Hoda asked Nahla, while passing her the last of the fattoush.

"Hoda . . ." their mother cautioned. While Nahla was only supposed to stay the weekend in Montreal, it was now nearly the end of March break. With each day that had passed, Nahla felt relief to not be alone in the empty manor. However, family dinners around their chipped linoleum table were only calm as long as no one mentioned Nahla's job.

"Come on, she should be able to answer the question," Fatmi countered. Their father pushed back his chair, exited the room, perhaps fleeing his own anger.

"Patience, habibti," her mother murmured.

Nahla muttered under her breath, "Do you tell him he should have patience, too?"

"Look how you're hurting him. Do the right thing and move back. You've forgotten that you're Muslim. Lebanese. You're acting like a Canadian," Ali barked.

"She has a job. She can't just leave it," Hoda countered with calm and logic, as was her way. Nahla met her sister's gaze, grateful.

"You can be Muslim, Lebanese, and want to live away from home, too," Fatmi added, defending not only Nahla, but also her own still undisclosed future plans. "We live in Canada now. Get with the program."

"Shut up. Go clean up." Ali waved his hand, dismissing them. He lit a cigarette.

"How dare you talk that way? We are your elders! You are not even out of high school, little brother!" Fatmi stood and leaned over him, and he blew smoke in her face.

"Khalas!" Their mother pushed apart her warring children, then rose to clear the table.

"Kalbe," Ali cursed under his breath. He followed his father's well-worn path to the front porch.

"Stupid little boy thinks he is a big man," Fatmi said, in a low voice.

"It's how he's been raised. To believe that he's more important than us, his sisters. Women." Hoda shook her head.

"It's the culture. It entitles them to be this way," Nahla lamented. Then she thought about Michael, his unforgivable behaviour. *Did every culture raise men to take whatever they wanted from women?*

That last night in Montreal, the three sisters stayed up late, whispering in the dark. Nahla finally told them about reporting a teacher for having an abusive relationship with a student. Not wanting to worry them, she didn't talk about the threatening messages. She also neglected to mention that he was the same person she'd dated earlier that winter.

"What kind of people do they hire at your school?" Hoda asked.

"There was an article in the *Gazette* last week about a local case just like that. The teacher went to jail, even though the girl defended him, insisted she led the teacher on," Fatmi said.

"In our case, they both denied it."

"So, how did they prove it, then?" Hoda asked.

"There was a lot of indirect evidence, but no direct proof. Apparently, there had been other complaints over the years. Plus, the headmaster thinks he hadn't been marking, just handing out random grades."

"A pervert and a lazy teacher, to boot," Hoda said sleepily. Nahla cringed at the word "pervert." She'd been kissed by that pervert dozens of times, gone to bed with him twice. Pined for him for months. Sometimes, not often anymore, she even missed the pervert.

At Montreal's bus station, Nahla inched forward in a loud and long line of people who were either leaving home or going home. As the bus pulled out, she wasn't sure to which group of travellers she belonged.

Hours later, she strode up the hill to the residence, enjoying the sunshine and the five degrees of warmth it offered. Her bags were heavy with her mother's namoura and Middle Eastern grocery staples, so when she reached the first cross street, she paused, set them down, and rested a moment, tipping her chin toward the sun. A car pulled up to the stop sign, and she waved it forward absentmindedly, but when it didn't move, she met the driver's gaze and saw that it was him, in his char bleu, watching her, jaw set, eyes hard. She reflexively picked up her bags, as though they might offer her protection.

He rolled down his window, his expression friendly. A charming mask.

"Get in, I'll drive you." His voice was as smooth as satin, and she was reminded of that autumn night when they kissed the first time.

"No thanks, I prefer to walk." Her hands made fists around her luggage's handles.

"Don't be silly. Get in." His tone turned hostile.

"No." When he didn't drive away, she turned right instead of crossing, going down a one-way street to avoid him. A few minutes later, back on the main road, she sensed a car creeping behind her, following, lurking. Her heart raced, and she picked up her pace, speed walking, the smell of gasoline in her nostrils. *Why hadn't she worn the rape whistle around her neck?* She considered pulling it from her purse, but that would mean stopping and so she kept walking. Finally, she saw the residence ahead, fifty metres away. A car farther back honked.

Then, his car was within inches of her, its heat like rage. She veered off the narrow sidewalk and onto the muddy shoulder. Tires squealed and sprayed gravel at her. She heard more honking. And then he drove off.

The road behind was now deserted. The honking car hadn't stopped. No one had checked to see if she was safe.

She quickly crossed the street and once she was halfway down the manor's long driveway, she put down her bags and wiped the hot tears that now ran down her cheeks, all the while keeping watch for the char bleu.

Leesa

At the Four Seasons, cutlery scraped against china, dissonant percussion to the Celtic music playing in honour of St. Patrick's Day. Leesa and her mother had just finished their Cobb salads, and in a few minutes, they'd take a limousine to Belltown. Leesa understood she was being hand-delivered, but her mother insisted that she wanted to spend a few days with her daughter on her old stomping grounds.

Hours later, the limo turned off the highway, and the nostalgia tour was well underway. "Oh, it hasn't changed much since I dropped you off in grade 7!" After that trip, Leesa had made the rest on her own. She would have liked to have been picked up and dropped off in grades 8 and 9 — most Thornton parents did that — but by grade 10, she no longer cared.

"Yeah, it's the same nothing town it always was." Her mother ignored her.

"Look, there's the old mill!" Leesa ignored her mother.

They passed a residential area, and Leesa stared out at little clapboard bungalows, similar to Michael's house. Missing him was a full-body ache.

They drove through the three-block downtown core. She recognized a few Thornton students coming out of a store. How separate she felt from them; she was no longer a child, hadn't felt like one in a long time. The limo turned onto a smaller street and then slowed to a snail's pace.

"Sunday driver," their driver crabbed. Then he craned his neck. "What the heck?"

Leesa and her mother looked, too, noticing the car ahead driving beside a pedestrian. Leesa squinted, recognized Michael's car, the back of his head, and . . . on the sidewalk, a woman walking quickly.

"What's going on?" Her mother asked. The limo driver honked, and the car ahead accelerated and disappeared down a residential street. They passed Miss Naim before turning into the residence's driveway.

"That's the French teacher, the one who told lies about me," Leesa said, nausea rising from her belly to her throat. *What was Michael up to?*

"And who was that following her?"

"I don't know." She swallowed bile. "She's known for bringing men into the residence. Maybe a jilted lover."

"Well, I plan to meet with Headmaster Lowery tomorrow, so perhaps I'll raise that. I don't know what's happened to the morality and safety of this school."

"Besides that, she shouldn't be a French teacher. Terrible accent. I need to get out of this car. I'm so carsick."

Later that day, when her mother left to settle into her hotel, Leesa dialled Michael's number. Ten minutes later, they met two blocks from the residence.

After a month apart, she expected it to be different. She leaned away from him, feeling off, like a tire losing its air, the puncture invisible, hard to patch. She studied the springy hairs sprouting from the back of his long fingers.

"What's wrong?" He exhaled smoky, stale breath and pulled over at their spot.

"Nothing." Maybe she just needed time to warm up to him again. *Hadn't she felt a little like this in September?*

He unzipped her coat and reached under her blouse. She felt the chill and pulled her coat tightly around her. There was so much to talk about. Yet only one question came to mind.

"Why were you following Miss Naim today?"

"What do you mean? I haven't seen her since I left Thornton." He stroked her hair. She pulled away.

"I was in a car behind you."

"Oh, that." He chuckled like a comedian needing a laugh track. "I just wanted to scare her, you know? She got me fired."

She exhaled. Revenge made sense, perhaps more than stalking her because he wanted her.

"Did I tell you I'm gonna sue for wrongful dismissal?"

"Yeah. Did you speak to your lawyer again?"

"I had to fire him; he wasn't any good. But I'm looking for a new one." He grabbed her hand.

She remained quiet.

"But maybe this was the sign for me to move on and finally focus on art. I'm free."

"That's a good way to think about it."

"And now that I don't have to worry about losing my job, we don't have to sneak around anymore."

"But *I'm* still at Thornton."

"Remember, we'll tell everyone we started up after I was fired."

"But no one will believe us. No one will understand. It'll be embarrassing."

"Embarrassing? Are you embarrassed to be with me?"

"No, that's not what I meant." He started the engine. "What are you doing?"

"I don't know what you want from me, Leesa. I'm taking you home. Or some non-embarrassing distance away from the residence."

"Stop, please. Don't you realize that if we go public, everyone will see me as some kind of victim? And my parents will take me out of

251

Thornton and back to Paris?" She exhaled. She was not a victim. She would not be seen that way.

"Okay." He turned off the engine. "Okay."

He reached for her, and this time she allowed him. He kissed her roughly. A month ago, that would have sent tingles through her legs, but now, they were numb, heavy. She kept her eyes closed, but heard his car door open, shut, then the back door open.

"We don't have much time." He got into the back seat.

She complied, but her body was like a piece of driftwood, bobbing in a lake's tide, barely afloat. She couldn't find pleasure in his grabbing hands and desperate lips. She pushed him away.

"I think . . . I think maybe today's not the best day for this . . . too much on my mind."

"Just relax, Babe." His voice and hands were making her sink to the bottom, and so she stopped trying to breathe, and succumbed to the deep water's darkness.

Zahabiya

"God, I wish I could've gone somewhere warm," Mei grumbled after Sunday's dinner.

"Mei, you look . . . really good." I couldn't put my finger on it, but something about her had changed over the break.

"True. You're not as 'alternative' as usual." Marie laughed.

"What's with the turquoise sweatshirt?" Lavinia joined in.

"Hey, I'm just diversifying my fashion." Mei held up her hands in mock-defence. "But yeah . . . March break was . . . good. And . . . my grandparents asked me to live with them next year."

"So, you told them?" Marie prodded. We all leaned in.

"Yeah. They never liked my other grandfather. And they believed me. They're really mad at my parents for dumping me here."

"They should be," I said. Finally, someone in her family had her back.

"But does that mean you're going to leave us next year?" Lavinia asked.

"Yeah, we can't break up our Benetton ad!" Marie protested.

"You can get one of the Hong Kong girls to sub in for me," Mei joked. Then growing serious, she said, "I might live with them. I have the rest of term to decide."

"I might not be back next year, too." I looked at my palms, studying my curving life and love lines, tearing up. "My dad says it's too much money."

"Maybe it won't be so bad? Your family seems nice."

"I guess . . ." They had been nice today. And yet, I didn't want to go home. A lump like a wad of gum formed in my throat. "But I like it here . . ."

"I'm with Lavinia. Have some perspective, Zahabiya. And your father is right: this place is stupidly expensive," Mei said.

"Wow, everything's gonna change next year." Marie shook her head.

"Well, it's only mid-March," I said, disregarding Lavinia and Mei — they clearly didn't understand. "I have three months to figure out how to change his mind."

"It'll be okay," Marie said, slinging an arm around me.

"Knock, knock." Miss Naim came in and shut the door behind her. "Welcome back." We said our hellos, but I sensed this wasn't a social visit.

"I wanted to check on you all. I know Headmaster Lowery asked you to keep everything private, but I know that's a lot."

"I'm okay," Marie said.

"Yeah, not a big deal," Mei added.

"We've had each other to talk to," Lavinia said.

"And Mr. Stephenson's gone, so that's good," I said.

"We hope so. He's been banned from school property. But that's all we can really do." Miss Naim's body shuddered involuntarily, and she rubbed her arms in response. She didn't look right.

"Miss Naim, are you okay?" I asked.

"Eh. Oui. I mean, yes! I'm fine." She smiled wanly and left us alone.

"She's not telling us the whole story," I said.

"Yeah. I wonder what's really going on?" Lavinia said.

"Has anyone seen Leesa?" Marie asked. "Do you think she's calmed down yet?"

"Not likely. Her cronies called me a 'smelly Chink' this afternoon."

"Wow, they're getting racist now," I said.

"They probably always were racist." Lavinia grimaced.

"Still, makes no sense." Marie frowned. "What's her motive for getting them to bully the two of you? I should have been the target, right?"

"Well, the room toss was maybe a message for all four of us because we all hang out here," Mei said.

"And they couldn't toss my room or Marie's because our roommates are Barb and Carrie."

"I'll bet the ongoing insults are serving as a distraction," Mei said.

"From what?" I asked.

"From Leesa. Has to be. From Leesa," Marie said.

Later that evening, as I passed the front lobby, strong floral perfume tickled my nose. I sneezed.

"Gesundheit." A woman with high heels and a long white wool coat stood near the doors. With her flawless makeup and Princess Di hair, she looked like she'd stepped out of a fashion magazine.

"Thanks."

"I'm Leesa's mother. I used to be a Thornton girl, too." Her look of expectation told me to introduce myself, so I did.

"Mom, I'm ready." Leesa stopped short when she saw us talking. Her eyes narrowed, a mismatch with her chirpy tone. "Oh, I see you've met my mother."

"Yeah, nice to meet you, Mrs. Allen," I said, starting to walk away.

"You know, Zahabiya, I'm so lucky to have my mom." Leesa sidled up to her mother and stage whispered, "The poor thing, her mother died."

I fled out the front doors, but the mist of Leesa's mean pity and her mother's perfume had already settled on my skin. Shivering in the cold, I looped around to the back door. *How did Leesa know, anyway?* I never told her. A cat crossed my path, Clement, the headmaster's pet

255

who prowled the neighbourhood. When I opened the back door, he slipped inside.

"Hey, you shouldn't be in here." I tried to grab him, but he dodged me and got comfortable on the stairwell. I gave up and sat next to him and stroked his cold fur. Gradually, we both warmed up, and the sting of Leesa's comment faded.

I reflected on the interaction, and how it seemed like Leesa's words often felt calculated. Like she could never just let down her guard. Even with her own mother. I guessed she hadn't told her family the truth about Mr. Stephenson. *Had she told anyone?*

I couldn't imagine keeping such a big secret. I'd shared nearly everything about my life at Thornton with Zahra. And I'd started talking to Jason and my friends about my family. I didn't have a mother, but wasn't alone, and Leesa did, and yet seemed all alone.

Clement stretched and headed to the back door. I let him out and watched him trace a line of paw prints in the fresh snow.

Nahla

In the middle of Monday morning's grade 12 class, Mrs. Reeves knocked softly on Nahla's door. At the threshold, she whispered, "Headmaster Lowery would like you to come to his office. Mrs. Allen, Leesa's mother, wants to speak to you."

"Oh? But there's still twenty minutes remaining." She glanced at her students, who, glad for the interruption, were now involved in non-French chatter. Leesa eyed her.

"I'll mind your class. The meeting should be brief." Mrs. Reeves rolled up her sleeves as though preparing for a fight.

Nahla hurried to the main office, heart pounding. *What did Leesa's mother want?* She inhaled courage, straightened her spine, and knocked on the semi-ajar door.

"Bonjour, Mademoiselle Naim." The woman had a stylish haircut, a trim figure, blue eyes, and upturned lips that performed a smile; she was Leesa, a quarter-century older.

"Bonjour, bienvenue, Madame Allen."

"Thanks for joining us, Nahla. Mrs. Allen wanted to meet the teacher who raised the alarm about Mr. Stephenson."

"Yes, I did. Leesa says this is a misunderstanding. That nothing untoward occurred between the teacher and her." Mrs. Allen's tone was neutral, and Nahla couldn't tell what she believed.

"She reported the same to me." Headmaster Lowery straightened his tie, although it was not askew — and said, "We have questioned a number of students and a parent who supported our concerns. We can't say for certain what happened, but we were certain we had to take action. We have students to protect. A reputation to protect."

"My daughter also says there are rumours . . . that you bring many different men back to your flat. And that your claims against the teacher were some kind of revenge against him for rejecting you." Mrs. Allen looked at Nahla, her gaze steady as she sized up Nahla.

"Yes, I believe your daughter started that rumour herself. And Mr. Stephenson is the one being vengeful." Nahla sat very still, trying to contain the slight tremor in her fingers. "Headmaster Lowery, I need to update you. Mr. Stephenson was harassing me, following me, for several blocks in his car on Sunday. It was frightening."

Mrs. Allen said with a sigh, "I can confirm that. We were in the car right behind . . . Leesa said that . . . never mind. Ma fille est . . . stratégique. She sometimes tells . . . white lies."

"Madame, ce n'était pas un pieux mensonge blanc. This was a big lie, a hurtful one, designed to ruin my career."

"Oui, je suis désolée. And . . . thank you for reporting this to Mr. Lowery. I had no idea anything might be happening. I still wonder what exactly went on, how deep things got between her and that teacher — girls can be so precocious at that age."

Nahla bristled at the word "precocious." *Was Mrs. Allen suggesting that a relationship between an adult man and a teen girl was normal or harmless? And how could a parent not notice that her daughter might be in trouble, very likely for more than three years?* But she knew it was not her place, as a teacher, to ask such questions of a wealthy parent. She unclasped her hands.

"De rien. I am just . . . doing my job."

Headmaster Lowery raised his eyebrows and gazed at her over his bifocals; he had already emphasized that Nahla let go of the sort of monitoring Sylvie had started. She'd wanted to agree, but a voice in her head, a voice she knew was Sylvie's, told her to continue.

"By the way, such a lovely accent you have, Miss Naim. You sound just like a Parisienne."

"Merci, well," Nahla chose her words carefully, "of course, you know Lebanon suffered colonization by the French."

At lunch, Mrs. Allen sat across from her at the table reserved for faculty and special guests. The soup that day was cream of broccoli, made with fresh ingredients, rather than yesterday's leftovers, and the main course was roast chicken with scalloped potatoes. She'd heard that the cook upped her game when notified of parent meetings. One good thing had come from Mrs. Allen's visit.

She gazed out at the students, the hall abuzz with chatter. After seven months, she knew most by name. She saw Zahabiya in the midst of an animated conversation with Cyril. At the kitchen window, Marie and Jason, both their tables' waiters that day, loaded their trays with soup terrines. Lavinia caught Mei's eye from a nearby table and waved. And there was Leesa, in the middle of the hall, staring in her direction, as though studying a chessboard in play.

"Bon appétit," Mrs. Allen said, raising her water glass.

"Bon appétit." Nahla reciprocated the gesture. Leesa dropped her gaze. Nahla sensed she wasn't a girl who liked to lose and wondered how many more lies she'd tell, how many more times she'd be "stratégique" before she gave up the game.

Leesa

"You're avoiding me. We used to see each other at least twice a week, and it's been two weeks now!" Michael's voice was like a snarl, but Leesa detected the hurt beneath. She scooted closer to him on the pull-out couch, but he drew away, his mouth puckered into a pout.

"I didn't know my mom would stay so long—" she attempted.

"She left last Sunday. You could have met me any day this week."

"She made me join extracurriculars and gets Lowery to send her proof of attendance. I can't help it!" She looked him in the eye. "She says it's to help me get into a good university, but—"

"It's really to keep tabs on you. I get it." He sighed and let her knead his neck muscles.

"Plus, on the weekends I have to call both my parents to check in now." She left out that these phone calls weren't all bad; five-year-old Liam always asked to speak with her, so she made sure to call her father's house before his bedtime.

"They're treating you like you're a child."

"Yeah. It's all such a drag. At least Mallory and Jessica are in spirit squad, so it's kinda fun and a good workout. But debate club is so stupid. I mean, we debate about real issues, but it's not like we're actually doing anything about them. We're just talking." She glanced at him, hoping he didn't notice her overcompensation. The truth was that she'd joined debate club because Rodney was in it.

"So, when are your free days?" he grunted like an injured animal.

"Um, well, the spirit squad girls have been doing extra practice after study hall most days because the regionals are coming up . . . sometimes they decide at the last minute . . ." This was partly true, but something else made her want to hold back, not share too much. The dynamic between them was shifting. For most of their relationship, she'd been like a moon, orbiting him, but since he'd been fired, his gravitational pull hadn't been as strong. Or maybe they'd switched positions altogether, and she was his planet now.

"And fucking debate club is on Sunday afternoons," he snapped. "And when do you manage to see Rodney?"

"I barely see him anymore. I've been phasing him out." Had he seen them at the movies last night?

"You promised you'd break up with him." He frowned, and she wanted to smooth his brow, so it wouldn't turn into a permanent wrinkle. But his face had turned feverish-looking, and his eyes welled with tears.

"Michael. Listen, I'll do it later today. It's just been a really busy month, that's all. Don't be so upset." She grabbed his forearm emphatically to shake him out of his funk.

But her heart hurt for him; maybe she'd been selfish, inconsiderate, had lost sight of the bigger picture. After all, he'd suffered for their relationship — she'd never seen him cry before — and he needed her support more than ever.

She vowed to find more time for Michael in her schedule, to make him more of a priority, to be a better girlfriend. What she didn't understand was why this felt like a chore. Things weren't fun anymore.

After debate club, Leesa took a walk around campus with Rodney. He intertwined his fingers with hers, but she let her grip go slack. "Listen, Rodney, you know how my mom was here?"

"Yeah, she seemed nice." Leesa had kept their meeting brief, so that her mother couldn't ask him too many questions.

"Well, actually, she's a bitch. She's told me I have to buckle down this term, join clubs, pick up my grades. That I can't have a boyfriend."

"But . . . she never has to know, right? I mean, she's all the way in Paris." His tone was dismissive.

"She's asked Lowery to keep an eye on me. And Miss Naim, too." She'd prepared for this objection. "I'm really sorry, but . . . we can't keep seeing each other." There, she said it. It was done. She wanted to puke.

"We'll just have to be careful, so they don't ever see us together. Don't worry!" He reached for her limp hand again. She shook her head, registering the irony of the situation. "I don't understand. We're so great together!"

"No, Rodney. It's just too much pressure. Classes, clubs. Sneaking around. I can't do it. It's too much." She didn't mean to, but tears streamed down her face and she broke down into ugly, involuntary sobs.

"I don't get it," he said.

"I'm really sorry, but this is for the best."

He tried to hug her, but she pushed out of his embrace and rushed off. He called out after her, but she kept going. She rubbed her chest, trying to quell a burning sensation in her heart that later would become a lingering dull pain.

Zahabiya

"There, I think it's done." I pulled the sheath of papers together. Marie and I had spent the week coming up with the proposal, stacking it with arguments for why it was best for me to stay at Thornton next year. Now I read the first page aloud:

"*One. My education is far superior here.* He can't argue with that. I mean, my old school doesn't even have a chem lab."

"Know your audience," Lavinia said, but I could tell she was lukewarm about this project.

"*Two. I am learning valuable life skills that will come in handy when I go to university.* He wants me to learn how to be independent, right?"

"Maybe reorder and put that one last." Marie raised an eyebrow. I nodded.

"*Three. I am being exposed to new friends from all over the world, a truly multicultural experience that aids in my self-esteem development and can't be sourced in small-town Brock.*"

"Ha! I feel my self-esteem growing just listening to you," Mei joked.

"I know, that's hokey. *Four. It doesn't have to cost that much.* I am appending the payment plan chart." Marie and I had calculated that I could pay off 17 percent of the fees with earnings from summer jobs over the next three years. I even offered to go without my measly three-dollar weekly allowance, projecting future summer job savings and earnings from walking dogs with Jason. Except I didn't mention Jason.

"Do you think he'll go for this?" Lavinia's expression was doubtful. "I mean, my family was all about number one, but you're from a so-called First World country, so it's not the same thing."

"This is my only hope, short of Brock High School burning down."

"Arson can be our Plan B," Mei quipped.

Jason, Toby, and I walked to the mailbox at the end of our street the next afternoon. The trees were budding, and it was a balmy ten degrees, but it was hard for me to enjoy the good weather.

"This probably won't work. It's not fair!" I could hear the pitch in my voice and knew I sounded spoiled. But I also knew that Thornton had changed me, and my heart would break if I couldn't see Jason and my friends. I imagined my father opening the letter and rolling his eyes at my proposal.

"Let's wait and see." Jason held open the mailbox's door.

Toby howled, joining in on my misery.

"I can't take any more changes right now."

"Zahabiya. Zahabiya! You're jumping the gun! And listen, even if you have to go home, we'll make it work." His brown eyes shone with hope. He turned to Toby, who was still beagle-moaning empathy. "Shut up, Toby!"

Toby's ears flapped furiously as he shook off his distress.

"Here goes nothing." I dropped the letter in the box's yawning mouth and watched my fate tumble down into its cavern.

"Ugh. Why did *she* have to join debate club?" I whispered to Marie when Leesa rushed into the room. She was wearing a sweatsuit, as she'd done the week before, technically not allowed in debate club; dress code was our casual uniform because it was supposed to make us more "serious."

"Yeah, this used to be a safe place. A boring but safe place." Marie and I had joined during the winter term when Geraldine, the senior leader, had advised us it was an impressive extracurricular for future university applications. I'd included it on my resumé, hoping it might boost my summer job applications to Brock-area veterinary offices.

"At least her buddies aren't here." Thankfully, their harassment had stopped. Maybe Leesa and her friends had lost interest in us.

Leesa took a seat across the room. She leaned over to borrow a pen and paper from the girl beside her. Perhaps sensing we were talking about her, she looked up and glared. We averted our gazes, focusing on Geraldine, who was calling the meeting to order.

"I betcha she's still in contact with Mr. S." Marie's whisper turned the *s* into a hiss.

"Maybe, but what can we do about it?"

"First, there's an announcement from Mimi." Geraldine waved to her. I didn't know Mimi well; she was a younger girl who lived down the hall from Lavinia.

"Hi, everyone. I've started a petition? It's about Mr. Stephenson's termination. We're demanding that he be reinstated." She passed a clipboard to a girl on her left.

"Wow," Marie said. I reached over and squeezed her forearm. I looked at Leesa, who seemed just as surprised by Mimi's initiative. *Was this the first she was hearing of it? Or could she be behind it?*

Geraldine began taking attendance. I glanced back at Leesa, who watched the petition move around the room. She met my gaze and smirked. When it reached Marie and me, we passed it on without signing.

Nahla

In the teacher's lounge, Nahla checked her mail cubby. Her phone bill included a service fee for changing and unlisting her number. Well, the cost was worth it; the middle-of-the-night hangup calls had finally ceased.

There was a second envelope in her mailbox. On it, her name and address were neatly typed, the thirty-four-cent stamp placed perfectly in the right-hand corner, but the return address was missing. Nahla took a deep breath, sensing danger. She tore open the envelope and read:

> *"Does your family know who you really are? That you're a wine-loving slut who has sex on the second date? Tell them to expect a call from me."*

She crumpled the letter, her heart pounding from fear and shame. She couldn't add it to Headmaster Lowery's file; she'd only admitted to two chaste dates and had denied Leesa's claims of bringing anyone else back to the residence. She didn't need the headmaster questioning that.

"Nahla! Wanna go to Wong's for dinner tonight?" She hadn't noticed Maeve's entrance. "Joanne is busy with the girls' track team. And I just passed the dining hall and was reminded that Wednesday dinner is mystery meat."

"Sorry, I can't today. I promised to call my sisters after work." The excuse popped out, jumbling with her mind's frantic attempts to solve this new problem. She'd have to talk to Fatmi and Hoda, get them to intercept phone calls, and look out for weird mail. She dropped the crumpled letter into her tote bag.

"Hey, is everything okay? You look peaked or something." Maeve frowned.

"Well, I haven't been sleeping well," she hesitated. She wished she could share more; it had been lonely guarding this secret for so many weeks. "Been getting prank phone calls since March break."

"Really? Who from?"

"I don't know." She scribbled her new number onto a slip of paper and passed it to Maeve. "But the calls have stopped since I got a new number."

"Well, good. But geez this has been a weird year. I still can't believe Michael is gone. Did you hear that one of the students started a petition in support of him?"

"A petition?" Nahla held her breath.

"Yeah, started by Mimi Rogers. Ninth grader. She asked me to sign it today, but I wasn't sure if that would be seen as insubordination."

"But why her?" Nahla pictured the girl: a quiet, polite student. Lived on Margo's side.

"Dunno. But it has more than a hundred signatures already. Everyone misses him." She paused, perhaps noticing Nahla's ambivalent expression. "You must miss him, too. Although, I guess it's easier to recover from a breakup if you don't have to see him every day at work."

"Yeah, that's one silver lining," Nahla said. But her mind was on Mimi Rogers.

That evening after study hall, Nahla sat by her phone. She fished the letter from her bag and smoothed it out, rubbing her fingers along its wrinkles. She deliberately exhaled each time she placed her finger into the rotary dial, then waited for it to circle back to its starting point. Thankfully, Fatmi answered.

"Remember what I told you about that teacher who got fired?"

"Marhaba to you, too." Fatmi laughed.

"Marhaba. Listen, this is important." Fatmi was silent as Nahla gave her a summary of the harassing calls. Then she read aloud the anonymous letter.

"It's so crude! I can't believe someone would write something like that! But don't worry: if anyone contacts us, I'll tell them it's all lies — from the teacher you reported."

"Thank you." Nahla hesitated, wanting to tell her the whole truth, but her humiliation strangled her words. Maybe one day she would tell her, but not today; she needed her sister's unflinching sympathy.

"Sister, I know the sex part is a lie, but you haven't been drinking wine, have you?"

"No, no. I tried it just once a long time ago in university. That teacher I reported knows that detail."

"Good, good. I'll keep your secret," Fatmi reassured.

They said goodbye. Nahla opened her window and lit a cigarette. Well, she'd probably put out another fire. But then she remembered Mimi and her petition.

"Oh, Sylvie, how much more damage can that man do?"

The answer came in a flicker of a fuchsia coat, a flash of blonde tresses, as a girl ran toward the back doors, just in time for bedcheck. Nahla picked up the phone and dialled Headmaster Lowery.

Leesa

"Mimi Rogers?" He frowned. "Really?"

The fact that Mimi was a grade 9 student hadn't escaped Leesa. She'd only half-believed Marie's allegations; their implications were too difficult to bear, and denial was a simpler, if eroding, island for her to rest on. But still, over dinner, she'd questioned Mimi about her motivations for the petition. The girl had only said that he was a fun art teacher, and she wanted him back. She also complained about the suddenness and lack of transparency about his termination.

Now, Leesa studied Michael's innocent expression.

"Well, good for her! Glad to see a Thornton student fighting for me." *Surely that wasn't a dig?*

"She now has more than 150 signatures. And I overheard her saying that she's planning to nominate you for teacher of the year next month, too."

"Teacher of the year! But I'm not even there anymore!" He smiled wide.

"Well, it's a protest nomination." She got up to find her bra.

"You have to leave already? Why don't we spend the day together?" Michael pulled her back down to the lumpy pullout, his insistent fingers digging into her waist.

"Isn't your mother coming home from church soon?" She hooked her bra and reached for her T-shirt, stuck between the mattress and frame.

"Nah, it's not even noon." He pointed to the wall clock.

"It's almost 1 p.m.. Today's daylight savings. April 28. We sprang forward."

"Oh, that's why Mom left early, and you arrived early." He registered this with the wonder of someone without a schedule. "But anyway, it's not a big deal if she sees you here. We don't have to be so secretive anymore."

"No, Michael." She tried not to sound condescending, but it was hard. She bent to retrieve her pants. "We've talked about this already. Almost every week you bring that up!"

"So, let your parents take you out of that crappy school. Come live with me and do your final year at the local high school instead."

"Public school?" She did not know how to respond to that. She stepped into her track pants.

"Okay, okay. Anyway, let's focus on today. Why don't we go somewhere together, to a motel—" He grabbed her forearm, his hand a vice.

"I've got debate club." She could have added that she couldn't use her parents' credit card, and it was unlikely that with his mounting legal fees he had the cash, but she spared him that. She pulled away, grabbed her T-shirt.

"If not today, then at least let's get together over the week." He crossed his arms over his chest.

"I'll try, but I can't guarantee it. My schedule . . ." She was trying to be patient, but his clinginess was getting on her nerves.

"What? Is spirit squad more important than me?" He rolled his eyes while waving air pompoms, the dreariest cheerleader ever.

"Michael . . . this . . . isn't working for me . . . anymore . . . I'm sorry." She hadn't planned these words; they'd spilled like a sack of marbles, rolling across the floor and into places she couldn't reach. And yet she didn't want to chase after them because they felt true. As true as his blank canvases. As true as his selfish lovemaking. As true as his growing tower of empties. She reached an arm through her windbreaker.

"What are you saying?"

"I . . . I think we should take a break or something?" Just that week she'd read about breaks in *Vogue*, how they were a way to get clarity in times of confusion or to let someone go gently. As she zipped her jacket, the latter seemed most honest. *But how could that be?* Only a little while ago she would have been deliriously happy to get an extra half hour with Michael Stephenson. Her enthusiasm had diminished so gradually over these past few months, that she'd normalized her love's contraction, and had grown smaller to fit within its borders.

"What?" His eyes bulged. She pushed her feet into her sneakers.

"Not a breakup, just a break . . . I'm just so stressed, and I have no time for anything . . . and you want more from me than I can give . . . and this would be a good way for us to figure out what we both want."

"I know what I want! I want you! Don't you want me anymore?"

"Let's talk about this later. Please? I've gotta go." She tried not to look back, but when she yielded, his face was a tableau of shock and devastation. She hurried up the back steps and around the house, then down to the sidewalk. She broke into a jog, needing to release the adrenaline and pain that coursed through her.

"Look who it is."

The sneering tone was unmistakable. Leesa spotted Ashley and Carrie across the street, a six-metre stretch of pavement away. *Crap, had they seen her coming from Michael's backyard? But they wouldn't know it was his place, right?* She ran faster. It was a good thing she was wearing her sweats and running shoes, her costume for her "Sunday morning workout."

A block away from the girls, she glanced over her shoulder at their backs. *Wait, something was amiss. What was Carrie doing with Ashley? Were they friends now?* Come to think of it, these days, she hardly saw Carrie with Barb and Lauren. She'd have to keep them on her radar, make sure they didn't know where Michael lived.

Five blocks later, she slowed to a walk, shaking her head at her careless lack of vigilance; she usually scanned the street before entering or leaving his place. Well, maybe it didn't matter anymore. *Had she really just broken up with Michael?* She leaned against a tree, tried to catch her breath. Her stomach ached, and she was dizzy. *Had she made a big mistake?*

"Had a good run?" Jessica greeted her when she got back to her room.

"Nice and warm out today."

"You do look winded," Mallory observed, smirking. "Is that sex hair again?"

"Ha, I wish!" Leesa undressed, wondering if she smelled of sex. She could still feel their eyes on her. "Hey, I saw Carrie and Ashley hanging out today."

"Oh, yeah, that's old news. Barb and Lauren don't like Carrie anymore," Jessica said.

Leesa frowned. *Old news? Why hadn't they shared it with her?* Come to think of it, for the last few weeks, ever since she'd broken up with Rodney, she'd felt a slight change in them, their coolness subtle, but palpable. To make it worse, their boyfriends had sided with Rodney, and so when the larger group hung out, she'd been excluded. She had to fix this.

"It's been ages," Mallory added.

She headed to the bathroom. "Anyway, gotta run, debate club is in half an hour."

After the debate, Geraldine directed the students to form new groups of four. Leesa rushed to the chair beside Rodney.

"Hey," he said. Thankfully, his expression was friendlier than in the previous weeks, when he'd barely been able to make eye contact with her.

"Hey. I've missed you. I know I've got a lot going on, and my parents said I can't have a boyfriend, but I should never have ended things with you. Would you be open to getting back together?" She batted her lashes, but the wetness behind them was real.

"I don't know," he looked at her guardedly, "do you mean it?"

"Yes. I'm so, so sorry."

"You're not going to change your mind again?"

"I promise."

"I guess that would be okay."

"Oh, I'm so relieved." She flung her arms around him and felt his hands on her back, hesitant at first, then yielding. And she thought: *Back then, I should've suggested a break instead of a breakup.*

But what about with Michael? A break or a breakup? Neither felt right.

Zahabiya

"So, my father said he'd think about the proposal," I whispered to Marie at the end of the debate. Chairs scraped against the classroom's hardwood floor.

"Well, that's better than a 'no,' right?" Marie closed her Trapper Keeper and stood, following Geraldine's directions to form new groups.

"He still says it's too expensive. Even with me killing myself to cover 17 percent of the fees." I breathed into my glasses and wiped away smudge marks.

We scanned the room. The only incomplete team was in the far corner, Leesa and Rodney.

"Wanna skip out?" Marie eyed the door.

"Perfect, we have equal numbers," Geraldine called. "Zahabiya and Marie, join Leesa and Rodney."

"They're looking cozy," Marie whispered. "Real cozy."

"Yeah, Lavinia said they broke up, but . . ."

Rodney, oblivious to the tension, waved us over. We followed Geraldine's instruction, like lemmings to a cliff.

We took the seats directly opposite them, and Leesa nodded in greeting. Marie and I warily nodded back. They did seem to be a couple again, and I wanted to believe this was a good sign, a sign that everything with Mr. Stephenson was behind us.

"So, we have to brainstorm a list of issues." Rodney passed around worksheets on the environmental arguments for disarmament.

"How about we save time and split up the arguments and bring them back for next meeting? Rodney and I can do production, and you two detonation impact?" Leesa's tone was like an anchor-woman's: bright and reasonable. Marie and I watched her, searching her words for subtext, waiting for bad news.

"Okay," I said, glad to spend less time with her.

"Sounds good to me." Rodney kissed the side of Leesa's head. The pair walked away, hand in hand. We followed them down the hallway, a dozen paces back.

"Well, I'm speechless. Speechless."

"Was she actually civil?" I mentally reviewed the brief conversation. It was like Leesa had been body-snatched.

"Yeah. Something's up." Marie squinted at Leesa's back.

On the way into the residence, we passed Gerry, who was up a ladder, installing a security camera by the back doors.

"Hello, ladies," he said, flashing his movie-star smile down at us. I waved, a wash of embarrassment hitting me when I remembered thinking he was the abuser.

"Hi, Gerry. God, do they make you work Sundays, too?" Marie asked.

"Not usually. But Headmaster Lowery ordered cameras for all the doors and told me to install them as soon as they arrived. Guess he wants to keep you girls extra safe."

"Probably should have had them ages ago," Marie said. I nodded but knew cameras at the residence's doors wouldn't have protected her. Neither would they have safeguarded Mei or Leesa. They weren't the solution.

———

For most of the next week, Marie was preoccupied with Leesa's shift in temperament, testing it by randomly saying "hi" or talking about the debate with her in hallways or classes. Then she reported back to the rest of us, rating the normalcy and level of politeness. These experiments freaked me out, and I kept my distance from Leesa; I knew not to poke a bear finally in hibernation.

On Sunday morning, Marie popped her head into our room. "C'mon! Get your jackets on and meet me by the front doors! Quick!"

"Where are we going?" I looked up from my English homework. It was the second-last assignment of the term, and I needed an $A+$ to pull up my grade to an A.

"No time to explain! No time. But I think Leesa is meeting Mr. Stephenson. I heard her on the phone. I'll get Lav." She darted away.

"Well, I'm in." Mei slipped her feet into her sneakers.

"I don't have time for this." But I zipped up my coat and followed Mei out the door.

We split into pairs and stayed a long block behind Leesa so she wouldn't see us. It was probably a bad idea, but I joined in anyway; all of Marie's hunches had turned out to be true. Besides, all of us were already so entangled in Leesa's story.

We watched as she checked her watch and paused periodically as though lost. She didn't seem herself. But then, we probably looked pretty strange, too.

She stopped at the dairy. Lavinia and I caught up to Marie and Mei, who huddled along its back wall like a pair of spies.

"Should we be doing this?" Lavinia whispered.

"I don't know." I did know that Marie wasn't about to turn back. And I realized in that moment that I didn't want to, either.

Mei peeked around the side of the building. "And . . . she's on the move again."

"Let's go," Marie said.

"Hey!" Jason and Cyril came around a corner with Toby in tow.

"*Shhh*!" We ordered them, and the six of us reflexively backed into the dairy's wall and watched Leesa continue on. Toby looked at me with bloodshot eyes. I really hoped he'd keep quiet.

Nahla

"You've been . . . different, Nahla. Ever since March break. Please, tell us, what's going on?" Maeve had invited her over for Sunday brunch. "We're worried about you."

"I've just been really busy and tired. And I was getting all those prank calls." *What more could she say?* Headmaster Lowery had repeated his warnings to not share anything.

"I bet those calls were coming from that girl who started the rumour. Leesa?" Maeve passed her a plate of toasted English muffins.

"Yes, probably . . ."

"I will never understand the logic of bullies." Joanne, frying pan in hand, deposited an egg, sunny side up, on each plate. "Do you think she was part of Michael getting fired? Everything seemed to happen around the same time, right?"

"Speaking of which, I'm worried about him, too. I tried calling after he was fired, but we keep missing each other's calls." Maeve said.

Nahla poked at her egg yolk, the sluggish yellow stream traversing her plate and oozing into the bread.

"Nahla? Are you all right?" Joanne touched her shoulder.

"No, I'm not all right. Listen, I need you both to keep a secret." Maeve and Joanne nodded. "It is huge. And it explains the bully's logic."

Like her runny egg, Nahla spilled over — about Leesa, Sylvie's notebook, Marie, and Michael's dismissal.

"Oh my God . . . we were friends with the guy the whole time this was going on." Joanne rubbed her eyes and asked Nahla to repeat a few of the details.

"Wow." Maeve sat back in her seat, landing heavily. She connected the dots out loud. "So, that notebook . . . that disclosure from that girl in your wing . . . and Leesa! Holy moly! So, you reported it. . ."

"And now he's angry and acting out against you in scary ways," Joanne added.

"They both denied it. The relationship is probably continuing on . . ."

"It's so disgusting." Maeve put down her fork, pushed away her half-eaten breakfast. "And now Mimi Rogers is getting signatures for her petition."

"I've asked Headmaster Lowery to sit down with Mimi . . ."

"And what if there are others? And what if he *is* still seeing Leesa?" Joanne asked.

"There has to be something we can do," Maeve said.

The three teachers sat in silence for a moment, pondering the question. And then they brainstormed ways to get Michael over at Joanne and Maeve's place, have him drink too much, and confess. They thought about how to covertly open dialogue among students about abuse at the school. Joanne taught Nahla a few self-defence techniques, including how to easily crack a man's clavicle.

Nahla walked back toward the residence, her spirit lighter for having shared her burden. Bells from three nearby churches clanged, asynchronous, reminding her of the mosques in her old Beirut neighbourhood, their competing adhans mixing and melding. She paused to listen, her imagination inserting the muezzin's melodic call to prayer into the bell ringers' unholy noise.

When she was close to the dairy, she saw them: the four girls with whom she'd grown more familiar with since Valentine's Day, as well as Jason and Cyril. They stood rigidly against the dairy's wall, as though in a game of hide-and-seek. Then they slowly and silently split into pairs and began walking, a fractured, furtive parade. *What were they up to?* Instinctively, she held back and followed them through a dozen blocks to a residential area with tidy front lawns and swing sets in backyards.

She tried to remain invisible, but Jason, in the last row with Zahabiya, turned and glimpsed her behind them.

"Bonjour!"

Before she could ask what they were doing, Zahabiya put an index finger to her lips and pointed to where the other four were crouched beside a hedgerow twenty feet away. Marie removed her camera's lens and whispered to Cyril.

Nahla frowned in confusion. Zahabiya pointed again, and Nahla saw Leesa, stock-still on the sidewalk in front of a pretty white clapboard house with a picket fence. A blue hatchback was parked in the driveway.

Leesa appeared to be staring at the door, contemplating whether to continue up the path. Decision made, she slowly turned, and stepped onto the sidewalk. Just then, a man burst out of the front door in boxers, a T-shirt, and slippers. Michael!

"Leesa, come in, let's talk!" He called from the front porch.

"No, Michael, I just . . ."

"Please! We can work things out! Just come in and talk." Michael ran down the front steps.

Leesa shook her head, backed up onto the narrow boulevard, on the verge of something.

"Babe! Come on! Don't be silly! Come in!" His tone turned terse. Leesa seemed to hesitate. Nahla's stomach lurched.

She moved closer, a wind at her back pushing her to interrupt them. Him.

"No, Michael. No. I told you I needed a break." Leesa darted away, in the opposite direction as her audience. He rushed to the sidewalk and then spied Nahla, who now stood on the next-door neighbour's property, like a shocked lawn ornament. His eyes beamed rage. Then he turned, glanced at Leesa's disappearing back.

For a second, she considered fleeing, but before she could will her legs to run, he leapt at her, grabbed her by her shoulders, his grip clammy, his ungroomed fingernails digging into her skin.

"This is all your fault!" He yelled. He shoved her, and she lost her balance, falling to the ground, fresh-cut grass sticking to her skin. And then he was on top of her, straddling her, the weight of his body in the hands that encircled her throat. She heard screams. And then everything went black.

Leesa

Leesa heard his yelling from half a block away. *Was that Miss Naim? What was she doing at Michael's house?* She sensed danger, and this overtook her creeping jealousy; Michael looked like a maniac, pushing and yelling at Miss Naim. When she fell to the ground, him on top of her, Leesa broke into a sprint, her eyes locked on them. Without thinking, without questioning, she piggy-backed him, grabbing him from under his damp armpits, and used her body weight to roll him over, tumbling, tumbling. In her peripheral vision she saw a small crowd of Thornton students. She heard the *thwack* of bone against cement before she felt it.

Everything went dark and blissfully silent, the hush before the film began. She relaxed back into her seat, the camera panning over the strange scene from above.

"Yooooouuuuu okaaaaaaaaay?" Zahabiya was at her side, along with Jason and a howling beagle. The girl on the sidewalk, the girl who looked like her, couldn't make her lips move.

The camera shifted to the right, where Michael was being pinned down by Mei and a guy she recognized from school, but whose name she didn't know. Marie stood over Michael, cursing.

And next to them was Miss Naim, rousing, sitting up with Lavinia's help. The teacher rubbed her throat and neck, her hands sluggish, the skin under them red handprints. Michael's handprints.

The film panned away and switched over to a series of scenes of him, moving one frame at a time in slow motion: a lost and lonely man who'd gradually pulled a girl into his life, charming her with his false confidence, his kindness and pain, a pain that mirrored her own. And the girl had loved him, truly loved him, until she began to have doubts about him. Because she had so much to do still, like finish high school and go to university and have a career and travel the world and fall in love a few more times. And when he'd phoned that morning, pretending to be her father, so that a girl would run upstairs and fetch her, she'd listened to his pleas because he'd sounded so kind and so sad, and she'd felt compelled to go to his house, all the while uncertain if she should.

"Bon, so now you see." Leesa found herself in Mademoiselle Leblanc's flat, which smelled like a mix of Anais Anais and coffee. They were eating digestive cookies, the way they'd done many times back in grades 7 and 8 and 9 when she'd confided to her about her parents' marital troubles, in the days before Michael.

"Why didn't I see it before?" She studied Mademoiselle Leblanc. This version of the French teacher was uncharacteristically trendy. She was in a flouncy burgundy dress, with hoop earrings and lace fingerless gloves and her long grey hair was styled into a shaggy perm. Leesa only ever remembered her in baggy beige clothes, her hair piled atop her head in a messy bun.

"Because he is an adult, and you a child. Because you loved him. Et bien, l'amour. We can't help it. You know, I loved someone once, someone much older than me, and it was wrong. And then he rejected me, and well . . . ça m'a brisé le coeur, my heart forever fractured until the day it just . . . stopped. You mustn't let this happen to you,

Leesa. You're young. You can recover from this. You still have to finish high school . . ."

"And go to university,"

"Et avoir une carrière,"

"And travel the world,"

"Et tomber amoureux encore, many more times."

Mademoiselle Leblanc's image pixelated and disappeared, and then everything was silent and dark again.

Leesa came to, hearing sirens, in Zahabiya's arms.

Zahabiya

On the night of the formal. I asked Suneeta, a grade 13 Trini girl who lived in the new wing, to help me with my sari after my efforts yielded sloppy folds.

"I can't believe an Indian girl can't put on her own sari!" Suneeta laughed.

I ignored her teasing and focused on the blue-and-gold silk and the perfume that wafted from it, faint but still present.

Finally dressed, I shuffled back to my room, holding up the hem so it wouldn't brush the floor. I saw Carrie down the hall, coming my way, and I picked up my pace. Of all the girls in Leesa's crowd, she was the least worst. She hadn't actively participated in the name-calling, but still, she hadn't ever come to our defence.

"You look great, Zahabiya!" She cooed, her smile bright, maybe sincere.

"Yeah, you, too. Nice dress." She was in a long peach gown, her auburn hair in an updo, sparkly blue eye shadow brightening her eyes.

"Listen," she touched my elbow, and I stiffened. "I'm really sorry . . . for all that stuff . . . you know . . . after the dance? After, I started talking to Ashley more, and stopped hanging with those guys. I guess she helped me understand, you know . . . what they . . . what we did . . . was wrong. And . . . I'm sorry."

Her eyes were wet, tears threatening to dissolve her mascara. I didn't say anything. She tottered away, as fast as her six-inch heels would allow. I thought back to Valentine's night, our tossed room, the talks with Miss Naim and Headmaster Lowery, and the taunting that had ensued. Despite Carrie's show of emotion, her apology rang hollow. Maybe before, back in the fall, I would have felt the glow of her attention, and accepted the apology. I might have ignored my own feelings, forgiven her, trusted too easily. I exhaled, shook it all off, and walked tall. No. No one was going to ruin my night.

The girls were waiting for me in my room, glammed up in full makeup, long formal dresses, and heels.

"Wow, girl!" Lavinia exclaimed, her lipstick matching her ruby-red gown.

"Oh my God. I gotta get a photo." Marie had spent the evening in rollers, and now her hair was all bouncy curls. She ran across the hall for her camera, a blur of kelly-green silk and poofy sleeves.

"You're a goddess!" Mei wore a tuxedo with a ruffled shirt, sourced from a second-hand shop, her glossy black hair in a French braid.

"You're all so gorgeous," I said, scanning the room. Marie returned and set up her tripod and timer. We were gorgeous. Better than Benetton. I beamed at my friends, taking in the beauty of us.

After the dance, Jason and I lingered outside the residence, stalling the night's end. The reality that school would be over in two days, and I'd be going home for the summer, hung as heavy as the curtain of humidity that warmed our skin. I was still uncertain whether I'd be returning to Thornton in the fall; my father said we'd discuss it when I got home, but it didn't feel promising.

"What a great night," Jason whispered in my ear. He leaned in to kiss me, his soft lips pressing against mine.

"We'll have plenty more, I hope." I clung to him for a hundred heartbeats.

Top-forty music blared from the bedrooms, everyone tuned to the same station. With the last exams completed that morning, detention was now a false threat, and the party would go on for a while yet.

I found Marie, Mei, and Lavinia in our room, still in their formal attire, high heels kicked off as they lounged on the beds.

"You okay, girl?"

"Yeah, just a little sad the year's over."

"Me, too. Me, too." Marie flopped onto her back.

"Not me, I'm already packed," Mei deadpanned, and we laughed at her tough-girl lie.

I undid the safety pins securing the pallu and waist, dropped them in my desk drawer. A purple envelope caught my eye.

I opened it, my fingertips brushing against paper. Inside were nine one-dollar bills, four twos and two fives. I held them up for the others to see.

"Is that what she stole, girl?" I nodded.

"Wow. Just wow," Marie said.

"So, it's over then," Mei said.

Since the incident on Mr. Stephenson's lawn, the wall of tension between Leesa and the rest of us had finally collapsed. We weren't friends, but neither were we enemies. We'd all been questioned by the police and Headmaster Lowery, and she still hadn't admitted to Mr. Stephenson's abuse, maintaining a story about a friendly relationship. But this time, she'd done so half-heartedly, abandoning her righteous anger and disdain for us.

But we'd all witnessed the stark truth about his relationship with Leesa that day at his house. It was all the evidence anyone needed, including, perhaps, Leesa herself.

I put back the bills, closed the envelope, then the drawer. I said a silent "thank you" to Leesa for the money, for the end of the hostility. The weight of dread — the fear that Leesa would inevitably return to her intimidation tactics, a burden I'd been carrying for months — slipped off my body, along with yards of blue silk.

The hallway was quieter as we prepared for bed. Mei left to brush her teeth, and alone in our shared room beside the common washrooms, I pondered returning home. In a few days, I'd start my receptionist job at a local animal clinic. And if I had to go back to my old school, maybe it wouldn't be so terrible. I'd be a couple of hours away. I could keep in touch with my Thornton friends, maintain a semi-normal long-distance relationship with Jason. And maybe I'd make some new friends.

Mei yelled, "Flushing," and as I always did, I cringed slightly. I got into bed and mentally replayed the last conversation I'd had with my dad, remembering how earnest his expression had been when he'd said he wanted me home. And, for the first time, I didn't discount his words.

Last spring, when I'd applied to Thornton, I'd been so sure that I'd had to leave, and now . . . well . . . *What had changed in the course of a year? Had I? Had my family?* Perhaps all of us had changed — or changed enough.

Maybe I could let home be home again.

Nahla

Nahla stood in the lobby, supervising the procession of girls laden down with suitcases and garbage bags.

When Mei's grandparents came to pick her up, Lavinia, Zahabiya, Marie, and Mei huddled for a group hug, gesturing for Nahla to join them. When they broke the embrace, Mei promised to visit.

Soon after, a hired bus to the airport pulled away, and Nahla joined Zahabiya and Marie as they waved at Lavinia, who sat at the back. Nahla watched out for Leesa, but she didn't see her get on the bus.

She shook hands with Zahabiya's and Marie's fathers, who'd arrived at the same time to get their daughters.

One by one, the rest of the girls were picked up by families and driven away.

As she'd done hundreds of times that year, she wandered the hallways, now with doors wide open, belongings vacated and walls bare. Here and there were personal items forgotten or discarded, and she gathered a random sample: a neon-pink jelly bracelet, an unsolved Rubik's Cube, a bottle of blue nail polish. They comforted her; she imagined the collection of detritus might make the vacant residence feel less empty.

On the second floor, she peeked into the triad, half-expecting Leesa to still be there, but the room was unoccupied. She'd hoped to say goodbye, but she must have missed her. She stepped inside and sat on the bed that had been Leesa's.

"Allah ma3ak. Au revoir. Goodbye."

She closed the door behind her and went to her suite. With Sylvie's departure, the space felt lighter, brighter. While Nahla missed her, she guessed that Michael's arrest had allowed Sylvie to find peace and move on, to know that it was unlikely that he'd harm another Thornton girl.

Nahla, too, felt better after his arrest. But the assault had changed her. She was even more cautious now, more aware of her safety, and this fear would linger for many years. She had new panic alarms installed in the manor and a plan to check in with Maeve each morning and night once all the girls left for the summer.

She was also more certain: to stay, to change the school for the better, to be there for the girls on her wing.

And now with two months off, Nahla planned to rest, to sew new curtains, and hang coat hooks. For now, she wouldn't restain the bedside table, would allow that perfect ring from Sylvie's water glass to remain.

She checked her watch, prepared the rakwe, tidied her rooms, and put out a plate of cookies. Then she waited in the front lobby.

She spied the car, rose to meet it. Her mother opened the front passenger door, and from the back, Hoda, Ali, and Fatmi emerged. After a moment of held breath, her father opened the driver's side door, unfolded his tall frame, and stepped outside.

Leesa

Leesa stepped out of the taxi and crossed the street.

"I'm so glad to see you. Thanks for calling. For coming." Michael beamed at her from the porch.

Leesa gazed at the front of his house, his car, his face. The face that had been her sunshine for three years.

"It's good to see you too." He looked thinner, his hair greasy. He'd phoned the residence multiple times in the last six weeks, sometimes impersonating her father to get her to the phone. She'd mostly dodged his calls. Some of the girls who took messages started a weak rumour that he was in love with her. Somehow, the larger truth, witnessed and kept secret by half a dozen students, one teacher, a nosy neighbour, and two police officers, hadn't circulated among the students.

Not yet anyway. If this had been a scandal about somebody else, and she and her friends had caught wind of it, the entire frickin' world would know by now.

It was hard to fathom. After all, she'd been the biggest jerk to all of them, and they had no reason to be kind, to shield her from shame and embarrassment — feelings that woke her in the morning and slithered into her dreams at night — and yet they had shielded her. And she was grateful for that.

But no one could hold back the news indefinitely; certainly, after his court date, it would be out in the open.

"Listen, Leesa, there's something I want to ask you." His smile was crooked, a screen door falling off its hinge. In an instant, he bent to one knee, took her hand, held out a ring. Its stone was small, yet her stomach twisted, and her eyes became wet.

"Oh, Michael . . ."

"You're the most precious thing in my life. It's only natural for us to start our life together, put all this craziness behind us. Let's just do it, Babe." He squeezed her hand so hard it hurt.

"It's just . . . this is not how we planned it." She untangled her hand from his. The fantasy of graduating, then moving to another city had seemed wonderful. Now, all these months later, the idea was like a child's game of make-believe.

"No. We didn't plan on getting caught." He half-stood, but then, defeated by his own legs, settled back down on the stoop. This was the first time he'd spoken about his firing in this way; in his last letter to her, he'd still referred to plausible deniability, ridiculous rules, suing the school. He'd even claimed he could beat the assault charges. A part of her hoped that was true, that he could walk away from this mess and start over. But another part of her, a part she barely recognized, wanted him to be punished for choking a woman.

She sat beside him.

"But don't you see? Getting caught really has liberated us. We can do anything we want now." He stared at the ring. Sunlight danced off the stone.

"For now, I just need to be on my own. But . . . in the fall, we can meet up and talk about this again." She patted his arm reassuringly.

"Promise you'll call from Paris."

"Promise." She gave him a quick peck on the cheek and hurried down the steps and into the waiting taxi, trying to outrun her guilt about the promises she'd never keep.

As the car drove away, she directed the driver to make a short detour through downtown, then past Thornton's buildings, whose lonely halls she'd walked for the last six years. She wished she could have visited the horse that grazed in their farmer's field one more time.

As they turned onto the highway, she closed her eyes and said a final goodbye to Belltown, to the school, to the man she'd loved. Next year, she'd start fresh — in a new city, at a new school, and maybe, with a new love.

From here, the view is better.
But I promise you
— all my girls —
I'll visit.

Note: this book addresses child abuse, gender-based violence, body-image issues, and trauma. If this is happening to you, there are people you can talk to. Contact the Kids Help Phone: text 686868 or call 1-800-668-6868 or visit https://kidshelpphone.ca/.

Acknowledgements

First off, thanks to Shamoon Doctor, my good dad, who allowed me, when I was fifteen, to leave home for a year. As a middle-aged woman, I understand now how difficult that must have been for him. This novel is inspired by that weird year, but the events, setting, and characters depicted in this story are completely fictional. Although, like Zahabiya, I do stop to talk to every animal I meet.

Thanks to Dania Sands and Miriam Hookings for your private school memories and for reviewing early drafts.

Merci to Danyelle Boily for checking Mademoiselle Leblanc's notebook entries.

Niá:wen ki'wáhi and shukran to Sherri Vansickle and Reyan Naim for your sensitivity reading.

Rachael Johnson described "side head" to me on a summer night, at a bar in Derry and my life will never be the same.

I am indebted to Rachel Letofsky for her editorial support and for being my advocate and agent.

It's often difficult to discern what needs revision when you've been sitting with the same long Word doc for so many years. (*What to keep? What to kill? What to develop?*) Much gratitude to Pia Singhal for her keen and kind editorial eye. Thanks to Jennifer Foster for her stellar copyedit and to Jen Albert for her sharp proofreading.

To all the staff at ECW who had a hand or finger in this book, I appreciate you all. Thanks for making the publishing world just a little better.

Gratitude to the Ontario Arts Council and the Canada Council for the Arts for the financial support, which allowed me to have DIY writing retreats.

I am grateful to live by Lake Ontario, on Turtle Island, which is on the traditional territory of many nations, including the Mississaugas of the Credit, the Anishinaabeg, the Chippewa, the Haudenosaunee, and the Wendat Peoples, now home to many diverse First Nations, Inuit, and Métis Peoples. As a settler on stolen land, I call on other settlers to support the Indigenous-led Land Back movement.

As always, thanks to all my friends, family, and community who support my writing. I appreciate every little thing you do to buoy me up.

For all the early drafts, my canine companion, Maggie, was at my side snoring, or making me laugh, or encouraging me to get up and stretch. She was the best friend.

And how to describe the ways my partner, Reyan Naim, contributed to this novel? Your daily gestures of love and care are *everything*.

Entertainment. Writing. Culture. ————————

ECW is a proudly independent, Canadian-owned book publisher. We know great writing can improve people's lives, and we're passionate about sharing original, exciting, and insightful writing across genres.

———————————————— Thanks for reading along!

We want our books not just to sustain our imaginations, but to help construct a healthier, more just world, and so we've become a certified B Corporation, meaning we meet a high standard of social and environmental responsibility — and we're going to keep aiming higher. We believe books can drive change, but the way we make them can too.

Certified B Corporation

Being a B Corp means that the act of publishing this book should be a force for good – for the planet, for our communities, and for the people that worked to make this book. For example, everyone who worked on this book was paid at least a living wage. You can learn more at the Ontario Living Wage Network.

This book is also available as a Global Certified Accessible™ (GCA) ebook. ECW Press's ebooks are screen reader friendly and are built to meet the needs of those who are unable to read standard print due to blindness, low vision, dyslexia, or a physical disability.

FSC
www.fsc.org
MIX
Paper | Supporting responsible forestry
FSC® C103567

This book is printed on Sustana EnviroBook™, a recycled paper, and other controlled sources that are certified by the Forest Stewardship Council®.

ECW's office is situated on land that was the traditional territory of many nations including the Wendat, the Anishnaabeg, Haudenosaunee, Chippewa, Métis, and current treaty holders the Mississaugas of the Credit. In the 1880s, the land was developed as part of a growing community around St. Matthew's Anglican and other churches. Starting in the 1950s, our neighbourhood was transformed by immigrants fleeing the Vietnam War and Chinese Canadians dispossessed by the building of Nathan Phillips Square and the subsequent rise in real estate value in other Chinatowns. We are grateful to those who cared for the land before us and are proud to be working amidst this mix of cultures.